WOLF LIES

ROCKY MOUNTAIN PACK

LUCÍA ASHTA

WOLF LIES

Wolf Lies

Rocky Mountain Pack ~ Book Two

Copyright © 2021 by Lucía Ashta

www.LuciaAshta.com

Cover design by Sanja Balan of Sanja's Covers

Editing by Ocean's Edge Editing

Proofreading by Geesey Editorial Services

CHAPTER ONE

NAYA

SHE CAME TO WITH A START, going from a deep, all-consuming unconsciousness to her heart pounding, her breathing shallow, her fight-or-flight response prickling under her skin, making her want to scratch at it.

All at once, the memories of the last several days slammed into her like icy water, clearing the last vestiges of haze that tried to lure her mind back under: the dark mage with the red magic; the twin sister who shared her burden of being a descendant of Oak MacLeod; how her twin had taken her from her pack—Maverick and Clove would be frantic in their search for her—Bruno: how he'd been the first to realize she had at least one identical sister, how he stared at her like he was seeing straight through to her soul...

Naya's reference of him. Instead, he nestled close to what Naya realized was a cell phone.

"His job is to watch us and report everything we do. I'm pretty sure that if we relieve ourselves in that fancy bucket over there, he'll send a message about it."

"To whom? The mage who took us?"

Meiling nodded slowly. "Who else?"

"Not sure I want to consider that question..." Just because this mage, whoever he was, had taken them, didn't mean others weren't still after them.

They carried the precious blood that was to save all werewolf-kind. What hunter wouldn't be after them?

"No one has been by to see us since I woke up," Meiling continued. "Just this man, watching, always watching."

"Perv," Naya said loudly. The man didn't so much as flinch at her insult, only looked down at his phone, typing away.

"We tried to get through this barrier before the mage took us," Meiling said, eyes pinned on their guard the entire time she spoke. "And then I tried here. Both times, it knocked us out. It's not worth trying again unless something changes. Besides..."

"Besides what?" Naya asked.

Meiling cleared her throat and inconspicuously

one side of the building. A rectangle of daylight outlined the open entrance.

Naya tensed, rising from her seat to crouch low. She might not have a way to defeat her opponent— yet—but that didn't mean she wasn't going to fight with everything she had just the same. And she didn't need any of Meiling's many blades to cause lethal damage. She had her hands and feet and twenty years of martial arts and strength training in her arsenal.

The door shut behind the male silhouette outlined in light, and the warehouse plunged back into darkness—save that disturbing red glow, a constant reminder of how very fucked the two sisters were.

Steady paces echoed across the wide, open space, growing louder, until a man stood on the other side of the glowing dome, grinning at them.

That smile was depraved and wicked, and it chilled Naya's blood. She shivered in her exercise bra and boy shorts.

"Hello, girls. Glad you're finally up."

Naya was absolutely certain she and Meiling had nothing to look forward to, and when the mage dismissed the other man, replacing him on the couch, it took everything she had not to reveal her fear.

This man was a predator through and through.

He wore his power cloaked across him so clearly, it might as well have been a blinking neon sign. He evidently ranked higher on the food chain than wolves.

Infusing every ounce of bravado she possessed into her words, she snapped, "What the hell do you want with us?"

CHAPTER TWO

NAYA

THE MAGE'S grin spread into a feral line that had Naya's instincts sparking, urging her to tuck tail and run as fast as she could in the opposite direction.

Tilting her chin up, standing, she refused to look away from the man's eyes, even as a simmering red glow overwhelmed the dark of his irises.

He stared at her for so long that Meiling rose to stand beside her. When he finally flicked his attention at her sister, Naya bristled. His eyes whisked back to her when she tensed.

"Oh, this is going to be such fun," he said in a deep, steady voice she instantly despised.

"I asked you a question," Naya said. "What do you want with us?"

Settling further into the couch, he crossed an ankle over the other knee, appearing as relaxed as if he were preparing to watch a movie. He tilted his head to both sides, considering them. "I didn't have any plans for you ... originally. But I'm reconsidering."

"What the hell kind of sense does that make? Why'd you take us, then?"

He draped an arm across his folded leg and drummed his fingers across it. To her acute hearing, the repeated *parumm, parumm, parummm* was too loud. Too common a sound to irk her as much as it did.

"I took you ... as a favor. But now I think ... I might want you for myself instead." His habitual pauses while he spoke, like he had no worries in the world, only set Naya's nerves on edge. He might not have anything better to do, but she sure as shit did.

He uncrossed his legs and rested his elbows on his knees, leaning forward. Naya held perfectly still as she warred with her desire to flee. She might turn into a werewolf, but she wasn't the beast to be feared here.

"I didn't expect to find ... two of you. I was only supposed to take one of you."

"Nice. Then let her go."

"No way," Meiling piped up. "I'm not leaving without her."

The man slid back against the couch. "Aw, how

sweet. You're trying to protect each other." He smiled again, and that one cold gesture made it clear he didn't think there was any chance of either of them protecting anyone against his power.

"Let her go," Naya said, "and I'll cooperate."

"I don't need your cooperation."

Of course he didn't...

Naya changed tactics, doing what she could to ignore the feeling of being a defenseless insect under the lens of a microscope: "If you took us as a favor to someone else, who's the other person?"

When he only seemed to consider them both, Naya added, "Is it a hunter?"

"A hunter," he said with an amused chuckle. "Hunters are unimportant."

Her pack had evaded hunters since shifters first founded the sanctuary in the middle of the Rockies. Hunters had been their one and only predator during the last century of her pack's existence.

And this man—this *dark mage*, not a man, she reminded herself—didn't even take hunters seriously.

She swallowed around a dry throat. "If not a hunter, then who else would want us?"

"That's exactly the motivation I'm trying to figure out." He leaned forward again, and this time Naya felt Meiling's tension coat the air around her, briefly overpowering the crackling ozone the red dome around them released. But her twin didn't so much as twitch at his renewed proximity.

"You're both just wolf shifters, I think. Or werewolves. Either way..." He waved an unconcerned hand through the air. "And you're twins, but she only wanted one of you. So why would she want you?"

He seemed to muse aloud while Naya cataloged away the fact that a female of some sort was behind the scenes, orchestrating their capture.

"Does she *know* there are two of you?" he continued.

Naya wondered if there was a way to play on his ignorance. She assumed the woman didn't know she had a twin, or why wouldn't she have asked for both of them? Of course, it didn't help that Naya had no idea why she wanted her in the first place... It must be for her blood, to take her out so she couldn't have children and pass on Oak MacLeod's strong genes that made any of his descendants so readily able to accept werewolf magic without risk of rejecting it and dying.

If that was the case, and it seemed as if it had to be, then no way the woman knew there were two of them. If she had, she would have absolutely wanted to kill them both. Two for one, and take out the remaining survivors of Oak MacLeod's bloodline? Yeah, that was a good deal for some sadistic asshole who wanted to destroy any chance werewolves had at long-term survival.

Unless Bruno was telling the truth and Lara actually did exist. Then Lara could carry on the bloodline and inject hope into the future of werewolves.

"What can you girls do?" the mage asked. When Naya scowled at the vagueness of his question, he added, "Is there anything extraordinary about you?"

Like they were going to tell him a thing they didn't have to. He didn't look this stupid. Thick, dark, caterpillar-like eyebrows bunched over eyes that were clearly intelligent, even through the distracting dim red glow.

"She wouldn't bother with you if you weren't different somehow ... if she couldn't run some of her tests on you."

"Well, shucks, you sure do know how to make a girl feel all special-like." Naya followed that up with a fake, peroxide-blond smile.

But then the mage was on his feet and a breath away from the dome, staring straight at both of them. He moved fast. Too fast.

"What are you? What's special about you?"

Naya was already thinking maybe he wasn't as smart as he looked if he thought he could just keep asking them the same questions, hoping they'd tell him something he didn't know, when a strange compulsion overcame her.

Suddenly, she *needed* to tell him what she was. And she wanted to tell him so much more than that. The desire to please him welled inside her, equally as shocking, and disgusting her.

Breathing heavily from the effort of resisting the odd and unnatural urge, a jolt of self-awareness had her noticing that the red in his eyes was swirling hypnotically.

She immediately shut her eyes against it, and the desperate urge to tell him every single one of her deepest secrets waned.

He grunted, but it wasn't a sound of frustration, more of curiosity. She couldn't help but wonder if it was somehow worse to show she was capable of resisting at least some of his magic.

"Interesting," he muttered. "So very interesting."

With her eyes still pressed closed, she registered that Meiling hadn't uttered a single word since he started talking. She must be resisting his compulsion too.

"Are you a vampire?" she asked. He didn't seem like he was, what with his unusual magic and all, but they were the only supes she knew of capable of compelling another to do their bidding—though vampires could only influence humans. But this mage before them was obviously an exception to rules.

"A vampire," he snorted, and in his mirth she picked up an accent she couldn't identify. She pegged it vaguely as European, realizing fully she might be wrong even about that.

"I'd take that as an insult, but it doesn't seem like you know much about anything."

"I know that I don't like you." Naya didn't know why she bothered saying that, other than perhaps to keep him talking. The more he spoke, the greater chance there was that he might let something helpful slip.

"Good." He drew out the one word in an accent that sounded very much like that of a black-and-white Dracula movie.

Was he messing with her? Besides trapping her, was he treating her like she was the idiot here?

This time, she shut not only her eyes, but also her mouth.

"Open your eyes."

She didn't.

"Open. Your. Eyes." The promise of violence and death rode his repeated command. Even so, Naya didn't open them, and it appeared neither did Meiling.

"Fine. You want to play? Let's play. I was bored anyway."

A second later, Meiling screamed before strangling the sound.

Naya looked to where her sister stood. Red licked across her body as if it were flames. Meiling looked intact beneath the wave of red, yet her eyes shimmered with unshed tears wrought from obvious pain.

The flames of the mage's magic increased in an audible surge and Meiling whimpered, clenching her eyes shut, biting her bottom lip so hard a trickle of blood dripped along its swell.

"Stop it," Naya growled at the mage without facing him.

"No."

The red magic pulsed once more.

This time, Meiling's eyes fluttered rapidly under her closed eyelids. She panted while she curled her fingers into tight fists.

"Tell me," the mage said in a wheedling tone that sounded oddly playful, as if he genuinely were enjoying himself. "I can do this all day. I assure you, she cannot."

Again, Naya heard before she saw the effects of the mage's increased magic. Meiling grunted, then choked. The red of the mage's power licked across every inch of her body as if it were a consuming fire.

Her braids rose to stand on end and she began trembling. No ... *convulsing.*

Naya rushed to catch her as she fell wordlessly to the floor.

She lowered Meiling across her legs, hastily folded to one side.

Her twin's eyes opened only to reveal that her irises were rolling up into the back of her head. Naya saw almost all whites.

"Okay," she snapped, pulling the sister she had only just met closer to her, as if that would stop whatever immense pain had hold of her. "Stop this and I'll tell you what you want to know."

But the sadistic asshole didn't stop. He ramped up the voltage even more.

Incoherent groans gargled up from Meiling's throat as her entire body grew rigid, straightening across Naya's lap like a log.

"No," Naya cried out.

"I need to have your full compliance if you want me to stop." The fucker actually sounded bored!

"You have it," Naya whipped out.

"I need proof, or we'll just start this all over again."

"What proof do you need?"

"Look at me."

When Naya didn't hop to it, he pushed another

wave of his power through Meiling. A whoosh of even brighter crimson flared across her skin, doing nothing to harm Naya but causing Meiling more pain than she could handle. Her rigid torso convulsed until her teeth knocked into each other uncontrollably.

Naya didn't have time to consider whether it would better help her sister to continue resisting the mage's assault. She whirled around to stare at the mage while pulling her twin closer, willing the shaking to stop.

Her eyes gazed at his feet, but they were open. "You stop first, or I swear to you I won't do a damn thing you want me to. If you hurt her—"

"But I already have hurt her, haven't I?" The laugh that followed was so wicked that it made Naya feel hollow inside, until she shoved away the foreign feeling.

"And I'll keep hurting her more until I kill her..." He said it so casually that Naya imagined the mage tortured and murdered every damned day. "...or you stare into my eyes."

She knew it was a mistake even before she did it, but she couldn't be responsible for the death of the sister she hadn't even had the chance to get to know yet.

Slowly, she raised her eyes to his.

The red in his flared, capturing her mind in an instant. As if her body were far away now, she absently registered that Meiling continued to tremble. But Naya could no longer so much as check to see if the mage had stopped as he'd promised. She couldn't look anywhere but into the endless depths of his eyes that felt like pools of molten lava.

"Tell me why my ... associate ... wants you."

Naya could tell her will was no longer her own even as she prepared to answer. From deep inside, she prayed she could control herself at least just enough not to worsen their predicament.

"I don't ... know ... why this woman wants me ... because I don't know ... who she is." Every word she uttered felt as if she were pushing it through a solid wall. Maybe her will wasn't as overcome as she thought...

"Oh no, little girl. That's not how this works. You give me answers, not the other way around." He paused. "Though your resilience is unexpected." Bizarrely, he sounded almost pleased at the fact.

"Why does someone want you?"

Any hope that she could resist the compulsion he streamed through her vanished as she heard herself speak.

"Hunters are the only ones I know want me." Her pause offered her a flitter of hope, before hearing herself continue dashed it. "We're the last surviving heirs of Callan 'the Oak' MacLeod."

By the time she finished that one simple sentence, she was panting from the effort to resist. She'd just thrown the two of them under the bus. At least she'd managed to avoid mentioning Lara specifically, even though in her mind she'd included the potentiality of Lara into her plural statement.

The mage dropped his hands to his sides and Naya thought Meiling might have finally ceased her convulsing. She couldn't be certain though, not with the way his eyes bored into hers with all the subtlety of a drill used for cranial surgery.

"And why is it important that you're the heir to this MacLeod fellow?"

"Because his bloodline is the only one strong enough to properly accept werewolf magic. All over the world, there've been increasing problems with werewolves. More often than not now, the magic kills them before they can even go through their first shift, and if it doesn't kill them early, it almost always kills them when they're in their first shift. And if they happen to be one of the few to survive the initial transformation, then they have defects."

Dammit, she was all but giving him a dissertation on her deepest secrets!

"What kind of defects?"

"Debilitating weakness. Deformities of their wolves. Decreased magic. Senses that aren't consistently heightened as they should be. Shorter lifespans, we're guessing based on the fact that they lack the usual strength of werewolves. We don't have the same advantages as wolf shifters, but we do have their same power when we're in our wolf forms."

"Greater even, wouldn't you say, when you're under the power of the moon?"

"No, I wouldn't say that."

"You can't lie to me. I've seen it."

"Well, I haven't."

"So you're telling me that you and your twin here are supposed to breed so that you can provide offspring strong enough to properly process werewolf magic?"

Her jaw hardened in rebellion. Her heart thumped as she tried not to answer. Sweat pricked her scalp. But in the end, she grunted out her answer anyway.

"Yes."

"And this is why the hunters are after you?"

"Yes."

"Is there anything else that would make you a specific target?"

"No."

"You're the salvation of the werewolf beast," he

said without inflection, but Naya still was urged to answer.

"Yes."

Then he did the most unexpected thing of all. Whisking his eyes across her twin and then absently around the storehouse, he began laughing.

Laughing.

His mirth rang out across the expanse of the warehouse. Naya scowled viciously at him before realizing this was her chance to check on Meiling.

Her sister's body was finally still and relaxed. She appeared to be melting into the aftereffects of so much tension and pain.

"You okay?" Naya whispered to her.

Meiling opened her mouth to answer, but when no sound came out, she nodded instead. She didn't, however, open her eyes.

It wasn't perfect, but it was definitely better.

Naya winced at the thought of the steep cost of sparing her sister more pain. Now the dark mage, who had more power than any sorcerer she'd ever heard of, knew that she and Meiling were the singular hope of werewolves. Lara, at least, was safe.

The mage's amusement devolved into rumbling chuckles when the door opened once more and another man, framed in daylight, entered swiftly, making his way over to the asshole with a penchant for causing pain.

"What is it, Matthias?" the dark mage asked.

"I received a call from Édouard." Matthias, a man in his thirties with tight curls, then cast a questioning glance at Naya and Meiling.

"Continue. They're irrelevant."

Acid swept up Naya's body to burn at the back of her throat. Irrelevant? That couldn't be good.

"Cassia is on her way, and she's angry."

"Oh?" For the first time, the mage's interest sounded truly piqued. "Did he say why?"

"No, not directly. Édouard guards her secrets closely."

"Yes. Quite annoying of him."

Matthias nodded once in acknowledgment of the sentiment. "He did, however, infer that she just experienced a serious disappointment having something to do with"—Matthias' attention swept over the sisters for the first time—"them."

The dark mage faced them once more. "Well, well, well, isn't that something?"

"I believe so," Matthias said, though it was clearly a rhetorical question.

The mage whirled around to face Matthias so quickly that the other man flinched, then immediately attempted to conceal his reaction.

"Did you tell Édouard that I captured two of them instead of the one?"

"No, Master, I did not. Édouard only knows that you completed the one mission with success."

"As was expected."

"Yes."

"And were you able to glean anything else from your conversation with Édouard that might help us understand why Cassia wants the one girl so much?"

"No, but I do believe they're traveling back from someplace in the United Kingdom."

The mage stilled, and Naya could all but feel the wheels turning in his mind.

"Édouard sounded like he was on her private jet, and I overheard someone talking, saying something about how dreary the weather always is in the UK."

"Very good, Matthias. Very good indeed."

"Thank you, Master."

Naya was surprised the man wasn't bowing and adding, 'I aim to please.' He appeared ready to lick the mage's shiny shoes—happily.

"Be sure not to reveal to Édouard under any circumstances that there are two of them. I'll give Cassia one, as agreed, and then she can owe me a favor and her support for when I choose to move on one of the wolf packs."

The mage looked straight at Naya. "I'll keep the

other one. If Cassia thinks they're worthy of her secret experiments she thinks none of us know about, then perhaps she'll be worth mine."

Naya barely registered Meiling tensing in her arms over the way her own muscles tightened. When the mage tried to meet her eyes again, she wouldn't allow it, though this time it was as much so he couldn't witness her dread—or perhaps her defeat—as it was to keep him out of her mind.

CHAPTER THREE

BRUNO

WHEN THE DENSE darkness that weighed down his mind finally began to fade, with a panicked gasp, Bruno emerged from the spell the mage cast on him. He sucked in breath as if he'd been drowning, all at once remembering everything that had taken place before he'd been forced under.

Naya. Lara.

Whirling around as his heart began to race, he discovered Clove facedown in a small pool of her own drool, sleeping soundly. She snored softly as if she were purring.

The glowing red dome that had held them captive was gone. Not a trace of their prison remained.

"Clove," he growled, shaking her. The turmoil of emotions pounding through him made anything more civilized impossible. "Clove," he ground out again when she didn't move.

But no matter how much he jostled her or how loudly he called her name, she remained victim to the dark sorcerer's magic.

Jumping to his feet, he tilted his nose in the air and searched for signs of Naya and Lara. Oddly, he didn't find Lara's scent, but he did identify Naya's. The same one that clung to her sheets and bath towels and had enchanted his senses.

Briefly, he debated the wisdom of abandoning Clove in her current vulnerable state to follow Naya's trail. His thoughts firing quickly, he whipped down to her, slung her over his back in a fireman's carry, and jogged along the same path the mage had taken when he'd hovered an unconscious Naya and Lara ahead of him, stealing the women away.

Brother Wolf paced inside him, urging him to go faster, to save the women who meant more to him than any others. *He was supposed to protect them!*

All too soon, however, Naya's scent abruptly ended.

Bruno drew to a sudden stop, Clove's chin bouncing against his hard back. Spinning wildly in place, he sniffed the air. But there was nothing. Not even the scent of that foul sorcerer.

Grunting loudly, he searched for the sun from

among the sprawling tree canopies. Given that it was late spring in the Rockies, the way the sun had already dipped below the mountaintops in the distance told him that he and Clove had been out for several hours.

Even so, that shouldn't be enough time for Naya's scent to fade, not from a shifter like him.

Magic. The answer bubbled up inside him, causing another low growl to rip free.

A sorcerer as powerful as the man with the glowing red eyes could probably mask a scent trail with a single flick of his hand.

And if he wasn't just a wizard who'd given himself over to darkness ... if he was one of the immortals Zasha and Quannah warned them about...

Then a bad situation was so much worse.

If he couldn't follow Naya's scent, then he'd be better off regrouping and informing Maverick. The alpha would have resources he didn't have so far away from his pack.

As he set off at a steady jog in the opposite direction, back toward Rocky Mountain Pack territory, holding Clove's legs tightly against his chest, he wondered what his alpha could possibly be doing in the United States.

Lara definitely seemed flightier than what he'd seen

of Naya, but Bruno knew his alpha better than that. Lara might be almost fairy-like in her connection to the forest and all of nature, and while this degree of being in tune with her surroundings might suggest she was disconnected from the reality of pack politics and the danger of the hunters, Bruno knew otherwise. Lara was highly intelligent, extremely perceptive, and never rash. It was part of what made her such an excellent leader.

He couldn't think of a single reason why she'd abandon their pack to travel here while he was away. Tomás, the gamma of the Andes Mountain Pack, was plenty competent, or the pack magic would have never appointed him to the role, but he lacked the strength and power Lara and Bruno had. While Bruno was beta of the pack, it was only because the pack's magic had decreed it so. He and Lara both understood that his wolf was strong enough to rival hers.

Though their pack hadn't been under any particular threat when he set off for North America, an attack from hunters was always a possibility. They never stopped searching for them, pursuing them, looking to wipe all wolf shifters from the face of the earth. Lara would have never deprived their wolves of her protection while he was gone, and she especially wouldn't have traveled so far as to not be able to return in time to defend their pack if it became necessary.

He couldn't think of a single explanation for her presence, and yet it was undeniable. His alpha was here, and along with his mate, she was in grave danger.

Mate.

Bruno didn't bother denying the title that his Brother Wolf so vehemently claimed. There'd be time for that later.

First, he had to get Naya and Lara back.

He and his wolf wouldn't be able to rest until they were returned; he knew it already.

Tree limbs and brush whipped by as he increased his speed. Clove was petite and he sailed through the woods with her across his back. As soon as he was able to pick up a worn trail, he ran even faster.

It didn't take him long to reach the heart of the pack's complex. Even so, it was too long.

No one had to tell Bruno that each minute that ticked by diminished the chances that he'd get either woman back. He could feel time passing as if each second were carving into his flesh, leaving a bloody, gaping gash behind.

"Where's Maverick?" he shouted at the first shifter he came across.

Bruno didn't even slow down as the answer trailed behind him. *The Huddle.*

He trained his focus on the center point of the pack's complex, sprinting all out as if he were vying for a gold medal.

———

"AT LEAST WE know Lara is still alive," Bruno offered lamely after he'd finished recounting what went down to Maverick. Brother Wolf bristled at the fact that Bruno couldn't say the same about Naya. His wolf was certain she was his mate, yet until they bonded as such, Bruno couldn't know anything about her or where she might be more than any other schmo.

He growled, but nobody paid him much mind. He'd been doing lots of it, along with grunting and snarling, since he'd charged into the Huddle like he was on fire.

Maverick had been there, deep in discussion with River and Blake, the beta and gamma of the Rocky Mountain Pack. One glance at Bruno with Clove strewn across his back and Maverick had run to meet him, receiving Clove into his arms as Bruno's chest heaved—more from desperation than exertion. To find Naya or Lara, he could have run all night.

"I'm not sure the pack bond would hold with her in the Andes and me here, but with her nearby I'd certainly know if something happened to her."

Only, that wasn't entirely true; he recognized it even as he spoke. But Bruno couldn't bring himself to specify that he'd only feel it if his alpha *died* ... if the link that connected her to every one of her pack wolves were severed ... if the pack magic no longer ran through her veins because her heart no longer pumped. She could be tortured to within an inch of her life, but so long as she remained alive, he wouldn't know it.

Maverick, River, and Blake glanced at him from where they sat around a small table strewn with papers, sympathy blazing in their gazes, as if they knew the turn of his thoughts.

Clove, who'd risen like the dead from a grave with such a sudden start that she'd startled all four hardened men, huffed. "Enough with the wishy-washy shit. I get that this Lara's your alpha and all, but she's not my alpha, and she's not my priority. If we can grab Lara when we get my girl back, then dandy. I don't want anybody in that evil asshole's villainous clutches. He can eat glass and shit blood. But Naya's our focus. She's *my* focus."

The tiny woman was pacing ferociously along the open aisle that lined the dais at the front of the large room, the men atop the raised platform staying out of her way. Since she'd woken, she'd done nothing that didn't have to do with getting Naya back beyond wiping away the dried trail of drool along one cheek.

Maverick hadn't even tried to send her away. Bruno understood that any attempts would have been wasted effort. Despite her delicate stature, she reminded him of an untrained adolescent wolf pup with a bone she would *not* release.

"Don't worry, Clove," Maverick said. "She's our focus too."

Bruno tried not to react, but he flinched at the casual dismissal of his alpha.

Maverick rose from his seat to pat Bruno on the back on his way to stalk across the dais. "That doesn't mean we won't get Lara back too. They're together. We won't leave Lara behind."

"Good." The one word was a low, deep, gritty growl.

When Bruno got his hands on the sorcerer with the wicked red magic, he was going to rip him in half. He just had to find a way to get at him before he managed to trap him inside one of his crimson domes.

"So what's our plan?" Clove asked.

River and Blake tensed, though Maverick didn't.

Pack wolves were supposed to show their leaders respect, especially their alpha.

But Maverick was so distraught over Naya's disappearance that he either didn't notice Clove's possible impertinence or didn't care.

"We're going after her as soon as it gets fully dark."

"Wait, what?" Bruno sat up straight as his brow furrowed. "We have to know where they are to go after them." *Obviously.*

"And we do." Maverick folded his hands behind his back and looked at River across the stage. "Go check on things. Make sure the team's going to be ready to roll out in"—he consulted his watch—"an hour and twenty-three minutes."

River was clearly already aware of the plan. He stood and left the room.

Bruno glanced from his retreating back to Maverick, Blake, and then Clove. Only Clove looked as astonished as he felt.

"What's going on?" Clove asked, and again Maverick overlooked how she was questioning her alpha.

Bruno had been around some alphas who were brutal in their demands for the respect due their rank. In those packs, the wolves gave their obedience, but not their respect.

Maverick sighed before answering, but stared right at Clove as he did. "We finally got Naya's tracker to work."

"Uh, excuse me?" Clove said. "You put a *tracker* on my girl? Ever heard of motherfucking privacy?" But before Maverick or anyone else could say a word, she barreled right on. "Ordinarily, I'd be pissed about it. But right now, Mav, I could kiss you smack on those pretty lips of yours. Only I won't so no one accuses me of macking on our hot alpha."

It was like she had no filter to process her thoughts as they streamed toward her mouth...

Clove jumped onto the dais and hugged Maverick, pressing her face into his chest, where she rubbed her cheek repeatedly against his pecs and blatantly sniffed him before finally disengaging. He was regarding her as if he knew her too well for her behavior to shock him.

Continuing to encroach on the personal space boundary of ordinary people, she tilted her head up to take him in. "How'd you get a tracker on her? I'm sure she didn't know about it, 'cause my girl doesn't keep secrets from me. So how'd you do it?"

Bruno didn't overly care how Maverick had done it, just that he had; he was all but ready to kiss the big, muscled man himself. Standing, he waited for an explanation, something he was well aware the alpha didn't owe them even if Clove wasn't.

When Maverick began speaking, relief washed over him, temporarily trumping the anguish that continually churned his insides.

"It's in her necklace."

Clove's jaw dropped before she whipped it back up and started moving it. Her eyes were wide. "In the wolf head charm you gave her when she was a baby? The one that's from her mom?"

"Yes. The one the woman gave me when she brought Naya to us."

"You sneaky bastard. Why the hell didn't you tell us this before? It would've saved us from running around like lunatics until the asshole caught us and pulled us under ... whatever creepy magic thing he does."

"I've never had to activate the tracker before. And it's been a long time since I put it inside the pendant. Think of how many showers alone Naya's taken with that thing on. I had no idea if it'd even work."

Bruno's thoughts rushed toward images of a naked Naya in the shower and Brother Wolf whined inside. He had to get her back before they both went crazy.

"You still could've told me," Clove added, but for once she sounded dubious.

"And trust such an important secret to the biggest gossip in the pack?"

"Ach." Clove brought a hand to her chest, credibly mimicking offense, though Bruno wasn't buying it. For how brash she was, he didn't think she was deluded into thinking herself something she wasn't.

Maverick moved on, ignoring her theatrics. "It finally came online, thank fuck, and her captor will have no way of knowing the thing's drawing us to her unless he scans her for electronic signals, which he should have no reason to do."

"Especially since she was wearing nothing more than a bra and little workout shorts," Bruno added, his thoughts racing to this equally tempting image, then skipping to when she'd thrown him to the mat and pinned him there. Straddling him. His body had heated to her as if flames had coursed across her exposed skin.

"Uh, not a lot of places to hide things," he added lamely while working to rein in his thoughts.

Maverick continued: "Boone's mages are on their way, but they might not get here before we have to leave. Zasha and Quannah of the Smoky Mountain Pack are also going to help, but they're gathering an assault team from their pack and are going to join us later. They were going to help us when it was just Naya missing, but now that we know two wolves have been taken, and that the man who took them is likely the immortal they described, or at least one like it, they'll get here fast, I'd bet on it. Zasha and Quannah both have a debt to settle."

"And enough determination to make it happen," Blake added.

Maverick nodded. "Yeah, for sure. But we're not gonna wait on them. The longer Naya's beyond the pack's safety, the greater the risk. We're not waiting a second longer than we need to. As soon as we're under the cover of night, we're moving out. Naya comes home tonight."

"And Lara," Bruno inserted.

Maverick looked at him with shielded, cautious eyes. "I hope so, Bruno. I really do. Those two women mean more to the shifter world than what they mean to us. If we lose them..." He cleared his throat and absently scratched at his forearm. "If we lose them, we lose more than two amazing women and werewolves."

"We lose all werewolves," Blake offered softly, when nothing about the large, powerful-looking man suggested he could be that gentle.

"What we can't lose is hope," Bruno said. "We'll

get them back. Tonight." He needed to hear himself say it aloud. "How many are coming with us?"

"Less than half the pack. Around two hundred. The rest will stay to guard our home. Most of them will spread out into the background of wherever we find Naya, there just in case we need them or the situation is more ... complicated ... than we thought. I'm leaving River in charge here. We'll have a small assault team going in with Blake and me."

"And me," Bruno said, uncaring that he was giving another pack's alpha a command. He was going. End of story.

Maverick simply nodded, accepting.

"And me," Clove said.

"No."

"What, why not? You let this guy go and you barely know him. You've known me all my life."

"Which is why I know you'll be a liability if you come along."

She gaped, then pouted, her jaw sliding from side to side.

"You have many strengths, Clove, none of which lie in stealth and lethality of attack. When your ability to fly through the trees is an asset, or when I need someone to spot intruders in the forest that surrounds us, you'd better believe I'll be calling on you."

Clove's jaw relaxed—fractionally. But her eyes still blazed heatedly.

"If Naya shows up here for some reason, I want you to use the pack link to let me know immediately."

"Yeah, yeah. I got it. I'm gonna be the phone bitch. I get to stay behind and do a mani-pedi while you all do the real stuff."

"Call it what you like. The assault team going in tonight is going to kill on sight. I'm not taking any risks when it comes to Naya"—he glanced at Bruno—"or Lara. We slice and dice first, ask questions later. No one messes with Naya. I swore an oath to protect her from all harm. I intend to keep it."

Then the alpha faced Blake. "Let me know if Boone, these mages, or any of the Smoky Mountain Pack arrive before we leave."

"You got it."

"Meet me at my cabin in an hour." And with that, the alpha strode from the room, purpose vibrating through every sure step. Whatever he was leaving to do, Bruno had no doubt it was important.

Blake rose from his chair, rubbing his hands over his face, before studying Bruno and then Clove. "You might want to get some rest before we go. You both look like shit."

Clove scowled. "Gee, thanks, Blake. You're a fucking peach."

Bruno didn't bother to address the gamma's suggestion. There wasn't a chance that he could shut down his mind—or Brother Wolf—long enough to do any kind of resting.

"I want to help. Tell me what I can do."

Blake met his eyes for a moment, taking in the fury and determination there, before nodding. "Follow me, then."

"Before we go, have a pen and paper you can spare? An envelope too? I need to get a letter off to my pack before we leave. They need to know what's going on so they can prepare."

He left off the rest of his thoughts, his fears. *In case Lara doesn't ever come back.*

As beta of the Andes Mountain Pack, his responsibility was twofold: to the wolves in his pack, and to his alpha.

He wouldn't walk away from his alpha now, but even if Lara hadn't been a prisoner as well, he wouldn't have been able to walk away from Naya.

His loyalties were divided and he didn't even care.

He wasn't leaving until Naya was in his arms and Lara was safe.

Brother Wolf paced inside him, making Bruno's anxiety feel more pronounced than it actually was.

Too much was at stake.

Too much could be lost.

And also ... so much could be won.

Brother Wolf growled. Naya was coming home to him.

Mate.

CHAPTER FOUR

NAYA

THE TWO IDENTICAL women stood near each other as if their mere proximity could protect them from what was to come. Naya itched with the need to huddle even closer to Meiling, but revealing weakness wouldn't help either of them, and that's exactly how their captor would interpret their reliance on each other.

Besides, Naya didn't *need* Meiling. She'd gone her entire life completely unaware of her sister's existence. How could she suddenly need somebody she'd never known?

But their captor unnerved her, the way he looked at them with those cold, calculating eyes, the way they flared with red every once in a while for no apparent reason, making Naya dread the direction of the creep's thoughts.

Since the dark mage had arrived, he hadn't left, and the guard he'd had stationed watching them before hadn't returned. The man their captor called Matthias had come and gone several times, always to carry out the mage's orders.

The way Matthias moved revealed that he was a vampire—a very old vampire. His gait wasn't so much a walk as a glide, and he covered ground too quickly. He'd be standing next to his master, then Naya would blink and Matthias would be at the door.

His agility and speed suggested that he could withstand the sun, and that Naya and Meiling were in real danger of having every drop of their blood drained at warp speed. No matter how strong the two women were, and despite how hard they'd trained to endure any assault, the old vampire would be a worthy opponent, a challenge they might not survive. But an opponent they, at least, had a chance of taking down before he could kill them.

And yet the centuries-old vampire was the lesser threat.

The dark mage with the eerie glowing red eyes? Naya had no idea what he was capable of or how he might attack them.

She worked to control her reaction so that the mage wouldn't, at least, realize how much he was getting to her. She longed to have a conversation with Meiling, to see if her sister had come up with a plan for their defense. Beyond "fight for their lives with everything they had when the mage released them from the magical dome," Naya hadn't come up with a single thing that would help.

And that deficiency was burning a hole in her stomach like acid. She had to figure out something to do. They'd only get one chance at escape, if they got one at all.

Adrenaline pulsed just below the surface of her skin, making her body tense until she noticed and forced her muscles to relax—only to have the same process begin anew all over again.

Beyond telling them that this woman Cassia was coming for her, the mage hadn't told them much. When he spoke with Matthias, he did so softly; with their preternatural hearing, Naya and Meiling could make out every word he said. But the mage and the vampire clearly knew each other well. They spoke to each other with the truncated commands and utterances of people—*creatures*—who understood what went unsaid as much as what was spoken aloud.

So it took Naya a moment to realize that the mage was talking to them, with Matthias at his side, returned from who knew where, looking down at his master on the couch, the dim red glow of the mage's eyes illuminating the vampire's lean, strong frame.

The mage's words filtered through to her mind with a delay, and when she finally registered what he'd said, she jerked before she could stop herself.

He laughed the same low sound she'd come to despise in the brief time since he'd taken them.

He had said, "Cassia will be here soon. It's time to separate you."

"You're right to fear her," he said. "Maybe that fear will manage to keep you alive. Maybe, but not likely."

Naya felt Meiling stiffen beside her as the mage once more laughed at their predicament.

Only, he'd misinterpreted their reaction—at least he had Naya's. She hadn't feared a woman she hadn't yet met.

The need to defend her sister, her identical reflection, waged inside Naya, making it difficult to concentrate on what else the mage was saying. But she made herself listen closely.

"Cassia has fairly earned her nickname, *Filema Thanatou*. Do you know what it means?"

"Kiss of death," Meiling said, surprising Naya, and the mage.

He arched one of his dark, caterpillar eyebrows. "And how is it that you know Greek? You don't look

Greek. Though it's true that looks sometimes deceive."

"Why is it so surprising that I might understand Greek?" Meiling asked, addressing him for the first time since their capture. "Many scholars do. Or perhaps I know Greek the same way you do."

That second dark, furry eyebrow rose to meet the other. "Because you've lived for over a thousand years and were around when people were still refined and cared to actually educate themselves? Modern day universities are a joke compared to the gatherings of ancient philosophers."

"Which you wouldn't have been around to see. That was way before your time if you're only a thousand years old."

Only a thousand years old? Naya felt like crying out, but she schooled her face into impassivity instead. Meiling was smart! She was drawing information out of him that might prove useful. Already, it was likely he was one of the immortals Zasha and Quannah of the Smoky Mountain Pack had come to Colorado to warn Maverick about.

Vampires could reach a thousand years old, though it was highly uncommon, to Naya's understanding. The bloodsuckers were acutely territorial, becoming enemies to their own species as they competed over hunting grounds—and waged war against each other to gain or maintain them.

The dark mage didn't seem like a vampire. For the undead, he possessed unheard of magic, and he hadn't once eyed either of their jugulars, whereas Matthias had checked out their pulse points multiple times in subtle flicks of his attention. Naya wasn't even sure the vampire had noticed; it was like a tick with them.

Crimson flared in a rapid burst, obscuring the mage's dark eyes for a moment. "You have no idea what you're talking about, little girl," he told Meiling, a dangerous undercurrent tugging at his tone. "You could only dream of the people I've met over the centuries."

Meiling scoffed in a manner most unlike her. "If you're suggesting you're a thousand years old, then you were born in the medieval ages. I have a pretty good idea what your surroundings were really like. People dumping bodily waste in the streets with no thought to hygiene. Right next to the piles of horse manure. Chamber pots instead of indoor plumbing, all that shit airing out while people slept. Probably a lot of mouth breathing going on, huh? No one showered. They used perfumes to mask body odors, of which I'm sure there were a great deal. And clothes probably never came clean with how soiled they were when they were finally washed. Were your clothes stiff enough to walk off on their own?"

Naya couldn't decide whether to applaud her twin or clamp a hand over her mouth to keep it shut.

The red glow in the mage's eyes sparked like embers as he stood, his ire wafting off him so tangibly that Naya briefly wondered if it could be part of his magic.

"Ignorant girl, those were the commoners." His upper lip curled with his distaste, revealing bright white teeth, and a slightly crooked bottom row. "There is nothing common about *me*."

"The Sun King Louis XIV took two baths during his lifetime. Same for Queen Isabella of Castille. King James I never bathed, infecting the rooms he frequented with lice. Are you suggesting that these royals were ... commoners?"

The air vibrated with peril, and Naya inched closer to her sister.

"I have more examples I could provide, if you'd like. Perhaps some figures who lived closer to the time of your birth?"

The mage stared at Meiling. Just ... stared.

Matthias pretended to examine something on the sole of one of his shiny leather shoes, taking a step backward in the process.

Oh. Hell. If the centuries-old vampire was retreating...

Naya latched on to Meiling's forearm and pulled her away from the edge of the red dome. A meaningless gesture, really, since the mage had them trapped like insects in a spider's web. They couldn't go anywhere until he dropped the magic that held them contained. But Naya still felt better carving out some distance between Meiling and that blazing red stare.

The dark mage, who was likely an immortal, must possess immense power. While Naya hadn't actually met any witches or wizards in person, she knew they had to focus to maintain their magic, and all but the most powerful could only perform one spell at a time. But the immortal? The red dome didn't so much as waver while he held full conversations ... while he wasn't even in the building with them.

The glow diminished, and Naya was able to trace the dark irises of the mage's eyes once more. The cold, blatant lack of compassion wasn't much better.

"Are you two about to give me some girl-on-girl action, all huddled together and scared? Are you about to ... console each other?" He chuckled at his depraved joke, making Naya's skin crawl. This guy was grade-A pervy asshole, immortal or no immortal.

"It's been a while since I've seen twins go down on each other."

Naya swallowed down her revulsion with effort. "I guess you gotta try to get your kicks where you can. Probably no woman in her right mind will come anywhere near you unless you force her."

Her anger had pushed Naya to speak, but she should have thought it through first. Taunting a depraved immortal was plain stupid. She attempted to at least redirect his attention.

"I bet you were a commoner, and now you're just trying to ... compensate."

"Yeah," Meiling chimed in. "Did you hang out in Queen Elizabeth's court with a fancy powdered wig? Did the lice make it down to your pubes? I've heard crabs are a bitch."

Naya guessed that Meiling was ramping up the crudeness to incite him to focus back on her, and away from any sexual attention directed at them.

Meiling took half a step toward him while Naya tried to pull her back.

"It seems that I'll enjoy teaching you the correct version of events, little girl." Eyes trained on Meiling, he scoffed, the nostrils of his long nose flaring slightly. "It is so fun to deconstruct arrogance. Matthias, change of plans. We're taking this one instead."

Naya's blood froze.

"Yes, Master," Matthias responded right away.

"You know where to take her."

"I do. Shall I go now? Édouard tells me Cassia is twenty minutes out."

Without warning or a second to prepare, the immortal walked partway into the dome, which didn't so much as flicker as he passed through it, and clamped his hand around Meiling's wrist.

Plan or no plan, Naya wasn't about to let him take her newfound twin without a fight.

She pressed her fingers together, making her hand a straight edge, and struck his wrist hard and fast. While he released Meiling, Naya registered that her sister had pulled one of her blades. But Naya didn't stop. Sliding behind him, she punched, *one, two, three.* To the kidneys, to the spleen, to the spine, where she felt vertebrae break.

The immortal grunted and she heard more than saw Meiling slice into him with her blade.

Naya slid around to his side and slammed her fist into his junk. Vampire, shifter, immortal, men were still men, and with this guy, who overpowered them so easily, she had no problem fighting dirty. In fact, it was smart.

Meiling stabbed her blade under his ribcage and up, Naya figured, into his uncaring heart.

And still Matthias waited calmly on the other side of the red dome. There was no rushing to his master's aid. No call for help. No panic.

Which made Naya freak out a little bit.

While Meiling continued to slice and dice, Naya pulled his arm against her chest, holding it with both of hers, and yanked it in the wrong direction.

Several bones snapped loudly.

It was the last thing she heard as a red light flashed through her vision a moment before darkness swathed her in its depths all over again.

———

NAYA WOKE to the sound of whirring engines and opened her eyes, blinking up at a low, rounded ceiling. A glance to the side confirmed that she was on a plane, sprawled on the floor beneath a small plastic oval window.

"Oh good," a woman said in a voice that was as smooth and seductive as silk—it made Naya's skin crawl. "You can strap yourself in. We're about to take off."

A strikingly beautiful woman looked down at her. She had long, shiny black hair pulled back into artful braids across her head; smooth, unmarred creamy skin; and pale violet eyes framed in black lashes, making them pop as if they were backlit. Plump, cherry-red lips curled up in an attempt at a smile, which failed to convince Naya, though she imagined it'd dazzle anyone less wary.

This had to be the "kiss of death" woman. Her eyes were even harder and colder than the dark mage's, and Naya wouldn't have thought that possible when she was last with the dark mage.

"My name is Cassia, darling, and you are my guest. Come, sit next to me. Let's catch up."

Naya gently rolled to her side, and when the world didn't lurch at the movement, she rose to sit on the carpeted floor, hugging her legs to her chest.

"We need to get you some more appropriate garments. Tell me, did Cyrus take advantage of you and leave you in your undergarments?" She asked as one would ask if she had already eaten or if she needed dinner. Her little act was all a ruse.

"Assuming Cyrus is the immortal who took ... me"—Naya had almost slipped and included Meiling; her heartbeat picked up and she willed it to slow, unsure if this woman, likely also an immortal, could hear it.

Cassia nodded. "That's Cyrus all right. He loves touting his immortality, as if he did something to earn it." She smiled coldly. "In case you were wondering, he didn't."

Another fact Naya filed away, thankful that her mind felt sharp despite her recent unconsciousness.

"Well, then he didn't sexually assault me, thanks for asking." Naya's smile was as cold as Cassia's. "Am I a guest? Or am I your prisoner?"

"That depends on you, darling." Cassia spun the *darling* until it sounded like a threat all on its own. Naya noted that her accent was similar to Cyrus', a mixture of sophisticated accents that seemed to originate from several parts of the world. Or maybe it was Naya imagining things, trying to piece together crumbs to form a slice of bread so she could feel like she had some control.

She so wasn't in control.

Cassia's smile widened around her perfectly straight, perfectly white teeth, and Naya couldn't help but feel like a mouse trapped beneath a cat's paw.

"Come." She patted the cream leather captain's seat beside her. "Don't overthink things. We have much to discuss. I haven't seen you in ages, Meiling."

Naya was grateful she didn't so much as twitch at Cassia's error.

Until she could better figure out what was going on, she decided to play the game ... and hope the cat waited to devour its meal until it got whatever else it wanted.

Naya had to find out.

When Naya rose and approached the appointed seat, Cassia said, "Change first though."

Clothing was thrust at her from the side, and Naya whipped around to find a man with model-high cheekbones and perfect features.

No, not a man. A vampire. Naya heard no heartbeat behind that sculpted chest.

She took the leggings and a burgundy-colored tunic. The vamp tossed low-slung boots and socks beside her seat.

"Where should I change?" Naya asked.

"Here," Cassia said while the vamp retreated to the front of the cabin, where he joined five others, all staring at her.

"We wouldn't want you to run into any trouble in the lav, now would we?"

"What if I have to pee?"

"Do you?"

"Yes."

Cassia flicked a hand at the vampire who'd just sat, and he bounced back up to his feet. "Assist her," she ordered him, which Naya discovered meant: *stand next to the open door while Naya relieves herself.*

Yeah, she was a guest all right. One captor had just handed her over to another.

But this captor thought she was her twin for some reason.

Naya intended to find out why.

Finally dressed in real clothing again, she took the chair next to the immortal woman, stretching her legs out and getting comfortable.

If Cassia wanted to pretend she was a guest, then Naya was going to pretend all right.

"So, what kind of food do you have on board?"

Cassia flicked a hand again, and a second vamp jumped to his feet while the jet's engines roared and prepared for takeoff.

CHAPTER FIVE

BRUNO

THE HOUR-PLUS until the assault and retrieval teams were set to depart both dragged on and flew by, a contradiction that Bruno was certain had to do with the conflicting emotions whirling inside him. He was struggling to hold Brother Wolf back, who wanted to charge to the aid of his mate.

But Bruno's mind still hitched every time Brother Wolf insisted on assigning Naya that role. She probably had no idea his wolf was mating them whether they liked it or not.

Apprehension for Naya's reaction to him as a potential mate swirled inside him, along with concern for her safety. He simply had to get her back —and fast. He couldn't take this internal turmoil much longer. Used to possessing a peaceful balance, he didn't feel like himself. He hadn't even come together with his mate yet and already he felt different than he'd ever imagined. She was changing his life whether or not she was aware of it.

There was a lot to do to organize two hundred wolf shifters to secure Naya's rescue, but Bruno had to admit, Maverick ran a smooth operation. His own pack in the Andes couldn't have responded any better or more swiftly.

He, Maverick, River, Blake, and a few other wolves, men and one woman, crowded into Maverick's cabin, filling the suite that adjoined his modest living quarters.

Of everyone there, Bruno was the only one Maverick had tried to push out. When Bruno's wolf had reared and growled, Maverick had snarled back, before relaxing and rolling his eyes, muttering something about stupid wolves trying to claim mates that weren't theirs. That had only made Brother Wolf growl louder, but Maverick had waved Bruno in after that. Since then, he'd treated the beta as if he were part of the team, equally invested in returning Naya safe and sound.

Every man and woman within the wood-paneled space was armed to the teeth, blades, guns, and other assorted weapons strapped to every conceivable available surface on their bodies. Even so, Bruno would have bet that everyone there could kill just as expeditiously with their bare hands. They had the stoic, determined faces of warriors, of those who'd been hunted all their lives simply for being who and what they were, a detail they were powerless to change. Their eyes were the same haunted, hooded gazes he saw in his own pack, wolves who'd been raised amid a constant threat to their lives and to everyone they loved.

Maverick was leaning over a large glass coffee table in the center of the room, pointing to a large building circled in ominous red on a city map.

"This is where she is. The signal hasn't moved since it came online."

Maverick hadn't bothered concealing the fact that he'd placed a tracker on Naya without her knowledge. He hadn't apologized for his actions either. Every shifter there appeared relieved their alpha had thought ahead so they could find Naya, savior to the werewolves. The end seemed to justify the means.

They were getting their wolf back.

"The building's in an industrial zone, and it's largely abandoned from what we could tell. All the buildings nearby are big, like hangars and lumberyards, that kind of size, and only a few of the buildings in a ten-block radius showed signs of recent activity. Since we'll be going in when it's dark, we shouldn't have to worry about innocent bystanders in the area. And no one inside the warehouse will be innocent—no one but Naya."

A few growls rumbled through the room.

"We don't know one-hundred-percent for sure that the person who took her is an immortal, but it's likely. Either way, remember, the guy has magic, and a fuck-ton of it from what Bruno tells us. Powerful magic. Use all your senses, not just your sniffers. They snatched Naya right out from under us, without a single scent trail to follow. They're masking themselves, so make sure you don't get caught unaware 'cause someone managed to sneak up on you."

"Sounds like something the hunters would do, use magic against us," one of the wolves said.

"Yeah, fucking hypocrites," a woman added. "Got no problem crucifying us 'cause we got magic, but then they got no problem using it on us. All day long, they'll use magic on us."

Maverick leaned back from the table, sliding into the armchair behind him. "Can't be sure it isn't hunters. The immortal might be working with them. Why not? Though it's not really their style to just snatch one of us."

Blake said, "Seems like they'd have taken us all

out once they were in here. Maybe with some of those missiles Zasha and Quannah told us about."

"Or some silver aerosol," another male wolf interjected. "The fuckers. I'd like to shove a silver aerosol up one of their clenched asses."

"Get in line," the woman said. Her brown hair was pulled up into a severe, no-nonsense ponytail. Bruno had no doubt she could kick someone's ass so hard it'd end up ramming the back of their teeth.

Maverick said, "All we really know about the immortals is that they don't die even when you blow them up and hack them into little bits and pieces."

"So what do we do if it really is one of them?" the woman asked.

"I don't know yet." Maverick ran a hand through his hair before letting it drop heavily onto his lap. "Boone from the Northwestern Pack has some mages..." Every wolf beyond Bruno, River, and Blake snarled. "...that he says he can trust."

"That's an oxymoron," one of them said. "There are no trustworthy mages. They're all scumbags willing to sell their souls to the hunters," another added.

Maverick frowned. "Some of them, no doubt. But Boone swears by these guys, and I trust Boone. He's a good guy and a good leader. He'll be alpha of his pack someday."

Several of the wolves tensed as if they wanted to question their alpha; none of them did.

"He says these guys aren't like any other wizards we've met. They're on their way. It doesn't look like they're going to get here before we leave, and I'm not waiting for them. I'm not waiting a single second longer to get Naya back."

Nods circled the room.

"But if we run into an immortal, if an immortal took our girl, then we'll do our best to reduce the asswad to tiny, little bits. And then hopefully we can get one of these wizards to tell us how to kill him. For good."

Maverick signaled to River with a nod, and River said, "We've picked up between three and six heat signatures moving around inside the building. Several more outside, maybe a dozen. People coming in and out of the place."

"All of you in here will lead small assault teams. We'll park our vehicles far enough out that supes won't pick up on us, and then we'll go the rest of the way on foot. Before you leave, River will tell you each where to park and where to position yourselves. The rest of the wolves coming with us will spread out in the area around us," Maverick said. "They'll stay out of sight. Backup I hope we won't need, but won't hesitate to call on if we do. We'll approach the warehouse in stealth mode. Keep out of sight until you have no choice. We don't want them to know we're coming so they don't hurt Naya before we can get to her."

Tension crackled in the room, making the space feel even more cramped, proof of how important Naya was to this pack. As important as Lara was to his.

Bruno had assumed Maverick would inform the others that he and Clove had seen the immortal mage taking Naya *and* Lara with him, but Maverick had surprised him. The alpha had told only his beta and gamma, asking Clove to keep the information secret until he told her otherwise.

Bruno suspected everyone in the cabin would have easily protected the secret of Lara's existence, since they were so invested in protecting Naya, but the fewer people who knew there were two werewolf saviors, the better. And the greater chance they had at sparing the werewolves from extinction.

"Naya's tough as nails," the woman commented. "Even if it's an immortal who's got her, no doubt she's making him work for it."

"Which means that maybe she's pissing him off," Blake said.

That likelihood hung in the air, before he added, "We've gotta go." He exchanged an urgent look with

Maverick, who stood, patting down the many weapons stashed around his body, making sure they were still in place, before grabbing a tote bag beside his chair.

"What's in there?" Bruno asked.

"Backup."

Bruno arched his brows.

"Grenades, rocket launchers, machine guns, you know."

No, Bruno hadn't. Now that he did, he was glad he was to be riding with the alpha. Once they got Naya out, it would be cathartic to blow the place, taking out every supe who'd dared put their hands on his woman.

"Time to roll, everyone," Maverick continued. "I want cells on every single one of you, but you leave them in the car. We're going to be creeping up on supes, which means no flashing lights and no buzzing from vibrating cells. Before you ditch your phones, every car checks in with River via text. I want River to know who's parked and approaching, got it? He'll relay the info to me."

Since River was the beta to the Rocky Mountain Pack, he could use the telepathic link between him and his alpha and not be overheard by anyone else in the pack.

"Wait to approach until you get the go-ahead

from River. Keep quiet, even through the pack link. We all need to focus. But if it's an emergency, if you see something we all need to know to stay safe and get Naya out of there without a scrape on her, you don't hesitate to use the pack link. I don't care if every wolf from here to Idaho and Wyoming hears you, use it if you need it, but only if it's a real need."

"And what are we doing with the supes there?" Blake asked. "Are we taking hostages?"

Maverick hesitated. "If it's safe to every pack wolf to take hostages, then do it. We need to figure out how they found out about Naya. See how far the breach spreads and what we need to do to contain it. But..." Maverick paused to look every wolf square in the eye, including his beta and gamma, and including Bruno. "If it feels risky, if there's any chance one of us will get hurt, kill on sight. We'll figure out how to best protect Naya afterward. Number one priority here is to get Naya back home and safe, along with every single pack wolf." He paused again, jaw hard. "And if you have the immortal in your sights, you keep shooting and hacking and biting, whatever you've gotta do, you keep doing it until we can figure out how to blast the asshole to kingdom come. How fucking dare he take Naya from us!" His final snarl was echoed by every wolf there, even Bruno. Brother Wolf was ready to tear the immortal's head clear from his body for hurting his mate.

Mate.

"Get your assignments from River, then roll out. We're on our way. Bruno, you're with me."

Bruno right behind him, Maverick paused with his hand on the doorknob, looking back over his shoulder with a heavy expression as if he were trying to memorize everyone's faces just in case they didn't all make it back.

Bruno understood the look all too well. He was certain he'd sported it several times when heading out into the mountainous woods around his home to head off hunters that had come too close to his pack in their search for the wolves' sanctuary.

"Also," Mav said, "remember to be as careful leaving as coming back. Take the usual roundabout ways out of here. And always assume someone's watching. We don't want to lead hunters back here after getting Naya."

"Seems like the immortal already found us," the woman said.

"But we don't know his motivation or if he shared our location with the hunters. First, we get Naya back and then we figure out where that leaves us. If we have to uproot our pack to keep us all safe, I will."

Relocating the entire Rocky Mountain Pack

housed in Colorado's Moonlit Mountains would be a monumental undertaking. The pack looked to have been here for decades at least, what with all the infrastructure they'd built. No doubt this was the only home most of the wolves here had ever known. Bruno also had no doubt that if Maverick determined they had to move, they'd abandon it all to seek safety.

It was the way it was with all of them, no matter what part of the world they occupied.

Bruno knew the Rocky Mountain Pack had several satellite locations. They might have to move to one of those, though it was unlikely the other sites would be able to house so many of them.

"Don't worry about what comes next," Maverick said as if he could read everybody's mind. "Focus on the task at hand with everything you've got. We don't know what we're walking into, and every single one of you is as important to me as Naya is to all of us. You come back in one piece, you hear me?"

No one answered at first, as if too busy considering all that could go wrong when having a showdown with a being who *couldn't* be killed.

"You fucking hear me?" Maverick roared, alpha magic pulsing through the room. "You all come back here. Every one of our wolves comes home tonight. That's a fucking order!"

As the growls, snarls, and yips of assent rolled in, Maverick stalked through the door.

Outside, beneath the pallor of a nearly full moon, Maverick tilted his head back and howled.

The cry was loud and long, and sang to Brother Wolf. It was a battle cry.

Bruno threw his head back and joined the chorus, as wolves from all over the territory howled back at their alpha.

We are one.

We are pack.

For tonight, Bruno was one of them.

And they were bringing Naya home.

CHAPTER SIX

BRUNO

MAVERICK LED Bruno to a low-slung late-model Honda Civic that was as dark as the surrounding night. They tossed their extra weapons, of which there were many, in the back seat, where they'd be on hand in case they needed them en route to the warehouse where Naya and Lara were being kept.

The arsenal the pack had amassed was impressive, far greater than what Bruno's pack in the Andes had. His pack relied more on their shifted wolf forms for their defense, but then their circumstances were vastly different. Despite the fact that the terrain of their pack homes was loosely similar, both nestled in thickly forested mountains, Bruno's pack was so much more remote and inaccessible that they approached their defense in a guerrilla warfare style. They used the dense terrain to shield them and conceal their approach until they were close enough to ambush any enemies.

After what Bruno had learned from Zasha and Quannah about the hunters' newest toys, he'd have to discuss the solidity of their defense with Lara—just as soon as he got her back. Hunters played dirty; they always had. But if they were now attacking from the air with missiles and aerosols that dispersed silver far and wide, well, then guerrilla warfare tactics would prove insufficient. The hunters could wipe out the entire Andes Mountain Pack in mere moments.

He had to get Lara and they had to get back to their pack immediately. Until they did, every one of their wolves, men, women, and children, were exposed to a threat that killed without hesitation, mercy, or deliberation. When hunters considered an infant, they didn't see a life only just beginning, precious and worthy of respect and nurturing. They only saw a wolf shifter, a species they intended to raze from the face of the earth.

Brusquely, Bruno pushed away thoughts of his pack back home. There was nothing he could do to help them now, not from the other end of the world. But he could get their alpha back.

But his mate ... would he be able to convince Maverick to let Naya go with him once they rescued her? Because Bruno didn't see how Brother Wolf would accept his departure without the woman he barely knew but nonetheless needed as a part of his life.

Damn.

Brother Wolf insisting he'd found his mate was a complication he wasn't prepared for. He had other priorities than latching on to a woman who was practically a stranger!

He only noticed he'd growled when Maverick glanced at him as he whisked them down a one-lane road, driving fast, the engine purring. The alpha whipped them around dark corners, weaving this way and that, until they finally emerged on a dark, two-lane road.

Despite the number of shifters heading in the same direction, and the fact that they'd all left more or less at the same time, he and Maverick were alone on the road for a solid five minutes before headlights popped up behind them, far in the distance.

Like his pack, the Rocky Mountain Pack wolves were careful not to lead anyone who might be watching to their secret location. But...

"How do you keep hunters from finding you from the air? If you could find Naya and Lara from an aerial map, can't they do the same to you?"

Bruno's pack was all but concealed by the tree

canopy. Even if someone were to search for them by air, he didn't think they'd be able to spot them. Unlike Maverick's pack, they hadn't clear cut trees to make room for their dwellings, building around them instead, using all natural, local materials. Few modern supplies from the outside world made it to their homes.

Bruno noticed with a start that, while his mind had wandered, Maverick was hesitating.

"You don't trust me." Bruno didn't phrase it as a question; it was the only explanation for his delay.

Both hands locked on the steering wheel, Maverick didn't look at him when he vaguely shrugged. "You're not pack."

"That doesn't mean I'll betray you. I'm still a wolf shifter. I'm a beta of another pack. The pack magic trusts me to lead capably."

If not for Maverick's preternatural eyesight, there'd be no way he could fly down the narrow country road safely. He didn't even have his brights on. When he took another turn too fast, the tires squealed softly before he gunned the engine again. They lost the headlights that trailed behind them.

"If not for all those things," Maverick said, "I wouldn't have invited you into our home. You wouldn't be riding shotgun right now."

"Or am I riding shotgun because you want to

keep an eye on me? I'm the only non-pack wolf coming along on this rescue mission."

"I trust you as much as I'm willing to trust a wolf that's not pack. But you're riding with me because Lara is your alpha."

"And because I'm equally invested as you in returning Naya."

"Because you're deluded into thinking she's your mate. She's not your mate."

Bruno turned in his seat to stare at the side of the alpha's face. Illuminated solely by the dim lighting of the dashboard's gadgetry, his jaw was tight, his eyes hard and determined.

"Look, Mav..."

Mav's jaw clenched harder, but Bruno plowed on, refusing to adjust to call him by his full name.

"We're heading into battle together, for fuck's sake," Bruno said instead. "I'm not convinced Naya is my mate either."

Maverick flicked a look at him. The looming shadows of towering trees crept toward them.

"I don't want Naya to be my mate. I didn't come here to complicate my life. Existence as a wolf shifter is complicated enough already. I've done just fine without a mate all this time, I'm not in the market for one."

Bruno allowed a weighted pause to fill the tense air between them.

"It's Brother Wolf who needs convincing of that, not me. He's the one who's latched on to Naya and won't let go. Meanwhile, I barely know the woman. Yeah, she's beautiful and charismatic and alluring, all that. She also seems highly capable of taking care of herself—"

"Damn right she is."

"Despite how you all try to cocoon her in protective wrap..."

Maverick grunted. "Naya isn't just any werewolf. She's trained her whole life, and fucking hard, maybe harder than any of us, to make sure she honors the duty placed on her as a baby. She never asked for any of this. She never wanted it. But she handles it without complaining. She demands the most of herself, pushes herself as hard as she possibly can, all because of the responsibility she has to an entire race of shifters."

"I know, I know. I've seen the same in Lara."

"I doubt you've seen the same. I've never had the pleasure of knowing anyone so devoted to a cause at such a young age." He slowed, rolled through a stop sign, and took another turn too fast. "She's as much a daughter to me as if she were my own blood."

Bruno had seen that in how he'd interacted with

Naya. Their relationship was so much more than that of alpha and pack wolf.

"And you don't know me, so you feel like you can't fully trust me. If you did know me, we wouldn't even be having this conversation."

"I wasn't planning on having it. You brought it up."

"Actually, I asked how you prevented hunters from spotting you from the air."

Instead of finally answering the question, Maverick studied him again. "You're sure it's your wolf that feels Naya is your mate and not you?"

"What kind of question is that? I just told you so."

"I heard you."

"So why are you asking me again?" Bruno was working hard to keep the menace from his voice, but wasn't sure he succeeded. His wolf was as strong as this alpha's, a fact that Maverick must know as well. Wolves could instinctively feel the dominance of another wolf when they were in close proximity.

It was one thing to be wary of an outsider, it was another entirely to all but accuse him of lying.

When Maverick spoke this time, it was as if his thoughts were far away, oblivious to the aggression building within Bruno.

"If it's your Brother Wolf..." The alpha trailed off.

"Yeah? What if it's my Brother Wolf?" Bruno snapped. "It's not like I've kept that from you. I even implied it the night Naya was taken."

Once more, Maverick ignored the tension rolling through the beta. "If it's your Brother Wolf, then maybe he's right. I've never known our wolves to be wrong about a mate."

No. Neither had Bruno, which was why he found it all so damn unsettling. Couldn't Brother Wolf have picked a more convenient time to screw up his life?

"If Naya really is your mate," Maverick continued, "then you won't betray us, because if you betray us, you betray her."

Bruno took a few moments to drag in full breaths before replying. He was a beta of a pack. Part of his job as a leader was to remain calm when others didn't. He was supposed to be able to keep a level head no matter what.

But right then he felt like shifting and giving Maverick a discipling nip, biting him hard enough to leave a lasting mark as a reminder not to question him again.

"If you suggest that I am not a man of honor one more time, I won't let it slide. You've insulted me again and again, suggesting I'm a weasel without integrity instead of a wolf shifter, the most noble of creatures. So tell me that I'm not who I say I am, or that I won't do as I've promised one more time, and you won't like what happens next."

Bruno forced his nostrils to stop flaring. "Besides, shouldn't we be focused on getting Naya and Lara away from this immortal instead of your empty distrust?"

Brother Wolf, who took less kindly to the alpha's implications than the more rational-minded man, sat perfectly still inside Bruno. But Bruno wasn't fooled. Brother Wolf vibrated with pent-up tension. He was ready to charge and attack.

Always connected to him, always one with him, Bruno understood that this was truly Maverick's final chance.

As the alpha slowed the car and turned off the headlights, he said, "We have hackers in our pack."

"Excuse me?"

"Pack wolves who are highly experienced hackers. We realized long ago that we couldn't fully camouflage a complex the size of ours from air discovery. So our hackers alter the footage. I'm not sure of all they do because computers aren't my thing, but they point our coordinates to images of some other location ... or something like that."

"Wow. Fascinating." Brother Wolf relaxed, muscles uncoiling. "And they're able to imitate the terrain closely enough that no one notices?"

Maverick shrugged into the darkness. Bruno felt it as much as picked up the movement with his sharp shifter eyes. "Our territory is large, and we don't have buildings on most of it. They pieced together the forest and patched it over the buildings. I think. Either way, all anyone ever sees is wolves running around, maybe some people going for hikes, and that nut Clove running through trees. I'm guessing they'll think she's a monkey or a flying squirrel or something like that if they ever notice. She's concealed by the foliage."

"She's one ... unusual young woman."

"Unusual doesn't even begin to cover the half of it. You have no idea how crazy she can get. We're lucky she at least listens to orders and she stayed behind."

"That was a good idea. As invested as she is in getting her best friend back, I don't picture her being stealthy about anything."

"I'm quite certain she's not even capable of it. She lacks the requisite skill set."

The fine-tuned engine rolled nearly silently through dark streets, now wide enough to allow large Mack trucks to come through. Occasionally, a few bald bulbs illuminated the front and back of large, unadorned buildings.

They'd reached the industrial zone that, somewhere, held the two women most important to him in the world.

"Thanks for letting me know. Since our pack is so isolated from the rest of the world, it's good for me to learn how other packs handle things, in case it might help us better shore up our, ah ... *defensas*. How do you say—"

"Defenses."

"Oh." Bruno chuckled, the mood in the car quite different now. "So close to our Spanish word, and yet I couldn't think of it."

"Your English is excellent."

"Thank you. I've been studying the language for a long time. I'm the one who always travels when my pack has need to. English has become a sort of universal language in most places."

The aerial map Maverick and River had studied was accurate. The buildings, despite their imposing sizes, did appear largely abandoned. Perhaps some saw activity during the day, but at nighttime? Bruno saw absolutely no movement, though surely at least some of the structures must have guards on night-watch duty.

"How close are we?" Bruno asked, turning to

look out the rear window when he sensed more than heard another car appearing behind them.

"Close. I'll park as soon as I find a spot that feels right."

"Good. I'm ready."

Maverick's focus remained on the road, cruising along so as not to draw attention. Just because they didn't see activity didn't mean caution wasn't important.

"Do you think you'll have to uproot and move your pack?" Bruno asked, knowing the alpha must be dreading the consideration.

Maverick sighed heavily, the burden of his leadership position clear. "I hope not, but maybe. First, we get Naya. And Lara. Then we find out how far the immortal spread our location. If we can contain it, we will."

Bruno interpreted that to mean, "If we can silence everyone who knows, we can stay." All that hard work and investment of building up a territory to have the infrastructure the Rocky Mountain Pack did could only be secured by the immortal's silence.

And there was only one way to ensure the discretion of one's enemies...

"Does your sudden trust of me mean I have your blessing with Naya?" Bruno asked.

The alpha chuffed. "No, man, it doesn't. Don't push your luck."

"Don't worry. I'm saving all my luck for us all getting in and out without casualties."

"You and me both, buddy."

Buddy. That was definitely a marked improvement.

Maverick rolled the Honda down an alleyway behind outbuildings lined with discarded oil drums and parked. When he turned off the engine, the crackling as it cooled sounded too loud, but the area was deserted.

Bruno pushed open his door to confirm. No recent scents. He nodded at Maverick, and the alpha emerged from the car, opening the back door and loading up when Bruno didn't think the man could pack any more weapons than he already did.

The hunters usually hunted them.

This time, it was they who'd go on a hunt.

The beat of battle began to hum through his veins, echoed into Brother Wolf.

Even without Maverick's directives, Bruno would have killed on sight.

The stakes were too high. The hostages too important.

This night would end with their enemies' blood.

CHAPTER SEVEN

CASSIA

UNWILLING TO VEIL HER DISGUST, Cassia watched Meiling devour her third chicken sandwich, piled high with all the fixings and accoutrements Cassia usually enjoyed, a swath of olive oil pesto mayonnaise smudged on the girl's chin.

If Cassia hadn't already known Meiling was a werewolf, she would have realized it from her appalling manners. It wasn't as if she chewed with her mouth open, which would have been cause for Cassia to swing open the door of her airplane and push Meiling out—the steep price of disposing of one of her precious experiments be damned. It was more the way the girl threw herself upon the food as if she hadn't eaten in ages, as if she were a starved beast. A savage.

There was no place for savages in Cassia's life.

She barely tolerated her vampire minions after she'd seen how they behaved during a case of bloodlust.

Édouard, at least, had conquered those urges centuries ago. He was more refined than this girl ever had chance of becoming. He'd been a prominent figure in the French aristocracy before she'd found him, transformed into a bloodsucker and then abandoned on the streets of Paris, the seedy parts Cassia rarely had cause to visit, crazed with urges he hadn't been taught how to control. A few decades locked in one of her dungeons and he'd mastered them, returning to the disciplined and educated man he'd once been—who had to drink blood on occasion to survive. Otherwise, he was the same distinguished man of his previous life.

Cassia's lip curled at a particularly ferocious bite Meiling ripped in the freshly baked baguette and tender white meat as if it were raw, pulsing flesh, straight after a kill.

"Didn't they feed you at the monastery?" It was a rhetorical question, as obviously the crusty old vampires with the arrogance to call themselves masters and lord over a whole sect of warrior monks fed their disciples. Sure, they believed in consuming only bland foods—none of the Dijon mustard, capers, olive tapenade, or sweet relish and thinly sliced purple onion Cassia delighted in atop her chicken sandwiches. According to the vampire "masters," the blander what a creature consumed, be it their food and drink or their surroundings, the more easily it was for them to focus on the inner work, the inner progress, the growth the vampires claimed necessary for any and all enlightenment.

Cassia called bullshit when she heard it. There was no such thing as spiritual bliss or mystical transcendence. Wouldn't she have seen sign of it in the thousand-plus years she'd lived if there were? Over her long lifetime, she'd met gurus and prophets, mystics and religious devotees. Not one of them had attained Nirvana, eternal salvation, or whatever particular brand of belief they were peddling.

Humans and supernatural creatures alike were given this one life to enjoy or endure, their choice. Since it just so happened that her life would go on forever, she had every intention of savoring its every turn, its every gift—the chance to transform into a wild creature that, when she pleased, could allow her to feel free from the binds of human thought. Over the centuries, it occasionally grew tiresome to have so much experience and be forced to commune with those burdened by such limited understanding.

After the misguided teachings of her vampire "masters," Cassia supposed it was no wonder Meiling was ripping into her food with such wild desperation.

She'd probably never been offered food with condiments or real flavors before.

Deciding to offer the girl her ... understanding ... she stared out the window while she addressed her. "You were supposed to stay put at the monastery. Didn't Mage Li Kāng tell you? For your own safety, of course."

Meiling had the good sense to fully swallow before she spoke. "He did tell me."

"Then why did you escape?"

"I-I didn't feel safe." Meiling wiped her mouth with the cloth napkin one of her vampire minions offered the girl and slid back in her seat, continuing to eat at a more measured pace, snacking on the crudites nestled alongside the massacred sandwiches.

Cassia snapped her view from the window to the girl now seated across from her, far enough away that she couldn't accidentally touch Cassia.

"Why wouldn't you feel safe there? Did one of the"—she calmed the lip that wanted to curl so she wouldn't betray the true nature of the situation—"monks ... accost you? Nip at your neck?"

"Yes, that's exactly what happened."

Cassia waited before speaking, allowing the rage that pulsed through her all of a sudden to wane. One of her many secrets to maintaining and amassing so much power over the centuries was never to reveal the way her emotions threatened to control her at times. The only one who witnessed her lose control on occasion was Édouard, and he would never tell another soul. She'd made sure he'd ceased thinking for himself before she allowed him to escape her dungeons. And anyone else who knew ... well, she'd made sure they'd never have the chance to talk.

"The ... master monks dared to drink *your* blood?"

"No, not in the end. I didn't let them. But that's why I ran away. So they couldn't. Wouldn't." Meiling picked at her food, as if her appetite had vanished under the thought of so many vampires gunning for her special blood.

Of course, Meiling would have no way of knowing her blood actually wasn't any more special than any other werewolf's. That if not for the fact that she was one of a set of quadruplets, Cassia would never allow her to occupy space on her plane, eat her food, or waste her time.

But the vampire monks didn't know that Cassia had invented the whole Callan "the Oak" MacLeod story. All they knew was what she'd told them. Well aware of her reputation, they should have obeyed and respected the sanctity of Meiling's body as if the girl were an extension of Cassia herself.

She hadn't killed one of the vampire "masters"

since the summer of 1513. She'd made sure to make it a bloody affair, tearing the vampire limb from limb with her bare hands before ripping into his chest and removing his heart. She'd made a spectacle of eating the thing while blood streamed down her chin, rolled between her breasts, and coated her dress. The fear she'd fairly earned after that had lasted all this time.

It appeared another reminder of her dominance was now needed.

"Which of the vampire masters tried to drink from you?"

Meiling picked at invisible lint on the leggings Cassia had chosen for her. When the girl met Cassia's waiting gaze, her eyes vibrated with trauma.

The only person who got to traumatize her girls was her. She was going to make an example of whoever it was so that the other vampire cretins would never forget. This time, maybe she'd make the vegan monks eat their compatriot's flesh. Yes, that ought to leave a lasting impression...

"Don't feel afraid, darling." Cassia's tone was the earnest one she'd practiced for so long that it nearly managed to convince even her. "I'll protect you now. I won't let anyone else hurt you. Not ever."

"T-thank you." Meiling's voice was tremulous.

Hell, the vampire monks had softened the girl until she was all but useless. It was a good thing that

Cassia didn't need her to be particularly strong of character, but she did need her to be strong of body, which was very often the same thing.

"Tell me who it was," Cassia entreated, "and I'll make sure they never hurt you again."

"Are you going to kill them?"

For a moment, Cassia deliberated whether to tell the truth to the girl with those vulnerable blue eyes. But she was a werewolf, after all.

"Yes, I will kill him in a way the undead can't return from."

While Cassia waited for a response, she picked up the chilled small glass of grappa and downed it, relishing in the burn as the clear liquid slid down her throat. She rarely indulged in the less refined drink much anymore, but she couldn't quite shake the comfort of ties to her long-held Italian heritage.

Finally, Meiling said, "Who do you think it was?" Her eyes narrowed with ferocity.

Ah, so the girl did have some fight.

Cassia growled, uncaring that her minions on board would witness her visceral reaction. It was unlikely they'd survive for long. Besides Édouard, whom she'd taken the time to train properly, they rarely did.

"Master Ji-Hun attempted to drink your blood?" Her question was so low and dangerous that she felt the girl's fear scent the air. "Knowing that you're under my protection. My charge. My ward."

Meiling hesitated, then nodded.

The girl was still trying to protect the bastard! Well, there was nowhere the bloodsucker could hide where she wouldn't find him.

He'd be an idiot to still be at the monastery at the top of Shèng Shān Mountain, but far more intelligent men than he had surprised her by underestimating her.

Cassia leaned across the open gap between them, preparing to pat the girl's hand in comfort, only to withdraw the offer at the last minute. "Don't worry. We'll be at the monastery soon." Cassia smiled in anticipation of what was to come. "I'll take care of everything then. You won't have to worry about anything."

Only, Meiling appeared even more worried at her uncharacteristic reassurance.

Cassia felt her brow furrow and forced it to relax. "What bothers you now, child?" she snapped when she hadn't meant to.

"I don't want to go back there. Never again."

"We won't remain long. Just enough for me to take care of Master Ji-Hun, confer with Li Kāng, and settle a few other minor matters."

"So what do you want with me, then?"

Meiling's eyes had cleared entirely of their previous weakness, and Cassia debated whether she should discipline the insolent child who didn't recognize what an honor it was to serve her wishes.

But no. Not yet.

Cassia smiled, feeling the edges of her mouth curl up though she didn't feel a speck of mirth. Meiling had no idea about the special destiny Cassia had bestowed on her. And she wouldn't know. Not until after Cassia's attempt at infusing her with immortality magic took hold.

The last time had been such a disappointment. Davina had been a strong, spirited girl, believing the story that she was to be savior of all werewolves until the very end. She'd trusted that "Gabrielle" was her parents' friend from long before their untimely deaths, and the girl had been just so willing to hand over her trust.

Such a foolish, innocent thing she'd been.

When Cassia had pressed her mouth to Brea's, infusing her with her immortality magic—a great gift since Cassia had never shared it before with anyone —the girl had appeared to accept the vast power. At first.

But she hadn't made it past the first five minutes before violent convulsions devolved into seizures that overheated her brain.

She died before Cassia's scientists could finish drilling into the girl's cranium to control the overheating and give Davina a chance to survive.

To grant Cassia the dual nature she deserved. The freedom she craved.

To be the only immortal wolf shifter in all of existence. In all of history. An honor that was to be hers and hers alone.

"How is it that you know me?" Meiling asked, interrupting Cassia's thoughts.

She huffed in annoyance. "When you were a baby, it was I who delivered you to the monastery. It was I who saved you from certain death and made it possible for you to survive. It is I who has given werewolves the chance to endure for many centuries more. Possibly forevermore."

Through her. Through Cassia. Through the immortal that would take the beasts and elevate them into something more, so much more, so much grander than anything they could possibly strive to be without her intervention.

Meiling's mouth popped open to ask something else. Cassia waved her hand with a snap, and Meiling shut it.

"No more questions now. Eat, sleep, and replenish, darling. I'll wake you when we arrive at the monastery. You have nothing to worry about now that you're in my care."

Then Cassia turned to stare out at thick cumulous clouds so she wouldn't have to see Meiling's face any longer.

A reminder of her failure with Davina.

Cassia had to find another way. This time, passing her immortality magic on to Meiling would work.

It had to. Her immortality magic was a part of her. She'd bend it to her will, just as she did everything else.

CHAPTER EIGHT

BRUNO

HE AND MAVERICK had been waiting, concealed within long, deep shadows, barely moving for more than twenty minutes. The large building that housed Naya and Lara sat a few hundred meters away. From the outside, the industrial structure suggested it was abandoned, but even without confirmation that heat signatures were within the plain, corrugated steel building, he'd have known. He and his Brother Wolf shared a tense anticipation. Bruno hadn't seen any movement from the building, with its sealed doors and boarded-up windows, but he could *feel* the creatures inside it.

Every single instinct warned him to flee from the darkness that was milling inside. He could sense the immortal mage as if he were standing next to him.

The man's energy was strong enough to overpower the women's.

This close to them, Brother Wolf should be picking up on his mate's energy signature as well as his alpha's. But Brother Wolf wasn't.

Bruno steadfastly refused to allow his fears to take over. Were they too late? Had the immortal decided he had no use for the two women after all and dispatched with them to cover his tracks? Had Naya and Lara pushed him too far and sparked his rage? For as gentle as Lara was with nature and its plants and animals, she had no patience for those who were cruel and mistreated others. Bruno had never known Lara to keep her mouth shut in the face of a wrongdoing, even if it put her in danger.

And Naya ... though Bruno had spent far too little time with her, it had been sufficient to identify the flame that burned strongly inside her. He doubted she'd remain quiet and play it safe either, not when others were in peril.

Not for the first time since their wait began, Bruno dismissed his worries, forbidding himself from focusing on all that could go wrong when they were this close to Naya and Lara.

He'd wanted to ask Maverick if he was sensing Naya inside, as he should as her alpha, but he didn't. Speaking at all was a risk when they were this close to a building occupied by supernaturals with advanced abilities. They couldn't do anything that would tip off their presence and eliminate the element of surprise.

Besides, Bruno could tell Maverick was busy receiving messages from River and likely telepathically coordinating final details with his beta.

When Maverick finally reached over to touch Bruno's shoulder, giving a silent nod, Bruno understood two things. Firstly, everyone was finally in place. Even though Bruno couldn't see or hear them, he could sense the presence of wolf shifters all around. The small assault teams were ready to charge the building, and the backup teams were in place, where they'd continue to wait until they were needed—if they were needed. And if Bruno could detect the many wolves surrounding the steel structure, most supernaturals would be able to as well if they were paying attention. And the immortal hadn't struck him as foolish or careless.

The clock had already begun ticking; they didn't have much time to act.

The second thing that Bruno realized was that Maverick didn't perceive Naya inside the building after all. The alpha didn't say or do anything to express this concerning detail, but Bruno could tell.

The man's eyes were heavy with anguish, with fatherly concern.

Bruno swallowed a fresh surge of fear and forced it to stay down. He needed to focus. Get in, grab Naya and Lara—he hoped—and get out.

He nodded back at Maverick, who immediately picked up the weapons bag and pressed it tightly to his chest to avoid any rustling or clanking. Already the grenades, rocket launcher, and whatever else the alpha had in there were secured to the sides of the bag and surrounded with padding. Maverick slunk around the side of the alleyway at a fast walk and Bruno followed, revolvers loaded with full magazines of silver bullets strapped to both hips, and silver blades concealed all around his body.

It was strange to rely on weapons when, had he been home, he would have shifted and gone in with nothing more than the force of his powerful body and sharp teeth and claws. But wolves couldn't open doors, and his wolf wouldn't be able to kill the immortal—though Brother Wolf would certainly give his best effort. If the dark mage could survive all that Zasha and Quannah's pack had thrown at him, they needed manmade tools to kill something so unnatural.

When he and Maverick rounded the corner of the building that had hidden them, forced to walk out in the open, Bruno spotted two of the other assault teams, one led by the woman, the other led by a man, each with three shifters following close behind them. They too moved swiftly, clinging to the long shadows roving across an open scraggly field and then a vast patch of cracked asphalt. Despite their dark clothing, the moon was nearly full, making it impossible for the night to completely swallow them up, no matter how camouflaged they were.

When the building that Bruno still hoped housed Naya and Lara loomed closer, he had to work to keep his heart from beating too quickly. To keep calm.

Yes, neither his Brother Wolf nor Naya's alpha had picked up on her presence inside, but they were dealing with magic here. With as little as they knew about this possible immortal and his strange ways, that he was using magic was all but guaranteed. This would also explain why Bruno wasn't picking up on his link to Lara.

Así es, Bruno told himself reassuringly. The immortal had masked the presence of the women inside with his magic. Why wouldn't he do that? It was a logical move. The immortal wasn't aware of the tracker Maverick had planted on Naya, so he'd think the only way Naya's pack could find her was through pack links. *Of course* the immortal would use his magic to interfere.

It's what Bruno would do if he were a sick, depraved fucker with too much time on his hands and a general lack of respect for life.

Even so, Bruno couldn't help but pulse his awareness outward, hoping to pick up on either of the captives.

When they were within a hundred yards of the building, Maverick set the weapons bag down at the base of a broad, solitary tree. In this industrial zone, they'd cleared most of the foliage; this tree stuck out and would be easy to find later. Bruno expected Maverick to load up with more weapons, but he moved on with barely a pause.

For all the waiting and the slow progress they'd made, now that they were within sight of the building, everything sped up so much that Bruno no longer had time to overthink things—a relief.

Running across the barren lot separating them from their target, they clung to every shadow, but there weren't enough. The moon was too bright. Too round. Too close to full.

If the immortal had lookouts—and why wouldn't he?—they'd have spotted them. Maverick didn't speak, but Bruno knew he must realize the same fact. He didn't stop, Bruno trailing directly behind him, until they reached the building.

As they crouched beside a set of double metal

doors, Bruno spotted the other two assault teams taking positions at different entry points to the building. The team led by the woman crouched under a window that bordered bay doors big enough to drive trucks through.

Bruno watched Maverick, waiting for his signal. It didn't arrive. Instead, Maverick stood and pulled gently on the handle to one of the doors, in case it shouldn't open and clank against a lock.

The door opened easily. With it ajar an inch, Maverick took a deep breath, yanked it more fully open, and disappeared inside.

Bruno slid in behind him and froze for a second.

It was a second too long.

He dove to the ground an instant before a beam of red light sliced a hole into the door directly where he'd just stood. As easily as a laser, the immortal's magic cut through metal like it was soft butter.

While the hole smoked, a crash sounded from somewhere in the building. Another red beam zoomed in its direction. Then another crash, another blast of a red beam, and then Bruno lost track of what everyone else was doing and focused only on himself. Only on finding Naya and Lara.

A red dome, exactly like the one that had contained Clove and him in the forest earlier, except for its larger size, stood in the middle of the vast warehouse, which was apparently empty except for the dome and a single couch in front of it. And within that dome was Naya. Or Lara. One of them.

Just one of them.

Only one.

Acid burned his throat as he did his best to ignore the sudden chaos around him.

Shots fired. The crash of magic hurled as a weapon. The cries as assaults met their intended targets.

There were a few dozen of the shifters while the immortal was there with only half a dozen men. But they weren't men, and that was a problem. Beside the immortal were vampires. One moved so quickly that Bruno could hardly track him, which meant that he was old. Very, very, old.

The vampires formed a protective circle around the immortal, who stood, an eerily placid look on his face, red light crackling across his open palms.

Every one of the shifters advanced on them.

The red dome behind the immortal and vampires provided the only steady illumination within the space. Like a beacon calling him, Bruno made his way to it with single-minded focus.

Naya or Lara was inside it.

He knew from experience that he couldn't touch it or otherwise cross through the shield. And though the dome didn't waver, it certainly would once they managed to kill the immortal, and if they couldn't manage that, surely there was some way to interfere with his magic enough to retrieve the lone woman.

Bruno rounded the back of the warehouse, placing distance between him and the rest of the fighting. When he heard a rustling and a clank, he looked over. Three of the wolves had shifted into their animal forms, their clothing and weapons a now-silent pile on the bare cement floor. Their wolves would be a formidable weapon against the vampires, who moved too fast for their human forms.

The woman seemed to sense Bruno. Her attention previously fixed on the fight in front of her, she turned, watching him approach.

When he reached the red dome, he didn't touch it. The immortal wasn't concerned about his prisoner, which had to mean there was no way he could get inside, nor the woman out of it while the mage still lived.

A scream rent the crackling air, but was then muffled by a crash, a snarl, and the unmistakable sound of flesh ripping and tearing.

But the shifters outnumbered the vampires, and already one of the vamps lay lifeless on the floor, his head separated from his body. One wolf clamped onto another vamp's leg, while a second tore flesh from the back of the thigh, and a third leapt and knocked the vamp to the floor.

The immortal lashed out with his magic, slicing through the hindquarters of the leaping wolf. The creature whimpered and fell heavily to the floor, where he lay panting, the bottom half of his body attached only by a few threads of sinew and bone.

The captured woman followed Bruno's line of sight. "Oh no," she gasped.

Though Bruno's every instinct urged him to remain at her side, he couldn't. "We'll get you out of here."

He began to round her prison, then turned back around. "Any ideas how to take the immortal down?"

The woman grimaced, making her beautiful face appear exhausted and burdened. "I wish. But no, I haven't observed any vulnerabilities."

"We'll figure it out," Bruno said reassuringly, but he wondered if his promise sounded as hollow as it felt.

As he moved to back up the shifters, his heart sank to somewhere around his boots.

The woman looked like Naya and Lara. *Exactly* like them.

But she wasn't.

Her voice was different. Her sad smile was new.

And when she looked at him, there was no recognition to light up her burdened blue eyes.

Whoever the woman was, she was identical to Naya and Lara—only she wasn't them.

How could there possibly be another one of them?

And where were the women who mattered more to him than anyone else in the world?

With a reckless desperation he'd never felt before, he shot a vampire in the head and then the heart, then launched himself at the immortal, drawing his second gun as he went.

CHAPTER NINE

BRUNO

THE PASSING of time distorted as Bruno allowed his body to move solely on instinct. There wasn't time to think ahead or process all that was happening around him. He leaned into the thousands of hours of training he'd put his body through. He relied on muscle memory, ingrained habitual responses, and pure animal instinct. Brother Wolf moved along with him, close to the surface. Man and beast became as much one as they could be, short of an actual shift.

Bruno shoved the vampire he'd just shot out of the way, fully aware that a silver bullet to the head and heart wouldn't kill him—but it would slow him down.

He emptied the rest of the magazine into the immortal's skull, mindful to aim so that any bullet that shot straight through would hopefully embed itself into one of his vamps.

With how blurringly fast everyone was moving, hitting a friendly was a real concern. Bruno shot without pause until the gun went *click*. He stared at the immortal's head.

Or what was left of it.

Half his face slid off the bone as if flesh were melting, and a sizable gap in his cranium revealed brain beneath dark hair, damp and matted with blood.

And still the immortal fought Maverick, whose left arm hung limply from his shoulder. Even so, Maverick had a hunting knife stuck in the immortal's chest, half the mage's heart carved out.

The vampires were too overcome to properly defend their master anymore. Only two of the vampires were upright. Just one of them, the oldest and therefore the fastest, continued his attempts to defend the immortal instead of himself, several bullet holes already through his shirt, one straight through his heart. With two wolves attached to either of his legs, he struggled to reach his master.

The immortal's hands flared red once more and he pointed the beam of his laser at Maverick's neck, slicing quickly through flesh.

"Noooo," Bruno roared, tackling the mage to the

floor, dislodging the aim of his magic from Maverick, whose head was now only precariously attached to his neck. And yet ... not a drop of blood slipped down his chest. The immortal's magic seemed to have cauterized the wound even as it sliced.

Maverick wobbled on his feet, but the woman shifter noticed the opening and ran to help Bruno pin the immortal down. Securing him flat on his back, she rammed her knee into the artery running down his arm, and Bruno did the same.

Red sparked in the immortal's open hands ... but it didn't coalesce into the lethal pointed beam he'd been using against them.

The shifter woman looked up and met Bruno's waiting stare, and they reached an unspoken agreement.

While Bruno leaned all his weight into pinning the man down, the woman yanked Maverick's blade from the mage's heart—probably hoping wildly that he might bleed out once she did since she had an identical serrated hunting knife strapped to her thigh —and began hacking off the mage's arm she held down.

Instead of crying out in pain, which Bruno would have expected of anyone, no matter how hardened, the immortal met Bruno's eyes while his own blazed a terrifying red.

"*La puta madre*," Bruno mumbled, though his mother was most definitely not a whore. "Hurry," he told the shifter woman. "He's..." *Freaking me the hell out.* But Bruno didn't say that last bit aloud.

"Got it," the woman grunted, holding an arm aloft. Blood streamed down her own arm ... and still the creepy immortal said and did nothing in reaction.

"He's a tough motherfucker. I'll give the asshole that."

In the next breath, the asshole did something Bruno wouldn't have thought his body capable of.

He yanked his arm out from under Bruno's very precise and very secure hold. Bruno weighed nearly two-hundred pounds of solid muscle, but the immortal tossed him like he weighed twenty, throwing Bruno onto his ass.

Immediately, Bruno jumped back to his feet, but by then the immortal had wrapped his one remaining hand to the woman shifter's head and was in the process of wrenching it from her neck.

"Noooo," Bruno cried out again, throwing himself wildly at the mage, trying to at least dislodge his hold in time.

But the immortal was too fast. *Too strong!* He shouldn't have been able to do that! Not with a single hand and the rest of his body battered.

The woman's head was in the process of falling

to the bloodied floor at her knees, the open-mouthed scream of shock frozen forever on her face—

When the immortal just up and ... vanished.

Simply ... disappeared in a quick flash of red.

One instant he was there, the next he wasn't.

The momentum of Bruno's body kept going when he didn't hit the mage as he expected; his arm and chest slapped painfully against the cement. Far worse, he landed in a pool of blood—the woman shifter's and the immortal's—her body, now headless, still gripped the immortal's arm.

"*Mierda*," Bruno grumbled, hearing his words as if from far away through his shock.

"Where the hell'd they go?" a panicked male voice cried out. "The vamp just fucking disappeared."

That's when Bruno understood that the immortal took the old vampire with him when he vanished.

Bruno wiped absently at the blood coating one side of his face while he took inventory, aware that he was moving as if in a daze.

Short of the one vampire who'd escaped, the rest lay unmoving, truly dead now that they'd been relieved of their heads. If Maverick was anything like Lara, he'd also order their heads and hearts burned, just to be certain.

And Maverick ... he was alive. His neck sported

an angry red line across where it had already begun to repair itself, and his head still wasn't fully attached to the rest of his body, but he'd heal.

For a few moments there, Bruno wasn't sure the alpha would make it.

But *he was alive.*

The woman and another of the shifters were not. The man's head also lay beside his body in a pile of congealing blood.

A stunned silence descended upon the survivors, especially noticeable after the chaos and din of battle. All Bruno could hear was the thumping of his heart, his breathing ragged when it shouldn't have been. He'd been in fights before where death had been one of the predominant outcomes. Violence was an unfortunate part of shifter life.

But he'd never fought someone he didn't know how to kill. And he'd never been so close to saving someone and failed, right before his very eyes.

His empty hands pulsed as if they still had the chance to capture the immortal.

Remembering with a start that Naya's lookalike was within the dome powered by the immortal's magic, he whipped his head around so fast that it kinked.

Naya's twin was still there.

The red of the immortal's magic continued to

hold strong, unwavering, despite the fact that he was missing an arm and was no longer physically present.

Slowly, even though he intended to move quickly, Bruno reclaimed his feet and offered Maverick a hand up.

They surveyed the damage once more, then walked over to the dome together.

To make the acquaintance of the woman inside the magical spell that should have failed—and yet hadn't.

———

"GIVE ME A MINUTE," Maverick said when they reached the dome, as if he weren't yet ready to confirm that the woman inside the dimly glowing red magic wasn't Naya. Or Lara.

"Let me reach out to River first. Get us some help."

"Of course," Bruno said. "Do what you need to do. I'll figure out what's going on here."

After a final sharp study of the woman with the familiar blond hair, pretty blue eyes, and limber athletic body, Maverick nodded at her and stepped to the side. And even though he didn't pull out a cell phone, relying on his telepathic link to communicate with his beta instead, he tipped his head down as if needing privacy.

Bruno wondered if the man just needed a solitary moment to process all that had just happened. He'd lost members of his pack. That always hit hard. A pack was so much more than an organization of like-minded supernaturals. Packs, when run right, became families.

Maverick would be feeling as if he'd lost sisters and brothers.

And worse, they hadn't even achieved their desired goal.

The longer Maverick went without confirming the identity of the prisoner, the longer he could hold off on the weight of all that loss, of concern for the fact that Naya was still missing.

Naya was gone. And they had no idea how to get her back. All their leads delivered them here.

Swinging his attention back to the dome, Bruno realized that the woman was studying him.

"Hello," she said simply, as if their little world hadn't just experienced a major catastrophic event.

"Hello. I don't believe we've met before."

"No, I don't believe we have."

When she didn't supply more information, he offered, "My name is Bruno. I'm the beta of the Andes Mountain Pack." Ordinarily, he wouldn't just offer up this kind of information. But his instincts told him he'd have to trust her if he wanted her to trust him. And right then she was their only tie to Naya.

"You're a long way from home."

"And from your accent, I'm guessing that so are you." Her accent was subtle, as if she'd been conscious of its development and worked to minimize its effect. Bruno suspected she'd been raised in Asia, despite her blond hair and light eyes.

Her cheeks flushed just enough to tell him that he'd been right about her desire not to have an accent. "I..." she started, then stopped. "Naya told me about you." She said it as if to justify placing her trust in him.

But Bruno startled. "She did?"

"Yes. She told me that you were the one to identify that there are more of us than just the two of us."

Bruno knew it was stupid, but his heart still flopped. And here he'd been thinking that Naya mentioned him because she was drawn to him as he was her. That in the middle of a life-or-death situation she'd be confiding in her newfound sister about her crush, like a foolish schoolgirl.

He scowled at himself before saying, "So she told you about Lara? My alpha?"

"She did."

"So what's your name?"

"Meiling."

"And where have you been all this time?"

"Hidden away in a vampire-run monastery atop Shèng Shān Mountain in China."

He felt his eyes widen. "Really?"

Free of all the agitation he felt, she nodded simply, as if unaffected by her current predicament and the surrounding bloodshed.

While they chatted, the shifters on the backup team were swarming in—likely on Maverick's orders, relayed through River—tending to the wounded. Already, they were carrying out the wolf whose flank was all but detached from the rest of his body. The wolf's eyes were closed, and he didn't so much as grunt when the others picked him up, though every movement had to cause brutal pain. Bruno suspected that his body was in a deep, restorative sleep, his healing shutting down his awareness to speed up his recovery.

Bruno returned his attention to Meiling, who hadn't looked away. Clearing his throat, he refocused. Her intensity was unnerving.

"How did you meet up with Naya?"

"I took her from her cabin on the pack's land."

"You ... wait, what?"

Meiling simply waited.

"You're the one who kidnapped her?"

"Yes, but only to protect her."

"And how'd that work out for you?"

"Not as well as I'd hoped. She's with the immortal woman."

Bruno's heart skipped an entire beat. "What immortal woman?" His question was so calm that it belied the panic rising inside him.

"A woman named Cassia. She came and took Naya while she was asleep."

"Asleep?" His brow bunched.

"She tried to break through our little prison here."

"Ah. And..." His mind was reeling so furiously, he was struggling to piece it all together. Did this mean that Lara was safe and home with the rest of his pack? Had she never left the Andes at all?

"Let me help you out a little here," Meiling said. "I can see that you're struggling."

Bruno pondered whether or not she was being condescending but couldn't decide in the end. "Go on."

"I took Naya because I'd gotten word that an immortal was about to take her. Yes, I realize that I ended up more or less delivering her to another immortal, but in my defense I didn't know there was more than one."

"Mmm," he said, because it was all he had just then. Dozens of the backup shifters were roaming the warehouse, taking in all the carnage. He could feel their sorrow. Every member of the Rocky Mountain Pack would be feeling the deaths down to their bones.

"When Naya was out, and Cyrus—"

"Who's Cyrus?"

"The immortal you were fighting. When Cyrus was distracted, preparing for the arrival of Cassia, I took Naya's pendant and put it on. They were about to separate us, and I wanted something of hers." She shrugged a bit timidly. "I've never had a sister before. I mean, I suppose I always have, but I didn't know it until recently. I wanted to feel her close."

Bruno took in the wolf head pendant Meiling's fingers alighted over, resting against the base of her throat.

Then she smiled. "At least Cyrus hid the fact that there are two of us from Cassia. I was standing right here next to Naya, but Cassia didn't seem to see me at all."

"Magic," Bruno growled.

"I'm sure it was." She glanced at the surrounding glow that tinted her face red. "As is this."

She let the statement hang. Bruno had no idea

how to set her free, not when either of them touching the magic would knock them out.

Bruno felt Maverick approach before the alpha stopped beside him, staring at Meiling.

"This is Meiling. From China," Bruno told him.

"Ah. And I see she's wearing Naya's necklace."

"I am," Meiling said. "Just until we find her again."

Maverick tensed. "Please tell me you know where she is."

"I think I just might. You're going to have to get me out of here first though."

"We're working on it," Maverick said, looking at Bruno. "Boone is on his way with the mages right now."

"What kind of mages?" Meiling asked, free of the prejudice toward wizards most shifters had.

"I don't exactly know," Maverick said. "But Boone trusts them, and I trust Boone. They'll be here in fifteen minutes. Until then, tell me everything."

One look at Meiling suggested that she wasn't in the habit of giving information freely, but she began to repeat the limited facts she'd already shared with Bruno.

He barely heard her. Brother Wolf howled inside him, a garbled cry that was half lament and half celebration. All he could think about was that she might have a way back to Naya.

Bruno had the feeling he wouldn't feel right until Naya was at his side.

Until he convinced her she was his mate.

After losing her once again, he was finished denying Brother Wolf's truth.

Every part of Bruno now understood what she was to him.

And all it had taken was having her snatched out of his reach. His heart tore and mended all at the same time.

They'd find Naya. And then he'd make her his.

CHAPTER TEN

NAYA

FOR PERHAPS AN HOUR OR TWO—NAYA had no exact way to measure the passing of time on Cassia's private jet—she resisted sleep, despite Cassia's orders. Now that Naya knew they were headed toward the monastery in China that was Meiling's home, she couldn't stop worrying.

She and Meiling were identical, but in appearance only. And while Cyrus had been correct in assuming that Naya wouldn't reveal Meiling's existence out of a desire to protect her newly discovered sister, surely someone at the monastery would discover that Naya was an imposter. Just because they looked alike didn't mean they acted the same. Besides, Meiling had a slight, elegant Asian accent while Naya didn't. Naya moved with strong, swift, assured steps, like the lifelong athlete she was, but Meiling moved as if she barely touched the ground, as if the elements bent to her will and she all but hovered above the earth. Surely one of her mentors at the monastery would pick up on the subtle yet important differences between them. Any attempts to imitate Meiling's gait or grace might just lead to Naya behaving strangely and drawing Cassia's attention.

Though Naya knew little about the woman who'd taken her captive, she was certain of one thing: the less of the woman's attention she received, the better.

By this point, though Cassia hadn't said so explicitly, Naya believed Cassia was another immortal of the kind Zasha and Quannah had warned her pack about. Given how Cyrus spoke of the woman, Naya was all but certain.

Cyrus had overpowered Naya and Meiling with frightening ease. With a lazy flick of his hand, he'd captured them both. Without any visible effort on his part, he was able to maintain the magical dome they couldn't escape, which was powerful enough to knock them unconscious with the slightest touch.

Despite all that, Naya was more wary of Cassia than she'd been of Cyrus. It wasn't as much what the woman said and more what she didn't. Her gaze was calculating and uncaring. Naya imagined she could actually see the machinations whirring like gears in her mind. If this was truly the woman who'd delivered Naya to Maverick as an infant, then that didn't bode well for any of them. Naya's Sister Wolf was on edge, warning Naya not to trust a thing that came from the woman's seductive cherry lips. If Cassia had come to retrieve Naya now while aware of Naya's ancestry—and she absolutely was since she'd been the one to inform Maverick about it—then Naya truly feared for the longevity of "the Oak" MacLeod's bloodline. At least now Meiling and Lara were out there to carry it on if Naya couldn't. Assuming Meiling could escape Cyrus...

Despite the frenzied thoughts buzzing through her mind, Naya did her best to remain completely still in the leather seat that was more like a lounge chair. She'd leaned it back and kicked her feet up onto a matching footstool that popped out from one of its sides. However, every inch of her wanted to get up and *move*. To pace. To work out the energy whipping around inside her like a tropical storm, desperately trying to discover a solution when she didn't comprehend the rules of the game.

And Naya *was* playing a game: Cassia's game, where the woman made the rules, not her.

As if Cassia's presence across the wide aisle from

her weren't enough to keep her wired, there were half a dozen vampires on board with them.

Werewolves and vampires didn't typically get along. They moved in separate worlds, their goals different. Vampires needed to remain near humans to feed from them; werewolves fled human populations that seemed to only ever want to hunt them.

Despite a vampire's innate speed, Naya was strong enough to fight them, but she'd have to do so in her human form, with limited advantages. Unlike a wolf shifter, she couldn't transform at will. The advantages of her wolf form remained out of reach until the next full moon.

It was one of the reasons Naya had trained so hard her entire life. Despite her duty to survive for all werewolves, the only skills she had to call on in her defense were those she cultivated on her own.

Vulnerable as she was, with her eyes closed on a plane when her only fellow passengers were enemy predators, she all but squirmed with the need to watch them all. Even a fledgling vamp could move quickly enough to have her head off before she could react if he managed to sneak up on her, and that vampire that Cassia called Édouard smelled old. Which meant he was fast. Too fast for comfort. And strong, as vampires grew with age.

If Naya fell asleep as commanded, she wouldn't be able to scent any of them before they were too close. But then, either way, the lot of them could overpower her, trapped as she was in this tin can, vastly outnumbered. Not exactly the way she'd pictured taking her first ever flight...

Finally, Naya grew wearier of her racing mind than of the myriad unknowns and what-ifs. If Cassia were going to kill her, she'd have done it already. Or if she had reason to wait, Naya suspected there wasn't much she could do to stop the woman. Though Cassia hadn't revealed magical powers as Cyrus had, no one possessed the woman's level of confidence without reason for it.

Fatigue began creeping over Naya, dragging her down. The stress of being continually on edge, adrenaline coursing through her from the constant tension, left her muscles spent.

The flight from the United States to China would be a long one. She had no doubt she'd need her strength once they arrived.

That was the last thought she had until exhaustion finally claimed her and she drifted into a deep, restless sleep.

———

BRUNO'S naked body was as glorious as she'd imagined. He stood facing her, legs leaning against the bed, all tanned, hard planes. All defined muscle.

Dark, twisting tattoos wove across his body like vines, making her want to trace and follow each and every loop and line. Preferably with her tongue.

He was all hers. *Hers.*

She leaned back on the bed and openly studied him. Unabashed. Unapologetic. This was what mates got to do. There'd never be another man for her ... nor another woman for him.

His body was hers to worship, to admire, and to *devour*.

Warmth pooled between her thighs, making her desire him more than she'd ever wanted anything else in her life.

Greedily, she sat up to trail both hands across the ridges of his flat stomach, up to his chest with its fine dusting of hair, teasing across taut nipples, following the lines of the tribal symbols tattooed on one forearm, tracing the head of a wolf—his true nature on display, never hidden—down his trim sides, across narrow hips, to his muscled thighs, which she squeezed, pulling him closer, so that his legs bracketed hers at the edge of the bed.

He groaned, pushing his hips forward, further

toward her. The animalistic sound almost made her come, and he hadn't even explored her body yet.

He wove his fingers into her hair while her own hands slid back up, slowing, savoring, trailing across bare skin some more, teasing, whispering over the body she wanted to explore until she knew its every detail as well as her own.

He nudged his hips forward again, moaning another time and, once more, she almost came undone.

Licking her lips, she dismissed the slow movements, reaching for the erection that was level with her mouth, the tip thick and engorged, glistening with early wetness, promising every pleasure.

She wrapped her fingers around his hard length. So thick, so ready for her. Pulsing with need. He'd fill her as much as she could ever be filled. As much as she wanted. *Needed.*

Electric tingles zinged between her thighs before racing across the rest of her body, leaving her feeling more alive than she'd ever been.

With one hand, she stroked him from base to tip. With the other, she cupped and squeezed his taut balls.

He moaned again, deep and prolonged, and she echoed the sounds of his pleasure.

She glanced up. Bruno's eyes bore into hers, hot, blazing, keeping her pinned to the bed—as if there were any other place she'd rather be. For several moments she lost herself to the greens, blues, and browns that swirled through his irises, to the faint forest green glow that was the color of his pack's magic, before she couldn't help but close her eyes.

She stroked him again, down and up, up and down, placing all her focus on how good he felt in her hands, how amazing he'd feel inside her, as deeply as anyone could touch her.

He guided her to lie down on the bed and her eyes popped open. Again, she met the molten colors of his irises, discovering devotion there, unquenched desire—urgency. He caressed her shoulders before circling the swells of her bare breasts with the tips of his fingers.

Her breath caught and she arched her back, pushing her breasts upward toward his mouth.

He chuckled, a deep hoarse sound that made her growl in return. "Not yet, *peligrosa*. We have all the time in the world, and I want to watch you melt."

His fingertips continued to trace her breasts, forming smaller and smaller concentric circles, until his light touch *finally* marked her areola. Until her nipples were hard and straining. Until her thoughts were pleading for the kiss of his tongue.

"Mmmm," he muttered, little more than a grunt overcome by passion.

Naya moaned and wrapped her legs around the back of his and tugged. Hard.

His knees buckled against the edge of the bed and he landed on top of her, bracing his fall with his hands to either side of her shoulders.

She grinned and dragged her teeth across her bottom lip.

He stared at her, eyes ablaze with green, consumed by her. "Peligrosa indeed," he said, the words as much a growl as spoken.

Naya didn't know if she was as dangerous as he kept saying she was, but she did know she was desperate to feel him fill her. Every nerve in her body was alive, yearning for him. *Needing* release. *Needing him.*

Wantonly, she spread her legs wide for him, uncaring that she'd never made love before, that he'd be the first. Now, with more certainty than she'd ever felt for anything else before, she knew she'd been right to wait for the right man, for the right fit. For the person and wolf that perfectly matched her own.

Her arousal pulsed through every inch of her body, leaving her slick and wet at the apex of her thighs.

"Inside me. Now," she grunted, incapable of

explaining more. Of telling him to be careful, that he was her first.

She hadn't even learned his full name, but she knew all she needed to know.

His response to her command was to grunt and groan as if he were incapable of forming words anymore.

He lined himself up exactly where she wanted him ... before withdrawing suddenly.

She shot up in protest, but before devastation and painful longing could swoop in, he guided her back down to the bed, slid his strong hands beneath her thighs, and dragged her to the very edge of the bed with one strong pull.

He spread his legs wider, hooking her calves over his shoulders, and in the next instant his hot, wet tongue slid up the length of her folds and she forgot everything but his touch. She forgot her name, the loss of her parents, her duty as savior to a whole species. She forgot every single fucking thing as all she could do was *feel* the trail of his tongue, the way it swept up and down her wetness before dipping inside the tunnel that led to her very depths. She whimpered as his tongue filled her with several insistent thrusts, and she almost wept when he withdrew ... until his tongue lapped up her essence as if it were the nectar of the gods, before settling on her clitoris.

Her entire body tensed for a moment, her back arching, her thoughts completely blank—

A hand jerked her shoulder ... when both of Bruno's hands gripped her thighs.

She eased into the heat sweeping through her body with each flick of his tongue—

Fingers dug into her shoulder, shaking her hard.

Naya's eyes popped open in the same moment as she registered the loud hum of the jet's engines.

"Shit," she muttered groggily as she blinked up into Édouard's face, blankly registering his dull eyes, pale hair, and the stern line of his thin lips. Disapproving. Annoyed.

Well, she was far more annoyed than he was just then, *guaran-fucking-teed.*

He stepped back as she sat up from where she'd been slumped in her seat. She took in the many sets of eyes studying her, while trying to force herself back fully to the here and now—a challenge when she felt as if she could still reach Bruno if only she closed her eyes again.

How she wanted to be with him instead of where she was...

She took in how the other vampires appeared aroused, their eyes a bit glazed, even for the cold creatures. Several of them adjusted the front of their pants, attempting to hide burgeoning tent situations.

Several of their gazes sought hers, but she didn't meet their waiting eyes.

The temptation to reach for Bruno again was strong. Alluring enough to have her considering it.

Instead, with great reluctance, she sought out the greatest predator in the cabin.

Cassia sat where Naya had last seen her, across from her, lounging in her seat like an elegant jungle cat who knew she could strike and kill in seconds. Cassia's body draped with evident relaxation, one leg crossed over the other at the knee, expensive and feminine-looking red leather boots suggesting that the woman had changed while Naya ... slept.

Naya couldn't help the plunging disappointment that gripped her as she accepted, with unreasonable devastation, that everything she'd just experienced had been nothing more than a dream. Irritated at the illogical loss, she shoved the regret away.

Her life was at stake, and within her existence she held the fate of an entire species. She had no right to dream of a life shared with a man she barely knew and who couldn't be her mate.

She scoffed. Her *mate*. What the hell was wrong with her? Bruno wasn't her mate.

At that, Sister Wolf growled an objection, long and sustained, deep inside the well of her being.

"That must have been quite the dream," Cassia said, interrupting her thoughts. The woman's voice was a seductive purr.

When Naya finally made herself meet the woman's eyes, she was surprised not to find the previous coldness there, but a simmering fire ... as if the woman ... desired her.

Of all the fucking places to have a sex dream! Naya admonished herself.

She didn't know if immortals or vampires could scent arousal, but werewolves and wolf shifters sure as shit could. Though she'd only dreamt of her time with a naked Bruno, her body had responded as if the experience had been real. She could scent her own arousal, heavy in the air around her, and she adjusted uncomfortably in her seat, hoping she was the only one.

From Cassia's responding smile, she thought the woman was following her line of thought.

"I've been alive for a very long time," Cassia said. "And I have a particular interest in the erotic arts." Her smile turned coquettish; Naya had to force herself not to visibly cringe.

"I'd enjoy teaching you what I know," Cassia continued, a flush to her cheeks. "Keep that in mind."

Naya feared she wouldn't be able to forget the

promise, which she interpreted as a threat, and swallowed down her revulsion. If this woman thought Naya would allow herself to be even more vulnerable with her than she already was, then the woman was out of her mind.

When Naya noticed Cassia was waiting for a response, she forced her voice steady so as not to reveal any of her internal thoughts. "I'll keep it in mind."

Cassia's smile turned devilish, and Naya cursed her mind once more for where it had taken her at the very worst possible time. She lived alone in her cabin, for fuck's sake. She slept completely alone in her big, empty bed every single night. Any one of those nights would have been fine—hell, she might have even welcomed making love with Bruno in her dreams. But here? Now? Naya couldn't shake the feeling that, somehow, she'd landed herself in even more danger.

"I wonder who the lucky man ... or woman ... is," Cassia said.

Naya's stomach sank. "I'm single. There is no lucky anyone."

"I see," Cassia commented, and the way she said it, Naya could tell the other woman saw through her bullshit.

Bruno was no more her mate than Naya was herself an immortal. But any more explanation on her part would only make things worse.

Without turning her head to speak to him directly, Cassia commanded, "Édouard, bring Meiling a cold drink. She needs to cool off."

"Yes, Mistress. Right away."

Then to Naya, Cassia said, "We're about to arrive at the base of Shèng Shān Mountain. Are you excited to return?"

"No, most definitely not. I wish we didn't have to come here at all." At least in that, Naya was able to tell the truth.

"We won't remain long. Then we'll proceed to our next part of the journey."

"Which is?"

"Oh, we'll go to one of my estates."

"And where will this estate be?"

"I haven't decided yet. Rest assured, wherever we go, it will be exciting."

Naya's gut churned for a whole different reason. Alone with Cassia and her minions was even worse than with Cassia at a monastery filled with master vampire monks.

How the hell was she going to get herself out of this? Without an answer, Naya accepted the glass and bottle of sparkling water from Édouard, wondering if Maverick had found Meiling. If she was safe.

And where Bruno was and whether he'd ever thought of her in the same way she dreamt of him.

CHAPTER ELEVEN

BRUNO

HEAT WASHED through Bruno's body in a sudden rush, startling him.

"What happened? Are you all right?" Meiling asked him from the other side of her red glowing prison. Its integrity hadn't diminished in the least, despite the fact that the immortal was both injured and long absent. The immortal and the one surviving vampire had disappeared more than an hour before. There had been time for the backup team of Rocky Mountain Pack wolves to help the injured members of the smaller assault teams away and back to the pack's home, where their healers would assist the shifters in their recovery. Those who were capable of recovering anyhow.

Another of the wolves had died on site, his body

tangled with the corpse of the vampire who'd killed him.

Bruno hadn't known the shifter, but a tangible heaviness coated the air like an unpleasant odor that couldn't be shaken—even now that most of the shifters had left, carrying away the body of their fallen comrade.

Some of the other wolves were also gravely injured. Their recuperation would take days, perhaps weeks, even with their advanced healing. The one wolf had been nearly sliced in half—and had still lived.

Bruno shook his head, trying to clear the sudden thick haze that had arrived out of nowhere, and seemingly without reason. "Sí. Yes, yes, I'm fine."

Meiling peered at him suspiciously. Though she looked exactly like Naya, her expressions were often different. Naya had never regarded Bruno with narrowed eyes like this, as if attempting to unravel a puzzle and all its secrets. Then again, Bruno had barely spent time with Naya. For all he knew, she gave unsettled wolf shifters the squinty-eyed third degree all the time. It was only Brother Wolf's insistence that Naya was his mate that made him feel an otherwise unreasonable closeness to her.

"Then why'd you jump like that?" Meiling persisted.

Because he felt as if warm liquid were sweeping everywhere through his body, pooling in his groin, making him feel aroused when there was absolutely no reason for it. Because he should have been sharing in the heaviness the others were experiencing instead of feeling suddenly light and ... excited.

He stared back at Meiling for a few beats, grateful he stood alone with her while Maverick paced, speaking into his cell phone, far enough away across the expanse of the warehouse not to be overheard, not even by the acute hearing of a wolf shifter. Several other pack shifters remained outside, on guard, just in case the immortal should choose to return—though what any of them could do if that were the case, Bruno had no idea. In the end, they'd been fortunate the mage had left and taken his vampire minion with him. Until they understood how to kill him, any encounter with the mage was a great risk, especially when his power was sufficient to maintain a large magical prison dome that didn't waver no matter what they threw into it, trying to disrupt it.

"What made you jump like that?" Meiling asked again.

Bruno groaned under his breath. She was persistent, he'd give her that. "I have no idea."

Only, he did. It just made no damn sense!

Even now, his skin tingled all over with the whisper of Naya's caresses—he was certain it was her touch. It could be no one else's. Her energy made Brother Wolf respond in a way he'd never responded to any other woman before.

When Bruno closed his eyes, he could practically feel her touching him all over. As if she were standing right there beside him, her hands and lips exploring every inch of his body, trailing across his bare skin, leaving a tantalizing trail of tingles pricking at him, making him wish he could rip his clothes off and follow the path of her touch with his own hands so he could make her exploration that much more concrete.

When he opened his eyes again, it took real effort. He wanted to stay in that place within his mind, where he could easily believe Naya was there with him, desiring him. Where he could believe he wasn't crazy for thinking she was his mate despite barely knowing her.

Where his fantasies could come to life...

But her twin sister was staring back at him with bright blue eyes that seemed to see too much, to comprehend what he didn't want her to. He didn't even understand this, but he did wish to keep it private, to keep this connection to Naya, whatever it was, even if it was just him imagining it, to himself.

But he was in the middle of a vast, empty warehouse that had seen so much violence and darkness that it left a permanent mark on the space.

And Naya was still gone. He still needed to find her—and he would, the very second he freed her sister.

But she's here with you now, a voice murmured from somewhere deep inside him.

As if to confirm this whisper of—what? His intuition? A mate connection when they hadn't even had the chance to bond yet?—he couldn't deny the zing that raced straight to his dick, instantly hardening it, as if Naya's hands were directly squeezing him.

He grunted before he could stop himself, remembering that Meiling was watching him.

Smiling tightly at her, in a hoarse voice that croaked when he felt another squeeze around his genitals, he said, "I'm going to sit."

Unceremoniously, he sat right where he'd stood, on the hard concrete floor next to the glowing dome. "It's been a long, exhausting day." That part at least was true. His whole body had been wired from concern for Naya and Lara, and then even more tense with the disappointment of realizing Naya wasn't here, but still missing.

He brought his knees up, leaning his arms on them to appear relaxed despite the fact that now he was anything but—but mostly to disguise his engorging erection. At this angle, Meiling wouldn't be able to see how the front of his jeans were straining—at the most inopportune of times.

The pressure that he imagined was from Naya's hands vanished, but arousal continued to pump through his body as if he were about to make love to the woman.

"Something is definitely going on with you," Meiling said. "Why won't you tell me?"

Because what would I say? That I'm about to make love to your missing and identical sister ... in my imagination? Yeah, that sounded nuts even to him.

"Tell me," Meiling insisted. "If this has to do with Naya, you have to tell me." She paused, before her voice became gentler, wheedling even. "I need to get her back. I only just was getting to know her."

Yeah. That's exactly how he felt too.

Another shot of pure arousal rushed through him like a hot, blazing wave.

Okay. Maybe that wasn't *exactly* how he felt.

But perhaps Meiling had a point. What he was experiencing felt too strong, too real, to be simply a product of his imagination. Yes, his imagination was plenty vivid, and yes he'd found himself fantasizing about Naya many times since the first time he'd allowed himself to follow that path. But he wouldn't have allowed himself to do that here, and certainly not now, not when so much was still at stake. Not when they still weren't certain they'd be able to free Meiling at all, when Naya was in more danger perhaps even than before, now that even more unknowns surrounded the woman who'd taken her this time.

He swallowed hard as his dick throbbed, straining against the waistband of his boxers and his jeans, pushing them both out, making him grateful the front of his t-shirt was tucked in to conceal that fact at least. His voice strangled despite his efforts to steady it, he said, "I think I'm connecting to Naya."

And he had the feeling he was trying to make her come. That thought alone made his erection almost painfully hard. Images of her sprawled out on a bed, legs wide and hooked over his shoulders flooded his mind's eye. He saw himself going down on her, licking and sucking her all over.

He had to stop himself from coming in his pants, shaking his head again, this time violently in an attempt to clear the imagery. He wasn't a pubescent boy. He had more control than this.

Usually. When his thoughts weren't on Naya. When she wasn't invading his mind, his thoughts, overtaking his body...

"What do you mean you're connecting to Naya?" Meiling asked.

"I mean, I can feel her. As if she's here with me right now."

Meiling seemed to think about that for a moment. "Oh." Then her eyes widened as she took him in, sitting on the floor, face probably flushed, eyes perhaps even glazed. "*Ohhhhh.* I see."

Bruno feared that she did indeed see.

"You're *feeling* her." At least she didn't sound coy or like she was holding what felt like a shameful secret against him. He'd about jizzed in his pants in the middle of a crisis, when his thoughts should be on freeing Meiling and finding Naya and getting her back. On making sure the werewolf bloodline was safe and would continue on far beyond the lifelines of these identical women—now *three* of them.

He'd have to tell Lara when he got home. She'd be shocked.

"Yes," he finally said after he decided that Meiling was trying to work out the mystery of *why* he was feeling Naya instead of invading his privacy merely to satiate her curiosity. "I'm *feeling* her. If I didn't know better, I'd swear she was right here with me."

"Hmm." Meiling began pacing the length of her prison, a hand absently touching her face as she considered. "And why do you think you of all people would be connecting with her?"

The answer was on the tip of his tongue—Brother Wolf was urging him to say it, to share the good news with his mate's twin—with the entire world!

But Bruno hesitated, his inner deliberations seeming loud in the cavernous open space that stretched perhaps forty feet over their heads.

Meiling turned back around to face him, stopping just at the edge of the dome, so close that it almost singed the tip of her nose, yet didn't touch her. Her eyes were bright and sincere. "Look, I know we don't know each other. And I understand these are dangerous times. But you can trust me. I promise you that I won't use the information you share with me for anything more than to return Naya to us."

To us, she'd said, and Brother Wolf liked that, chuffing happily inside Bruno.

Bruno stared hard at Meiling, and in doing so he realized with a start that the sensations of Naya being with him, opening herself up to him, inviting him to make love to her ... had ended abruptly. He no longer felt her touch, her lips, the warmth of her moans and devilish smiles. He felt cold all over, wishing he could hold on to the memories of her body against his...

But she'd never touched him at all, and the images of her with him were quickly fleeing, like long shadows giving way to the descending dark of night.

As his body settled, he sat up a little straighter.

Meiling's eyes were sincere, and Bruno's gut *and* wolf trusted her.

"We're mates."

He had no idea that this belief had settled within him as fact until he heard the certainty of his voice outside of himself. There was no denying it anymore. Not after what he'd just experienced.

Brother Wolf was too sure, too possessive of her, for their connection to be anything less.

Meiling's eyes grew large once more, but she didn't speak.

"I'm not sure what happened or why, but all of a sudden I began feeling as if she were touching me. And it seemed so real. I would've sworn she was actually here with me. Only..." He paused at the unreasonable devastation that the admission delivered. "...she isn't here. We don't even know where she is."

"I told you before, I think I know."

Yes, of course! He and Maverick had put further discussion with her on hold earlier when the other pack wolves flooded in, discovering members of the assault teams more seriously injured than Bruno had realized. Amid their shouts, Maverick had run over to better assess the situation, and Bruno had done what he could to help. He'd only just had the chance to return, now that all the injured were gone and Boone was confirmed on his way with the wizards he claimed he trusted.

"Tell me absolutely everything you know," he told Meiling now.

"Yes, it's time." She took a seat on the floor next to the steady glow that kept her imprisoned. She crossed her legs in a lotus position, adjusted the sleeves of what appeared to be a martial arts gi, and leaned a hand on each knee. She opened her mouth to begin.

"You don't question me saying that your sister and I are mates?" Bruno spit out. He hadn't known he'd say it, but she hadn't said a word, hadn't much reacted at all at the news.

A soft chuckle bubbled out from between her lips. "Why would I?" When he didn't reply immediately, she added, "Just because you doubt doesn't mean I do."

"That's not..." He felt his brow furrow. "That's not what I meant."

"I know what you meant. I assume your wolf is telling you she's your mate? And that perhaps you haven't had the chance to have a conversation with her about it yet?" Her words were posed as questions, but still seemed more like statements. The young woman was almost eerily sure of herself.

"That's right," Bruno said slowly.

"I gathered, since she didn't mention you or a mate when we had the chance to talk."

Even though Bruno wouldn't have expected Naya to mention a mate, since she'd have no idea yet that she had one, it still pained him to hear Meiling confirm it aloud.

"Don't worry," she said with a smile. "We'll get her back. I think she's on her way to China."

"China? Why would she be heading to China, of all places?"

His voice had raised in pitch with his surprise, drawing Maverick's attention. He was off the phone now and heading toward them.

"Mav!" Bruno called, though he wasn't sure the alpha would like him using the familiar nickname. "You need to hear this."

When the alpha reached them, he stood next to Bruno, who'd regained control over his body and claimed his feet once more.

"Meiling says Naya's headed to China."

Maverick faced Meiling with a single arched brow. She heeded the silent invitation to continue.

"I was raised in a monastery at the very top of

Shèng Shān Mountain. It's an isolated region in China. The forests are dense around the base of the mountain, and the area is sparsely populated. I can tell from the looks on your faces that you're wondering how I ended up in Asia when I'm clearly not of Asian descent."

Both men had to be wondering, but neither interrupted, riveted, waiting, knowing more understanding would be the result of their patience.

"I was delivered there as an infant and entrusted into the care of the master monks. Vampires."

Bruno's jaw dropped open for a moment before he quickly regained his composure and closed it.

"What were you doing with *vampires?*" Maverick asked. "You're a werewolf, just as Naya is, aren't you?"

"I am. And as to why I ended up with vampires, I do not know. I've never met the woman who delivered me to the monks."

"A woman," Maverick whispered.

"Yes."

"A woman who told the monks about your rare and special ancestry?"

Slowly, Meiling nodded. "So you know."

"We both do. Bruno here is the beta of the Andes Mountain Pack, and he knows of Naya's special purpose as well. Apparently, it is a purpose you also share."

Meiling's unwavering eyes settled on Bruno. "Naya told me about Bruno and his alpha, who is another sister to us."

Bruno felt a weight lift at knowing he wouldn't have to keep Lara secret from Meiling. He hadn't yet decided whether he'd tell her. His loyalty was always to his alpha first, despite her connection to the woman before him.

"I didn't realize there were three of us," Meiling said. "I only recently learned of Naya's existence. Up until last month, I thought I was the only one to carry the burden of being Callan 'the Oak' MacLeod's last remaining descendant." She smiled wistfully. "It's nice to know I'm not alone."

"So why do you think Naya is headed toward this monastery of yours in China?" Maverick asked.

"Oh, I don't lay claim to it. I learned most everything I know while there, but that doesn't mean my time there was particularly pleasant. My training was ... hmm ... intense, shall we say?"

From the way she carried herself, Bruno could tell the woman could *move*. He'd bet that she was swift and lethal in battle. She had as many blades attached to her body as did any of them, and she seemed completely at ease with them there, as if this were her common mode of dress. Blades attached everywhere to her blue gi-style loose pants and shirt, creating tufts in the fabric where the banded sheaths pressed inward.

"When Cassia arrived here—" Meiling started, but Maverick interrupted.

"Who's Cassia?"

"I can't be fully certain, but from how Cyrus spoke of her, I believe she is another immortal."

Bruno's blood chilled in his veins, while Maverick followed up.

"And Cyrus is the immortal that we fought when we arrived here?"

"Yes. He referred to the woman as Cassia, and from everything he said, I think she's another just like him."

"Did this Cassia use magic as Cyrus does?" Bruno asked.

"Not that I saw. But she didn't appear intimidated by him in the least."

Great. "Well, then that doesn't bode well, does it?" Bruno said.

"Not particularly, no. But Cyrus didn't appear fearful of her either. He didn't defer to her, but he did treat her with a certain amount of respect that suggests she's as fearsome an opponent as he is."

Bruno ran his hand roughly through his hair. He had to get Naya back. Now.

"Something curious though," Meiling went on, her energy calm despite the topic. "Apparently, Cassia commissioned Cyrus to capture Naya and hold her here until Cassia could arrive. Of course, Cyrus didn't expect to find two of us when he caught up with Naya."

"And he only caught up with you both because *you* took Naya from the safety of our compound." Maverick's accusation was a rough growl that Bruno's wolf responded to. The alpha did have a bit of a point, and Brother Wolf snarled at how Meiling had exposed his mate to a greater danger.

Meiling wasn't flustered by either of the men's reactions. She smirked at them instead. "After having seen Cyrus in action, do you really think he wouldn't have been able to sneak into your pack and snatch Naya even if I hadn't shown up first? Besides, how was I supposed to know he was coming for her? *You* didn't."

The alpha had no response to that.

"I'd only just learned that I had a sister. After twenty-two years of believing I was alone in the world, I found out I had a twin. So when I heard she was in danger, I escaped my own prison and traveled here, to protect her."

"And you protected her by taking her away from her much larger, much stronger network of protection?" Maverick pushed.

"Yes. I know little to nothing about your pack. But I know my skill level intimately. It was a safe bet."

Damn, Bruno thought. It wasn't even arrogance, just genuine self-confidence. Her assertion that she was a match for a pack of wolf shifters, even though she was a werewolf who lacked many of the advantages of regular shifters, made Bruno wish he could see her fight. After sparring with Naya, he wanted to see both sisters in action. But mostly he wanted to see Naya again. To watch her move like a puma, sleek, strong, wickedly fast, and incredibly lethal.

"The curious thing is," Meiling continued, "Cyrus didn't know who we were at all. Yes, he expected there to be only one of us, but beyond that he didn't know why Cassia would want Naya. He knows now though."

"No," Bruno said softly.

Meiling frowned. "Cyrus is apparently capable of compelling others to tell the truth. He forced Naya to tell him about our heritage and why it's so important."

Bruno felt as if acid now burned through his

body. The fate of all werewolves was at stake, and now the evil immortal knew their secret?

"That's ... unfortunate," Maverick said, rubbing at his left shoulder absently. He'd had one of his wolves pop it back into its socket, but steadfastly refused to head back to the pack's home for focused healing—even with his head still not completely attached to his neck.

"Most unfortunate," said Meiling. "But more curious still, Cyrus hid the fact that there are two of us from Cassia. When she arrived—and she came with her own set of vampire slaves, by the way—he put a spell on me so that she wouldn't see me. He let Cassia take Naya alone."

"Naya must've put up some brutal resistance, then," Maverick said. "That girl can *fight*."

"She was unconscious when Cassia took her. Well, she ordered her vampires to carry her out. She didn't even touch Naya."

Bruno discovered himself clenching his fists, ready to do something about the situation already. The wizards had better arrive soon!

"So this Cassia doesn't know about you, then," Maverick said. Bruno looked over at the alpha. The man appeared exhausted, weighed down by the burdens of leadership when he had someone so precious entrusted to his care. His body was busy healing at its expected accelerated pace, but even so, Maverick still looked like he'd fought a bulldozer—and lost.

"Well..." Meiling touched a hand to the wolf's head pendant that rested behind her shirt, just above her breasts. Naya's necklace. "Cassia took Naya thinking she was me, and it has nothing to do with Naya's necklace I'm wearing. I don't think either one of them noticed it. I'm not entirely sure why Cassia thought Naya was me, given that she apparently asked Cyrus to find Naya..."

Meiling paused. "But from what I could tell, Cassia left thinking that she had me, and that I was the only one there was. I also heard her telling one of her vamps to make sure her jet was ready to go, that she had some business to take care of with the monks. Now, I can't be totally sure she meant the monks from the Shèng Shān Monastery, but since she thinks she has me, it's likely. And she needs a plane to get there, plus a whole hell of a lot of stamina."

"Meaning?" Maverick gingerly explored the gash in his neck that was busy suturing together.

"Meaning, once you get to the region of Shèng Shān Mountain, that only gets you so far. Like I said, the forest around it is thick and old, and there are no roads, just walking trails. Once you get to the mountain, the only way to reach the monastery at the top is on foot."

"Okay..." Maverick said.

"And it's more than four-thousand feet nearly straight up." She chuckled darkly. "Once, to punish me for not completing all my assigned studies in one day, one of the vampire masters ordered me to climb the mountain on my knees."

"*Mierda*. That's harsh," Bruno said.

"I was eight."

Maverick whistled. "We have to get to Naya."

"We have to get her *now*," Bruno echoed.

"I have one ally there," Meiling said. "His name is Li Kāng. He's a mage, and he's the one who told me about Naya."

"How did he—?"

But Bruno was interrupted. The door to the warehouse flung open loudly, and a shifter raced in, spotting his alpha right away and running toward them.

Maverick stalked toward the harried man. "What is it, Scooby?"

"Boone and the wizards are here. And..."

"And what?" Maverick barked, his impatience familiar to Bruno.

"Well, you gotta see it, man. They're, like, kinda dead ... or something."

CHAPTER TWELVE

CASSIA

UNLIKE WHEN THEY landed in Strathdale and the moody damp wind of the Scottish Highlands caught her by surprise, Cassia was bundled up against the chill of Shèng Shān Mountain. She'd traveled there enough to know that it was never entirely temperate, even when it was supposed to be springtime. Warmth didn't quite manage to reach the old vampires' abode, as if their seemingly endless strict rules wouldn't allow it. They openly rejected comforts, condemning them as marks of weakness among their acolytes.

A phantom shiver ran the length of Cassia's body in anticipation of the bone-chilling cold that permeated the large monastery, entirely constructed of stone. The vampire "masters" likely never suffered the cold, but their human slaves—with their blood-pumping hearts—definitely did.

For all the power and abilities that Cassia had amassed over her long life, she still couldn't control her body's reactions to the elements. Something she'd find the way to remedy someday, she was sure of it. She always got her way ... eventually.

An immortal goddess capable of connecting to air currents and riding them needed insulation from the cold.

However, the frigid temperatures weren't the only thing Cassia was dreading about this visit. The vampire monks reminded her of dusty old tomes, their covers embossed with gilded flourishes of letters that caught the light, promising an important, perhaps even sacred or enchanting read. But in reality, when the spine was cracked, the book's contents turned out to be pompous spewings riddled with a misplaced sense of importance, insufferable, however annoyingly necessary.

"Watch the girl closely, Édouard," Cassia said over her shoulder, causing the vampire to run a few steps to walk at her side.

"Of course, Mistress. Am I watching for anything in particular?"

They trekked across a narrow path, a well-worn seam amid dense old-growth trees. Clearly, the vampire masters, wholly unbothered by their many secret hypocrisies, continued to indulge in imported luxuries. The austerity of their monastery was solely for those ranked beneath them in the complicated hierarchy they'd invented.

A single-engine Cessna parked on the airstrip next to Cassia's jet confirmed her conclusions. The vampires had been smuggling in delicacies, since their errand boys had to travel the long distances on yaks.

Cassia lowered her voice as she answered Édouard. Not only did she not want Meiling to overhear—and the girl, despite being a werewolf instead of a regular shifter still must have acute hearing to some degree—but Cassia didn't want the other vampires aware of her true plans either. She'd learned long ago to keep her intentions to herself. Only then could she be certain they wouldn't leak out. But Édouard wouldn't dare defy her.

"I want you to gauge her strength, her agility, her prowess. Watch for any signs that her body is already reacting to the full moon tonight. Anything noteworthy, I want to know."

Édouard nodded his assent. A beam of sunshine filtered through tree canopies to glisten across the pate of his head.

"Will this girl be next to receive your generous gift?"

Cassia offered Meiling a quick glance. The girl walked alone at the very back of the entourage, save for one of the vampires assigned to watch her at all times. Meiling noticed Cassia's attention and looked up, eyes curious even as the rest of her features remained tight with evident trepidation.

Cassia scowled and faced forward again as they continued to walk. "It's likely that I will choose her, yes. She's here, and I've grown impatient. Davina let me down—all that time I invested into her, and for what? A total betrayal. A disappointment. Now I have but three more chances for my scientists to get this right."

"I'm sure they won't let you down."

"Not if they know what's good for them they won't."

"I believe their fear of you, Mistress, is healthy and strong. I pass on rumors of the legendary *Osculum Mortis* with regularity. They think that if they look at you too long, you will kill them."

Not all that far from the truth. If Cassia didn't need their skills, and if they weren't the top specialists in their fields, she would have punished them for letting her down in Strathdale.

"Good. Continue to do so. Fear is a healthy and important emotion."

In others, of course. Cassia had set out to vanquish her own fears centuries ago. Fears were a weakness unbecoming of her kind.

"Indeed, Mistress."

Cassia glanced upward to take in the full expanse of Shèng Shān Mountain and the monastery that sat daringly atop it as if placed there by a divine hand. From a distance, the structure appeared majestic, magical even, a wondrous feat of imagination and agility. A staircase carved from the mountain itself rose steadily from its base, climbing ever upward until the thousands of steps finally reached the monastery's entrance. Beginning about halfway up, snow dappled the treetops that crowded the mountain. Another quarter of the way higher and the trees gave way to the biting, bitter winds that whistled hauntingly around the mountain like the ghosts of the many humans who died there as husks empty of their life-giving blood.

"I will deal with that snake Ji-Hun as soon as I arrive. Then I must speak with Li Kāng." He alone would be able to tell her how Meiling learned of Naya's existence and how the girl was able to escape the monastery under his watch.

"And the book, Mistress? Will you retrieve that as well?"

"Oh yes. Those *bastardi* don't get to keep my payment when they haven't done their job. We will find out who betrayed me."

Because someone had. There was no other way for the girl to learn of her sister. She hoped it hadn't been Li Kāng, as she still had use for the mage with the unusual ability to co-exist so well with vampires. But if it was he, she could do without him.

She could do without anyone if she had to, even Édouard, though she'd miss him most. She'd invested so much training into him.

"And what of the girl? She will shift with the full moon," he asked.

Édouard's mind was sharp. He was able to keep track of the many lines that wove into her wide net. It nearly made her wish he could be her friend.

But friends were a liability. Their betrayal sliced deeper than she would allow. And a friend that was both family and companion? She shook her head to dislodge the sudden memory of her cousin's face. So many centuries after she'd forced Cassia to kill her, Cassia hardly thought of her anymore ... or of what she'd done.

Cassia cleared her throat, noticing how Édouard

was careful not to look at her then. Over the years in her company, he'd learned to read her moods.

"We'll use the monastery's confinement cell for the girl through the full moon."

"I shall prepare us to spend the night, then. Just as soon as I reach the top."

"Good, Édouard. I'll see you up there." She took a step off to the side, but then added, "And do hurry. I want your bloodsucking friends to witness what I do to Ji-Hun." Her smile spread wide in anticipation. She'd enjoy putting the stuffy vampires in their place again. Too long had passed without reminding the monks of her superiority.

She closed her eyes to feel the air as it whisked around her, ebbing and floating and speeding by, depending on which pocket of the element she tapped into.

Here, at the base of the mountain, magic was easier to feel, to access. The vampires had discovered a center of energy and claimed it by erecting their edifice directly on top of it.

The moment she felt the air whip beneath her, responding to her will already, she leaned into it, allowing it to carry her upward.

She opened her eyes and looked down twenty feet at Meiling. The girl's mouth hung open. Cassia nodded in approval at her admiration, felt herself light in the air, and pictured it moving her ever higher.

No other immortal in the world could manipulate air as she did. And soon she'd have something else none of them did.

A wolf's raw power as well.

Enjoying the way her body hung effortlessly in the air, she whipped toward the peak.

She had business to attend to.

———

Naya

The bitch was flying.

Motherfucking *flying*!

What. The. Hell?

No wonder even the vampires in her little fan club were terrified of her.

Naya had never heard of anyone flying. Sure, she imagined there was a mage or two out there who could do it by casting some spell or another, and she'd heard rumors of eagle shifters. But it was an entirely different thing to witness a woman just ... taking off. She didn't even need a running start. She simply ...

floated upward, as if she were in command of the air. And Naya thought she possibly was...

Naya's contemplation of escape suddenly seemed foolhardy as she took in the bright, pulsing waves of energy that surrounded Cassia as she flew.

Naya's ability to see energy was fickle. Ordinarily, she couldn't pinpoint why she could see energy at some times and not others. The ability seemed entirely random. This time, however, she knew. The closer they drew to the mountain, the more her entire body buzzed with a force she could only think to describe as magic. Whatever it was, it was real as it encircled the freaky immortal in iridescent shimmers.

Naya was certain that's what Cassia must be. An immortal. A supernatural being so powerful that not even death could interfere with the course she set.

Naya tilted her gaze down when she noticed the balding vampire waiting for her up ahead. His constant *Yes, Mistress* this, and *Why of course, Mistress* that, and *Shall I suck your proverbial dick now, Mistress?* had set her teeth on edge—and also alerted her that of all of Cassia's minions she should be most careful with him. The man clearly had no will of his own left.

She caught up with Édouard and he fell into

stride beside her, the vampire who'd been guarding her before moving on ahead to join the other undead.

"I take it we're going to be taking the stairs while *Mistress* uses the elevator?" Naya heaped a healthy dose of snark into her use of *mistress*, but Édouard didn't seem to notice, nodding at her approvingly.

If he believed she would be so easily brain-washed, perhaps there was a way to use that to her advantage. She couldn't think of one just yet, but still.

"The mistress is using her great power to travel on air currents. There is no elevator."

Naya blinked at the vampire. *Ohhh-kay.* So he left whatever sense of humor he might have had in whatever century he was born.

Naya forced an empty smile to cover the fact that she just thought of something.

This monastery was in China. *China!* What if they spoke to her in Chinese?

What was she thinking, and how had she not thought of it before? *Of course* they'd speak to her in Chinese.

I'm so incredibly fucked.

She didn't even know how to say *hello* or *namaste* or whatever thing vampires with a taste for Zen and human blood said to each other.

"You appear worried," Édouard commented with a slight and sophisticated French accent.

"No, I'm fine." She put her all into being convincing, pushing down the approximate ten million things that could go wrong with her ruse as Meiling chill-as-a-cool-cucumber monk girl.

"Don't worry," Édouard said with an emptiness that only made Naya worry more. "The mistress will take care of you."

Yeah, that's exactly what I'm afraid of, asshole.

"She has a plan for everything," he continued, only making things worse. "Whatever you're thinking of, I assure you, she's already thought of it. She thinks things out a hundred steps ahead of the rest of us. You'll never be able to figure out what she's planning." A wistful smile followed that statement.

Naya sighed. The man was gone, gone, goooone. Whatever free will he might have once had was nowhere to be found.

Craning her neck up to take in the monastery so far up, she had to squint to make out its details, even with her perfect sight: "So how far up is the place?"

"From the bottom of the first riser to the final step in the grand staircase, it is exactly four-thousand-two-hundred-and-forty-four feet. That's seven-thousand-two-hundred-and-seventy-seven steps."

Naya chuckled darkly. "That's it, huh?"

"Is that not enough for you?" He glanced at her, appearing serious. "I assure you, even with your stamina, it will be quite the challenge."

It was a challenge Naya was looking forward to. There was no better remedy for all the tension running through her than to move her body. She was exhausted from all the times she'd been taken against her will. She'd never gotten a shower after her last workout, in the gym with Bruno, which seemed like a million years ago, and she could smell herself—not a pleasant reminder of how long she'd been gone from her pack.

Maverick and Clove were probably out of their minds looking for her. And Bruno ... would he even be thinking of her? Would he even care that she was gone—and having sex dreams of him, in which she was crazy enough to consider that he might actually be her mate?

To dream of having a mate, she actually had to survive and get out of there alive.

And Meiling ... the *real* Meiling. Naya hadn't even gotten the chance to say goodbye.

The twin she'd only just met was alone with a scary-as-fuck immortal with the ability to magic things with the flick of his wrist.

She rubbed her neck, so over the endless looping of her thoughts. All it did was freak her out more, and

Naya wasn't used to being freaked out. She hadn't trained as hard as she had her entire life to be a victim. She was used to taking charge and kicking ass.

What she wasn't used to was flying fucks who scared the crap out of even old vampires. When the immortal man had discussed Cassia with his own minion vampire, he'd sounded grudgingly respectful of her.

Not a good sign.

But as much as an appreciation of how dangerous the situation was made her uncomfortable, the constant wariness and apprehension was worse. It was disempowering.

Naya decided right then and there she'd had more than enough of it. She might not have control over what Cassia did, but she *could* control her own thoughts. Her attitude.

She could and *would* refuse to cower at the asshole woman who believed she had the right to take people and do whatever she wanted with them. To behave as if she were a god.

Fuck. Her. Fuck her *hard.*

If Cassia tried to kill her, then at least Naya could go knowing she had sisters who could still spare werewolves from extinction. She wouldn't have failed an entire species for many generations to come.

Naya would resist with everything she had until her very last breath. And she had a whole hell of a lot of fight in her.

Cassia quite literally could walk on air...

Well, Naya had prepared her entire life to overcome impossible odds. She'd always known that powerful people would come after her. *Hunt her.* Try to take her out.

The specifics of her circumstances were a surprise, but not the fact that she was a target. *That* she was ready for. *That* she actually *could* handle.

It was all a matter of mindset.

Cassia had picked on the wrong werewolf...

She'd backed Naya against a hard, unyielding wall, and pinned her there.

Hell, Naya was about to tear that wall down, stone by motherfucking stone.

She'd pretend to be a kitty cat so that Cassia wouldn't realize she was a lioness—until Naya ripped her throat out. Bitch couldn't die? Unlikely. Everything had an end, one way or another.

Naya just had to find the way to end her.

Feeling better than she had since she woke up in a glowing red dome prison in the middle of a warehouse in Colorado, she breathed in the clean, crisp scent of mountains and trees and *hope.*

She ran the rest of the way to the stairs, passing

the other vamps, welcoming the familiar flow of her muscles. When she started up the stairway, she took the steps two at a time, welcoming the burn in her thighs.

The chance for her escape wasn't here yet, but it would come. Nothing ever went perfectly to plan, not even for immortals.

CHAPTER THIRTEEN

NAYA

SEVEN-THOUSAND-TWO-HUNDRED-AND-SEVENTY-SEVEN STEPS WAS a number worthy of respect. Of that, there was no doubt. Naya's leg muscles bulged and burned from the demands she'd placed on them, but every step she'd taken had felt like a goal accomplished. Her skin was pink and flushed. She felt as if she could climb four-thousand more feet, though she was relieved she didn't have to.

The air was thinner up here, making her lungs work harder than they were accustomed to, and it was crisper, colder, making her grateful she was at least dressed in a long-sleeved tunic and leggings over the workout bra and boy shorts she'd been wearing before. If she weren't a werewolf who grew up in the

Rockies of Colorado, she'd be freezing. Instead, the sharp bite in the air kept her alert.

By the time Naya reached the monastery, she'd convinced herself that she'd find a way out of this mess she was in. All she had to do was remain aware and ready. An opportunity for her escape would arise. It had to.

The monastery was a towering structure made up from endless amounts of gray stones roughly twice the size of bricks. It had few windows and those it did have were narrow. Most of the windows on the lower levels were angled openings so archers could shoot arrows at approaching foes while not permitting the return favor.

Its walls were smooth, with no more than subtle notches between each stone. There were no easy handholds, no obvious vulnerabilities.

The monastery of Shèng Shān Mountain obviously wasn't simply a place for spiritual enlightenment —or whatever version of monk-like teachings vampires engaged in—the monastery was a fortress carefully designed to ward off breaches. No wonder Cassia deposited Meiling here as a baby. Who would ever find a savior to the werewolf bloodline here of all places?

The stairs ended at a large landing that morphed into a courtyard. A pair of guards stood to either side of its entrance. As stoic and unmoving as statues, they didn't so much as blink at Naya's sudden arrival. Cassia had likely warned them she was coming, because these men weren't vampires, and humans wouldn't be able to sense her the way a supernatural could. Two of the men held spears, the other two curved swords. They weren't playing around; their weapons weren't even sheathed, as if they might need to use them at a moment's notice.

Maybe since the dangerous immortal lunatic is in the house. Naya itched with the need to get as far away from Cassia as she could.

High stone walls surrounded the courtyard on three sides, shielding it from the winds that whipped and whistled at this altitude. Several square patches of sand nestled between squat walls, and a couple of monks occupied two of them, tracing intricate patterns across the sand with long wooden tools that resembled rakes. Their movements were fluid and graceful, as if this were a meditation to them. At Naya's arrival, neither of them glanced up, even when her attention skimmed across them, with their long flowing robes and almost as long hair, held away from their faces in multiple braids. They traced spirals, circles, and waves into the sand, not a single straight line in sight.

Carefully manicured gardens occupied several

more sunken beds on either side of the sand pits. Delicate white flowers grew amid petite gnarled and twisted trees that reminded Naya of bonsais. A fountain in the center of it all gurgled soothingly, suggesting that though the monastery teetered so high up the mountain range, somehow the monks had managed to tap into a natural water source.

A sudden call from somewhere behind the monastery building itself guided Naya past the sand-raking monks, beyond more perfectly manicured gardens, and onto a path paved with stones that led around the side of the building.

"Dayum," Naya said under her breath, softly enough that she wouldn't draw the attention of any nearby vampires. As a general rule, she didn't particularly fear the undead bloodsuckers. However, she also wasn't foolish. Any supernatural creature deserved a healthy level of wariness until she could gauge their prowess.

There, in front of her, dozens, perhaps even a hundred, acolytes occupied a large, recessed patio that served as a training area. A monk in pristine white stood ramrod straight at the head of them, guiding the students, all outfitted in identical burgundy. They appeared to range in age from the prepubescent to teenagers who were nearly adults. Every single one of them had a full head of black hair that glistened in the sunlight of mid-morning.

With her long blond hair, Meiling would have stood out like a dove amid a flock of ravens.

The monk in white called out a command in Chinese, and at once every acolyte swung around to execute a perfect crescent kick. Another order, and they crouched into a low sweep meant to kick an opponent's legs out from under them. A third prompt, and they rose to perform a combination of fast punches and jabs that had Naya longing to join them.

Now this ... *this* was the way to train! Yes, she'd managed to become a proficient fighter herself within her pack, but she'd had to chase down each and every skill. She'd researched different fighting styles and hounded fellow pack shifters until they taught her what they knew. But largely she'd taught herself, her own drive responsible for the endless hours she spent perfecting her form.

Something about this rigid structure appealed to her—though maybe all the rules would have eventually driven her mad?

With a start, she noticed she was mooning, enjoying the comforting sight of so much order and proficiency. But Cassia's vampire underlings would be arriving. They'd lagged behind her and her punishing speed. Given what they were, it had been their choice. She suspected they made the most of whatever chances they got away from Cassia's ever-watchful eye.

Walking back to the entrance to the monastery, she glanced upward at the human-sized double doors that were set into another pair of larger doors sized for giants. Naya took a moment to hope there weren't any of those kinds of creatures inside. She'd never heard of or seen a giant. Didn't mean they couldn't be real. After all, she turned into a wolf on the full moon.

"Meiling," Édouard called from behind her. "You must wait for us."

All vampires had advanced speed. If the bloodies didn't feel like using it, that was on them.

She pulled open one of the doors and stepped inside, allowing it to shut behind her with a soft thud. Moving to the side of the doors, she flattened herself against the wall, waiting for her eyes to adjust to the dim lighting. It didn't take long. After all, she was a werewolf. When she was in her wolf form, she was as strong and fast as ordinary wolf shifters were—though with far less control. When she was in her human form, as best she could estimate she possessed only a fraction of their preternatural abilities. Her vision was far better than a human's, but not as good as a shifter's walking around on two legs.

High ceilings arched across the open space in front of her, several candlelit hallways branching off from it. Another set of gargantuan double doors cut into a wall a hundred yards directly in front of her. Hundreds of pillows, encased in fine silk fabrics, dotted the stone floor. Otherwise, there was no furniture at all to disrupt the openness, save a single long table like a bar against one wall, and hundreds of hooks on the other, with assorted items such as prayer wheels, drums, and weapons hanging off of them.

The door yanked open beside her, and in rushed Édouard, the other vampires close behind.

It took Édouard a moment to locate her pressed against the wall. "I told you to wait, *mademoiselle*."

Naya shrugged. "And I don't care what you said. I'm not your little puppet." Duh. She was here against her will, and Édouard didn't frighten her despite his clear age. Unlike his mistress, cruelty didn't vibrate from him with every move he made, every word he uttered, so potent that Naya could almost taste it.

One of the other vampires took a step past Édouard to hiss at her. He was handsome, with dark wavy hair and a body that nicely filled out his charcoal suit. His bronzed skin suggested he was at least old enough to withstand the sunshine. With his chiseled features and bright tawny eyes, he appeared better suited to the cover of GQ than to climbing up a mountain.

When Naya leaned around Édouard to glare at him, he hissed again. Like a snake.

"Fuck off, asshole," Naya said, talking over him as his hissing grew louder. "I don't pretend to control you. How 'bout you give me the same courtesy, yeah?" She smiled coldly.

His similarities to a GQ cover model evaporated as he bared his teeth and hissed even louder.

Naya, though human, bared her teeth right back, letting Sister Wolf rise within her to let loose a growl so vicious that the vampire ceased his hot-aired gesturing after that, averting his eyes.

"Knock it off, Ernesto," Édouard scolded, pointing an equally reprimanding look at Naya.

She rolled her eyes so obnoxiously that the older vamp couldn't help but notice, before walking up the aisle between cushioned seating on either side of her.

"Wait," Édouard called—just as shouts sounded from the other side of the doors that led beyond the vast room.

Naya ran toward the exit, yanked a door open before the vampires trailing could stop her, and rushed in.

She stopped, foot freezing in mid-step before she finally lowered it.

Oh shit, she thought loudly, thankful the words didn't slip past her lips.

The vampires crowded in behind her, taking in the tension in the room that all but crackled, rushing ahead of her and bowing—lowering to their knees and pressing their foreheads to the marble floor.

Naya hadn't even finished taking in the series of ornate thrones at the front of the room or the way men and women, all dressed in gi-like robes, lined the walls, hands pressed in prayer in front of their chests, heads bowed low. When Naya saw even Édouard hit the floor, she did the same, hoping that was what she was expected to do.

Because the scent of fresh blood tinged the air. She was in a room filled with vampires and the humans they fed on. And Cassia was at the front of the room, facing down the vampire who sat in the most grandiose throne, positioned in front of the others.

Clearly, he was the head honcho. His eyes were as black and lifeless as coal.

Those of a predator used to capturing his intended prey.

Cassia glanced over her shoulder at them when

Naya would have never, *ever* taken her eyes off Head Honcho.

Although he appeared to be in his early thirties, Naya would have been surprised if he didn't rival Cassia in actual age. Magic oozed off him, like a cloying, overly pungent cologne that would stick to her. Revulsion welled in Naya.

The vampire might be as bad as Cassia. Maybe worse. His power felt as dark as his eyes, and she already feared they might be capable of sucking out her soul. It was an irrational thought, but she still had it.

"Finally, my minions are here," Cassia announced to the assembly in loud, clear English.

Reeling from the shock of discovering herself in an even more precarious predicament than she'd anticipated, Naya didn't even react to possibly being included in that "minion" statement. Nor did she experience relief at the immortal's use of a language she could understand.

Naya knew enough of what Cassia had planned to have every nerve on edge—now that she set eyes on her intended target.

Naya was a minnow who'd believed herself a shark, only to discover herself in blood-infested waters with circling, hungry, great whites.

And she was an imposter who could be discovered with as little as a casual "kiss my slippered feet, bitch" in Chinese that she wouldn't know how to respond to.

Her heartbeat threatened to speed up. Her head dipped low, she forced herself to focus on her breathing. Every vampire could hear a heartbeat as close as hers was, even when she shared the space with humans. The older the vampire, the more precise their ability to discern which beat belonged to which body.

Who knew what a vampire as old as Honcho could do? She'd never met one. She was pretty sure not even Maverick had met one as old as he.

Without more than a passing glance at Naya, Cassia faced Head Honcho again. His long jet-black hair was braided in spirals all across his head—his hair stylist was a rock star. His robes were an indigo blue no one else in the room wore. His features remained placid, his almond-shaped eyes calm as a sea about to storm. But Naya didn't buy his nonchalance for a second.

Maybe this was how she got free of Cassia ... only to become a slave to a more frightening creature.

Honcho looked like he could slice the immortal's throat wide open with one of his sharp fingernails before the woman could twitch.

"You have betrayed my trust," Cassia announced

in a steady, even voice that rang throughout the suddenly silent room.

Not a pleat of fabric rustled at her announcement, though a few of the onlookers glanced up from the devotional press of their hands.

"You have broken our agreement."

More eyes peeked up at the scene.

The nervous energy in the room cranked up a notch.

"For that," Cassia sang out, "you will die."

This time, a few gasps interrupted the otherwise shocked quiet that followed the crazy woman's declaration.

Cassia did see that Honcho was flanked by six vampires, three on each side, who appeared nearly as formidable as he did, right?

But Cassia either didn't notice or care. "Shall I kill you here, Ji-Hun, or would you like to spare your slaves the task of mopping up your body parts later?"

The immortal chuckled, dark, low, and rough, like flint knocking against rock.

"Who am I kidding? You don't care about your minions. You enjoy pomp, and there is nowhere more pompous on this mountain than your throne room. This is where you'll want to die."

From the pocket of her jacket, Cassia withdrew a slim, elegant hair clasp adorned with small, pink-hued pearls. Then she slipped out of her coat, tossed it at some humans without looking, and wrapped her long dark hair up into an elegant bun. The clasp snapped as she locked her hair in place.

"I'll let you choose the weapons, though it is you who has betrayed me."

How fucking magnanimous of the woman...

But when Ji-Hun finally spoke, his long fingers gripping the dragons carved into the armrests of his throne, Naya didn't expect what he said.

"I've done nothing to betray you, *Osculum Mortis*. I am a man who values his life. Whatever accusation you have against me, I request the chance to argue my defense."

What? Ji-Hun was *deferring* to Cassia?

Naya brought her head up from the floor, needing to understand.

Cassia took two menacing steps toward the vampire. His body didn't tense in any visible way, but Naya sensed his fear like a metallic smell in the air.

"No, you may not plead your defense," Cassia said. "Your betrayal is undeniable. Choose the way of your death, or I'll choose for you."

This time, Ji-Hun's pale throat bobbed as he swallowed.

On Ji-Hun's far left, another master vampire, the

one who sat, rose to his feet. Back straight, chest puffed out, he said, "I offer my life as a sacrifice, in place of that of our highest master Ji-Hun. Great immortal, take me instead."

What. The. Fuck?

Cassia hmmphed in a quick grunt, then frowned. "You allow those beneath you to die for you, Ji-Hun? Where is your sense of honor?"

Ji-Hun laughed. "You are merely envious that my students are so willing to die in my place." His voice was accented in the same way as Meiling's, only more noticeably so.

Naya half expected Cassia to kill the ancient vamp on the spot—somehow—but she laughed instead, her tinkling seductiveness entirely discordant with the scene she so clearly commanded.

"You are perhaps correct about that, Ji-Hun. Good help is difficult to come by. That one fact doesn't change despite the passing centuries."

"Indeed, *Osculum Mortis.*" His light tone suggested they were friends, or at the very least, close acquaintances.

Cassia stalked toward the sacrificial master on the left, humans scurrying out of her way.

She didn't so much as glance at them.

Naya took the opportunity to rise and stand

beside the rest of the crowd, abandoning Cassia's minions in their sustained prostration.

"You're new," Cassia told the man with long hair shaved into a mohawk, then braided into a single plait that reached his waist. "What's your name?"

"I am Master Xiong." He dipped his head in deference to Cassia.

Naya chewed the inside of her cheek.

"How old are you?" Cassia asked him.

"I've walked this earth for more than seven-hundred years."

"And you are ready to die now?"

"There is no greater honor than giving my life for worthy Grand Master Ji-Hun."

Cassia smiled, and Naya tensed. A smiling Cassia seemed more dangerous than an openly angry one. "Then your character is more honorable than the man you seek to protect. I deny your request."

She spun to face Grand Master Ji-Hun, whose composure was not as even as it had been at the start.

"There is only one end for those who break their promises to me. Rise now or die where you sit."

It was only then that Naya understood with complete clarity that Cassia was more lethal than anyone else on this mountaintop. Perhaps than any other person in the country of China, even with its

Shaolin monks. Likely even more so than anyone on the whole continent of Asia.

Either Naya escaped her or she died at her hand.

If she was caught escaping, Naya would die.

If Cassia unearthed her lies, she would kill her.

It wouldn't matter that Cassia had saved Meiling and must know of her rare bloodline.

It was all at once clear. Cassia was death. Every moment Naya remained in her presence shortened her life expectancy.

Mind racing in a dozen directions at once, Naya suddenly realized someone was staring at her. She met the man's eyes from across the room, thought they were kind, and decided then and there that he was her path to salvation.

She had no idea who he was. But that didn't matter.

Not anymore.

Not when the stakes were as high as they were.

While everyone was distracted by the immortal with the gladiator spirit at the front of the room, Naya edged toward Kind Eyes.

There was no time to doubt herself or her intuition. She had to move fast.

She had to get out of here.

Before Cassia discovered the many ways in which Naya had already betrayed her.

She padded behind Cassia's minions on silent feet while they finally rose to back up their mistress— who clearly didn't need their support.

Cassia was managing to scare the shit out of an entire room quite well all on her own.

CHAPTER FOURTEEN

CASSIA

THE IMMORTAL SENSED the fear coating the inside of the throne room, imagined it dripping down the jade-lined walls like condensation, and relaxed. The many humans and newly turned vampires standing along the walls bled the emotion.

She'd last killed a master vampire of Shèng Shān Monastery nearly five hundred years before, but she assumed the story of how quickly and brutally she'd devastated him endured. She'd made a point of making the man's death gory and bloody for just this purpose.

Then, Ji-Hun had been an apprentice to one of the seven masters. He, like everyone else on the mountain, was raised under the strict and demanding tutelage of the Shèng Shān warrior monks. He would have been required to practice their martial arts, for which the monks were well known, every day of his life since his training began. And Cassia had seen toddlers being guided through basic strength and balance building exercises. The warrior monks had no use for coddling.

There wasn't much Cassia envied about the rigid and inflexible lifestyle of the monks, but she'd be a fool to underestimate their prowess or devotion.

She eyed Grand Master Ji-Hun as he descended from the dais that elevated his throne, more pompous than it had been during her last visit. Ornate and intricately carved dragons wove across the frame of his throne, their eyes a jade so bright that they resembled polished emeralds.

Though his posture was regal as befitted a self-aggrandized vampire, and his dark eyes studied her with unwavering intensity, he was frightened of her. She could tell. This truth was in the barely noticeable rigidity of his movements, the way his usual gliding grace hitched when he took the step down.

Molto bene, Cassia thought.

She traded in fear.

She relied on it to keep her alive.

Yes, she was a formidable opponent, of that there could be no doubt. Her father, despite his abundance of shortcomings, had seen that she learned to defend herself with blade and spear, and with the strength of her own body. He'd hired men skilled in the arts of battle to teach her how to compensate for her disadvantage in size and use her opponent's greater weight against them. She was strong and agile and wickedly fast. Plus, she knew her way around practically every weapon ever invented. Just because she'd had to kill her father didn't mean she rejected all that he'd taught her.

She kept up her training.

But she didn't practice from sunrise to sunset, every day of her entire life as the monks did. She didn't devote her every waking moment to thoughts of her advancement, both in body and spirit. What would be the point of living an eternal life if that's how she was going to squander it away?

As Ji-Hun sized her up, she returned the favor, doing nothing to hide her blatant scrutiny. The man was lean and wiry, and she'd seen him fight before; he'd already been impressive centuries ago.

And vampires didn't age or otherwise decline. He'd be stronger than ever before.

But being outmatched wasn't new for her. She'd learned long ago that illusions were as powerful as realities, and reputation was everything.

She heard someone whisper in Chinese some of the few words she knew in the foreign tongue she'd never had the desire to learn. *Kiss of Death.*

She swallowed a pleased smile, aware that Ji-Hun would have heard too. That he'd be cataloging the many horrors and brutalities attributed to that moniker.

"I have decided," Master Ji-Hun announced, silencing the buzz of murmurs circling the space with a clear, strong voice. "If there is a chance that I may die today, then I wish to do so outside. To feel the sunshine on my face one last time."

"Very well," Cassia said. "And what's your weapon of choice?"

Unblinking, unflinching, he met her waiting stare. "None. I am weapon enough."

At that, Cassia had to focus very hard not to reveal her apprehension about his advanced skills.

In all the world, very few people were aware of the existence of true immortals like her. Those who knew had no idea how to kill them. Cassia suspected not even some of her fellow immortals knew how to deal the decisive blow.

But *she* possessed the knowledge.

She had killed her father. The first immortal she'd ever met. The man who both blessed and cursed her with eternal life.

The grand master vampire before her might be able to ravage and devastate her body, but he wouldn't be able to kill her. Not without knowing the secret way to do so.

Fear was the only true weakness she could reveal, and so she clamped down on it with an iron will.

The vampire's blows might not be able to kill her, but she still experienced pain. It had been so long since she'd been human, but she didn't remember anything hurting as badly as it did in her immortal form. Every slice felt like a thousand, and every strike seemed to punish her very organs.

"Very well." Cassia forced a tight smile to spread across her face.

See? I'm not worried in the least. *Sono il bacio della morte.* I am the Kiss of Death.

She moved out of the way, gesturing with her arm toward the open doors behind her. "Lead the way to wherever you wish to draw your last breath."

"As you wish, but since you have decreed your will over mine, might you indulge me with a final conversation?"

Cassia hesitated.

"I have much of value to impart."

She'd already announced her intent to kill him. Even if he did have a valid defense, she couldn't back down, not with an audience. He would know this. A master of strategy as well as martial arts, he'd understand how someone like her, alone, had managed to survive as long as she had.

So what did he want to tell her?

She nodded with unnatural graciousness. "Walk with me, then. There will be time to fight afterward."

Walking half a step behind Ji-Hun so he could direct them, Cassia paused to tap Édouard on the shoulder. "Watch the girl. Do not lose sight of her under any circumstance."

"She is with Mage Li Kāng, Mistress."

Cassia flicked her gaze across the crowd, not seeing them, until she looked in the opposite direction, where Meiling's blond head popped out right away. The girl stood close to the mage, who appeared unassuming with his shaved head, odd tuft of hair emerging from the top to fall in a braid along the back of his head.

"So long as she is with him, she will be safe," she told Édouard. "But make sure that you do not lose sight of her regardless."

"Yes, Mistress." Édouard moved to stand, leading the rest of her vampire minions to do the same.

From the mage's reports to Cassia, Meiling had learned to trust him, considering Li Kāng a friend even. After the two had a chance to catch up, Li Kāng would be able to tell her how Meiling found out about Naya and how she managed to escape and reach the other girl. Naya might not be in a monastery at the top of a remote mountain in China, but her pack was well hidden. After Cassia had spun the story of the girl's werewolf bloodline, the pack alpha hid her as well as Cassia herself would conceal her. So how had Meiling discovered Naya's whereabouts?

Something was fishy in Ji-Hun's operation...

Cassia caught up to Ji-Hun while he ordered everyone else to remain behind. Then he led them out into an empty courtyard with a central fountain. Positioning them right next to its loud splashing, he stopped.

"No one will be able to overhear us here."

A multitude of eyes were on them, but no one advanced, crowding at the far edge of the courtyard to observe. Even the six other vampire masters waited at their leader's command.

"I must know why you've come into my home and threatened my life," Grand Master Ji-Hun said. "You owe me that much, especially if you truly plan to end me."

"I don't owe you anything," Cassia snapped. "You were supposed to care for Meiling as if she were one of your own. I paid you, and handsomely, we can both agree on that, to watch over her and make sure she never escaped. And yet I find her on the other side of the world. Out on her own, free, when that girl hasn't been free a single moment of her entire life."

He visibly blanched, and the vampire was already pale.

"What? You thought I wouldn't find out about that? You were just going to keep her escape from me until, what, you found her yourself and put her back hoping I'd never find out?"

From the way his skin lost much of its remaining color, she knew she was right.

"I didn't wish to bother you. I was going to tell you only after I'd returned Meiling."

"Did you know where she'd gone?"

He tilted his chin up before answering. "No, but that doesn't mean I wouldn't have discovered her whereabouts soon—"

"And by then I might have lost one of my most valuable possessions! *That* is why you have earned death. You have betrayed both my confidence and trust in you."

"It wasn't anything *I* did."

"Perhaps not, but it was most certainly something you did not do. You should have gotten word to me immediately."

"You know we don't muddy our ways with modern inventions. We have no telegraphs or telephones."

"Oh, I remember. You don't even have electricity. How could I forget? It is foolish to reject inventions of the modern day when they can improve your life. Have you ever even taken a hot bath?"

"Why should I have need of a hot bath when a cold one cleans just as well?"

"Because life, Ji-Hun, is to be enjoyed and well lived. If not, what is the point of it all?"

"To purify ourselves in this lifetime so we might ascend in the next. I devote myself in this life so that I may earn my afterlife."

Cassia scoffed. "Well, then you will be ascending soon."

"You have bigger problems than putting on a display of killing me. I did not release Meiling. I did not tell her anything of her true nature. I treated her at all times as one of our warriors in training. None of her escape came from me."

"That's no excuse that will get you out of your sentence. You run this place. It's your responsibility to ensure you keep your promises to me. I gave you *the book* in exchange for her safekeeping."

"A fair payment for how much care I've given the girl. She has wanted for nothing."

Cassia scoffed again. "Except maybe a hot bath."

Ji-Hun scowled. "You cannot take the book from

here. It is sacred. It belongs in a place where it will be revered and shown the respect it deserves."

"Monk, something is only sacred when someone believes it is."

"No, immortal, that is where you are wrong. Some things have a sacredness beyond the human world. The book does not belong with you." He held up a hand at her open mouth. "The book does not belong with any one person. Its truths are for the entire world, for anyone seeking to understand what this life is really about and what comes after it."

"The book is mine and so I shall do what I please with it. I entrusted it to you so long as you kept Meiling safe—for no other reason. You failed in your mission, and so it now returns to me."

"Instead of focusing on how Meiling escaped, you will take the book from its true home? From the one place it will be treasured and protected from all harm?"

"What makes you think I will do one or the other? I will take back my book, and I will get to the bottom of Meiling's escape. She will never be away from me again. She's too important."

"And why is she so important to you, immortal? You care little for the survival of werewolves, do you not? You've never told me why you are so invested in her survival and that of her kind."

"Then perhaps it is time you stop asking." She paused. "Is Mage Li Kāng still to be trusted?"

"I trust him with my life."

"That didn't answer my question."

"It should have. At my command, he has watched over the girl as if she were his own younger sister. There is no one better suited for the task."

"And yet he knows nothing of her origins or her rare werewolf blood?"

"Nothing." Ji-Hun dipped the tip of a long nail into the water pooling in the fountain. "If you kill me, you will lose an ally of great value."

"You don't even like me. I'm only your ally because I have what you want."

"So? Then you will not doubt my motivations. I want the book. If you allow it to remain here in my care, I will ensure Meiling can never leave here again. Must she retain full use of her legs? It would be helpful to cripple her. Then surely she can never escape again."

"I told you, from now on, she remains with me."

"So how else can I convince you to allow me to continue being the guardian of the book? I'm sure there is something."

When Cassia hesitated, Grand Master Ji-Hun added, "I will be in your debt. You will have my gratitude. That is a useful asset, even if you have no need for it now. Someday, surely you will. In a world where few live as long as you, I will indeed be of use. No one dares threaten my life but you. I will live many centuries more, thousands of years even. One day, you will have need of me."

Cassia, too, dipped her hand into the water of the fountain. It was frigid, likely snow melt runoff. "Ji-Hun, Ji-Hun," she said with a taunting lull. "I can't back down now. I've already announced that I will kill you. Besides, you drank from Meiling. Granted, that is not of the same importance, but she is still under my protection, and you should have never *ever* defied me by drinking her blood." As an afterthought, she added, "The blood that is meant to save all werewolves. Without her blood, werewolves will fade into extinction."

His obsidian eyes blazed like glass marbles. "I did *not* drink from Meiling. I have hundreds of blood slaves to choose from. Why would I ever choose her? I am not stupid, immortal, and only a fool would drink from the one person under your protection."

Cassia studied his eyes. Angry, yet still unreadable. Even so, she believed him.

"Meiling told me you did."

"Then Meiling lied." His accusation was a snarling hiss.

"Why would she do that? She'd know I'd ferret out any lies eventually."

"More reason to keep me alive, immortal. You need my eyes and ears."

Cassia flicked her fingers in the water, causing a small splash. "I have to follow through, Ji-Hun. My reputation is on the line."

"Then take Master Xiong. He offered, and under the rules of our kind, he is a valid replacement for me. He is a good man and would be a worthy tribute."

Cassia didn't appreciate how this "conversation" had turned into a negotiation.

"You can make another announcement, saying that I am a good ruler, and to preserve the importance of what we do here, you have decided, in your infinite wisdom, to accept my replacement. So the teachings of the warrior monks may endure. Something like that."

"Fine," she snapped. "But if I can't kill you, I'm going to make an example of him. It will be painful, bloody, and *memorable*."

"I'd expect nothing less of you, immortal. You will not regret your choice today."

"Be sure that I don't. Because next time there is nothing you can say that will convince me not to kill you."

"Noted. I am at your service."

"Yes. You are. And I'm taking the book with me when I leave."

Then Cassia turned toward the onlookers, calling out, "Send out Master Xiong."

CHAPTER FIFTEEN

BRUNO

BRUNO DIDN'T IMAGINE that Scooby's description of the wizards as "kinda dead" had any chance of being accurate. He was wrong.

The wolf shifter Boone walked into the large warehouse accompanied by two men who were obviously brothers, and who were equally obviously not fully alive. Or something...

The two men were translucent. Visible enough to be there, and yet not solid enough to be tangible to the touch—at least, that's what Bruno figured, itching with the desire to put his conclusion to the test, doubting he'd have the chance to.

The two mages glided instead of walked, hovering an inch above the floor, their feet invisible beneath dark, flowing robes.

Bruno couldn't help but stare. They appeared to

come from another time, or perhaps another place, one with mannerisms and traditions different from his own, as if the men had stepped out from the pages of an enchanted storybook.

Their hair was gray and divided into dozens of small braids, capped in beads that would have been bright and garish if not for the fact that their opacity was diminished. Even braided, their hair reached their waists. They wore identical long beards as well, similarly divided into plaits capped in beads.

Their beads tinkled softly as they drew near, suggesting the brothers were more solid than they looked—or at least their beads were. Their light eyes sparkled as they studied the red dome that encircled Meiling, holding her captive long after the immortal had disappeared.

Their smiles were child-like in their enthusiasm and seemed entirely out of place in the grim atmosphere of the warehouse. Blood stained the cement floor in dismal patches, and Maverick's neck still hadn't quite finished suturing itself back together.

Besides, Bruno felt every passing minute since he'd lost Naya as if it were a thousand. He all but twitched with the need to find her. Brother Wolf was restless, and Bruno knew his wolf wouldn't be at ease until he claimed Naya as his mate.

"Maverick," Boone called out to the alpha as he arrived to greet them. "I'd like to introduce you to Mordecai and Albacus, the great wizards of Irele that I've been telling you about."

Maverick, caked in blood from the neck down, extended a hand toward them before considering their translucency and pulling it back. "Thank you for coming so quickly. We really need your help. I owe you." He looked to each of them in turn, pausing to ensure they felt his gratitude. "Both of you."

Bruno had been hoping Boone would point out which of the mages was Mordecai and which was Albacus, but he hadn't, which meant that Bruno couldn't tell them apart.

One of the wizards waved his hand dismissively in the air. "We're pleased to help under such extraordinary circumstances. It isn't often that Albacus and I get to experience something so new and different." The man beamed. "Isn't that right, brother?" Bruno frowned and started toward them, leaving Meiling on her own within the red dome. She appeared as intrigued by the new arrivals as he was.

"Oh yes," the second mage bubbled. "That is certainly right, brother. This is quite exciting. We truly are happy to be here to help." Albacus smiled widely at Maverick as if the scent of death didn't hang in the air. "We should perhaps owe you for the opportunity to learn of immortal magic firsthand."

Boone cleared his throat, giving both the wizards an admonishing—yet fond—look before addressing Maverick. "They are generous with their time and vast wisdom. But they are the force behind the Magical Arts Academy and the Magical Creatures Academy, along with all the sister schools and locations, and these are unsettled times across the board. The supernatural community faces threats from many directions. I'm quite certain, Maverick, that it would be useful to be able to call on your pack at some point in the future."

Mordecai grinned, stuffing his hands in the pockets of his robe, causing something inside them to tinkle as the beads in his hair did. "*Oui, oui*, Boone. *Bien sûr*. Always looking out for us, aren't you, dear boy? A future favor would be well-received."

"And of course you shall have it," Maverick said. "On my honor."

Boone circled to clap Maverick on the back, seemed to notice the severity of his healing injuries, and only patted him gently. "Your honor is more than enough."

The wizard brothers floated toward Meiling, leaving Boone with Maverick.

The alpha leaned into Boone. "Thanks for

getting them here so quickly. We're not set up to deal with immortals."

Boone's brow furrowed. "You're sure that's who took Naya?"

Maverick started to nod but stopped, bringing a hand to his neck, rubbing thoughtfully at the angry red line that sliced fully across it. "It looks like we're dealing with two immortals."

Boone shook his head, his ponytail sliding across his back as he did so. "Holy fuck, man. Two of them? That's not good."

"No, it's not. We fought a single one and came close to losing. Everything Zasha and Quannah said looks to be spot on." Maverick turned toward the red dome, which held as strong and steady as when he and Bruno had first arrived at the warehouse.

"The immortal's been gone for well over an hour and look, his magic's holding strong even though we tore off one of his arms. He's gone and we still can't get through. It's some powerful shit."

Boone's jaw tightened, his hazel eyes blazing. "Damn."

"Yeah, it's bad." Maverick looked back at Boone. "Did you tell your dad?"

"Yep. He knows. He's readying the pack in case we need to go to war along with you all."

"Good. These immortals, wherever they came

from, they've hit two packs already. I don't think anyone's safe now."

As Boone and Maverick mulled that over, their foreheads scrunched in a similar grim set, Bruno joined them.

"Hey, man," Boone said. "Good to see you again."

Bruno nodded, shaking Boone's extended hand. "*Hermano*, glad you could make it so quickly."

In truth, it had felt like a small eternity of waiting until their arrival.

"I heard what you guys were talking about." The fact was obvious when dealing with shifter hearing. "Whatever magic this immortal has, it's powerful enough to knock shifters right out from a single touch. Strong shifters too." Like him. His shifter magic was dominant enough to rule packs, yet he hadn't stood a chance against the red glow of the immortal's domes.

"You really think these two guys can figure it out?"

Together, the three shifters glanced over to study the translucent wizards, whose grins had only intensified now that they floated beside the dome.

"If anyone can do it, they can," Boone said. "They've been around since the 1500s or something, and they've been badasses since then. All they do is study and practice magic. They're our best bet at figuring any of it out. And as you can tell, they're motivated."

They studied the wizards some more. They didn't seem to be doing much beyond admiring the glowing prison.

"Trust me," Boone said. "The dudes will knock your socks off."

"Good," Bruno said. "We need that."

"What's their deal?" Maverick asked. "Are they dead or alive?"

"Half and half," Boone said. "The one, Albacus, died. He lingered around as a ghost until Mordecai figured out a way to share his life force with him."

Bruno whistled his awe; he couldn't help it. "You weren't joking. That is impressive."

Boone nodded. "We're lucky they're on our side. They can do shit I've never even heard of other mages doing. If they ever were to go to the dark side, we'd all be fucked."

"It doesn't look like that will be a problem," Maverick said. "They're like little kids in a candy shop staring up at the dome."

"Yup," Boone said. "They're always a bit like this. Since I told them what was going on here, they haven't stopped talking about it. They were in the middle of war council discussions or something and just ditched to zoom over here."

"The arm!" one of them called over—*Albacus*, Bruno thought. "We're ready for it now."

Maverick signaled Scooby to bring it before he, Bruno, and Boone walked over to join the mages.

Scooby extended the severed limb toward the translucent brothers uncertainly, but one of them grabbed it without issue. He studied the arm intently, turning it this way and that in the dim glow of the dome, unaffected by the dangling ligaments hanging from the severed end.

"It appears just like normal human flesh," the one brother said to the other, unconcerned by their audience. "The anatomy is identical."

The second wizard joined his brother in studying the limb. "Fascinating. Perhaps these immortals have managed to secure long life as we have, then ... but no. We cannot access this specific magic they can."

"A difference that could be caused simply by the originating spell. Whatever elements went into the spell could account for the ensuing magic."

"Perhaps. But as you know, brother, we shouldn't ever—"

"Make assumptions based on a limited understanding of the unlimited."

The one brother scowled. "That's right. There might still be circumstances we've never—"

"Encountered before. This could all be fresh and new and establish an entirely novel set of operating equations."

The other brother's scowl deepened. This time his eyes also narrowed, deep lines crinkling along their edges. When he next spoke, the playful mirth was absent. "If we were to draw conclusions based on a limited parameter of analysis—"

"Our—"

"*Our* deductions could lead us astray."

Unperturbed by his brother's silent censure, the other mage said, "And we'd lead an entire magical community down an erroneous—"

"And dangerous..."

"And dangerous path."

"They always do this," Boone whispered to Bruno and Maverick. "Gotta just let them do their thing their way. It works out in the end."

Bruno certainly hoped so. If Boone didn't have so much faith in the wizards, Bruno would have already hurried them along. Every moment that Naya was in the hands of a terrifying immortal was a moment too long.

"There's only one thing to do," one of the

brothers announced, jiggling the pockets of his robes, where several somethings chinked inside.

The other wizard groaned and rolled his eyes. "No, Mordecai. Not the runes. Not now. This is not the time—"

"What better time is there for the runes than when we are in the throes of uncertainty?"

Albacus grunted and took a turn at frowning.

Mordecai added, "You'd think that after all these centuries you'd have learned to trust the runes as I do."

"I'd trust the runes if they were trustworthy."

"You know they are!" Mordecai said. "How many times have they saved our behinds? Or that of our friends?"

Albacus didn't answer.

"Exactly. I'm right."

"Just because you say you're right doesn't make you right. You do know that, don't you?"

"Of course I do. I'm right because I am. Because the runes are the correct move, and if you were to remain open-minded for once, you'd know it."

"I'm nothing if not open-minded," Albacus snapped so that the beads in his hair set to knocking together. "You're the one who takes after *that* side of the family, not me."

Mordecai sucked in an audible breath. "I do not. Take that back."

When Albacus didn't, Mordecai added, "Would I trap Sir Lancelot in a painting just because I didn't want anyone else to have him?"

Boone whispered to Bruno and Maverick, "Sir Lancelot is a talking pygmy owl who's been around for longer than these two have, if you can believe it."

"But is this Sir Lancelot important right now?" Maverick asked.

Boone chortled. "The little owl is always important—he's brilliant—but I get your drift." He moved his mouth this way and that. "If they don't come back around to the point soon, I'll step in. But best to leave them to their flow if we can."

Bruno would give them at most five more minutes, and then *he* was stepping in.

Mordecai had removed a small leather bag of said runes from his pocket and then plopped unceremoniously on the floor, proving both that he was solid enough and remarkably limber for a man who was centuries old—and looked it in most regards.

"Give me the arm," Mordecai told his brother, who groaned and rolled his eyes all over again, but did hand over the body part.

Mordecai tossed it on the floor next to him with a small splatter of blood that shook loose from behind coagulation, then jiggled the runes in his cupped hands across it, chanting softly in a French so old that Bruno struggled to make out the words despite the language's proximity to his native Spanish.

The arm began to glow slightly in response to whatever the wizard was saying. Bruno drew closer, wanting to better see what the man was doing.

"Truly remarkable," Albacus said, no longer frowning at his brother. His eyes were wide, his forehead crinkled into a dozen lines as he studied the arm's glow, reaching out to prod it with a fingertip.

"Go ahead," he said. "Throw the runes."

Mordecai, who'd been poised to do exactly that, paused with his cupped hands above the immortal's arm. "First, admit that the runes are a valuable tool in a wizard's arsenal."

Albacus snorted. "I'll do no such thing. Divination is a tool reserved for the superstitious and foolish. The only reason the runes work for you ... *sometimes* ... is because your subconscious is manipulating them. Your deep inner knowing, which informed from hundreds of years of study and discipline, modifies the runes' responses."

"Oh?" Mordecai shook the runes a tad violently. "Is that so? You think me so skilled that I can alter the result of a random throw?"

Albacus tsked, trying Bruno's patience. "It has

nothing to do with your skill, but rather your unconscious functioning. But yes, you hit on a great point. The runes are wholly useless since their guidance stems from you, a man fully capable of fault."

Mordecai jiggled the runes again. "How many times have the runes saved us and our friends? How about how they helped us with the Oliana situation?"

Albacus' shoulders drooped, losing their angry edge. "We didn't manage to save Oliana, now did we?"

Mordecai visibly deflated as well, slumping across his folded legs. "No, we didn't."

"What's happening?" Bruno whispered to Boone.

"I think Oliana's their sister. She died a long time ago, I think. But I'm not entirely sure. They don't share their secrets often."

Bruno, who was in the habit of respecting his elders, wasn't in the mood to follow rules. He crouched behind the two men, crowding them.

He couldn't help the growl that rolled through his words. "I'm sorry that you lost your sister, I truly am. But we're in danger of losing a woman who is very important to me *right now* if you don't take the shortcut to figuring this out." His tone softened. "Please ... if you could just put your argument on hold for a while."

The brothers stared at him for several beats before Mordecai chuckled. "It's an argument as old as we are. It isn't going anywhere fast." Then, without further comment, and while Albacus appeared a tad chagrined, he mumbled in that same old French above the runes, then tossed them to the side.

One of the small flat stones deflected off the immortal's arm before landing among the others, a mysterious etched symbol facing up.

Bruno, Boone, and Maverick leaned in to study the odd symbols that Bruno didn't recognize. Even Meiling from the other side of the dome tried to make them out, and Scooby, who stood off to the side waiting for any orders from Maverick, scooted closer to see.

"Well," Mordecai announced, "would you look at that..."

Bruno was looking all right. Were they Druidic symbols? Or perhaps another ancient language? Maybe even a system of Mordecai's own devising? He had no idea.

Thankfully, Mordecai seemed to have plenty. He murmured and grunted while he pointed at this rune and then that one, then signaled paths between the runes that appeared visible only to him. Even his brother appeared baffled at the method with which Mordecai drew his conclusions.

Bruno didn't dare ask for an explanation, eager for the wizards to move along.

"Mmhmm," Mordecai was saying, mumbling into his thick mustache and beard. "It's as I thought."

"What? What is?" Albacus asked eagerly, undermining his earlier doubting of the runes.

"The magic connected to this arm is ancient," Mordecai said. "Logically, it would have to be, wouldn't it?" But he didn't wait for his brother's input anymore. "The magic is connected to a spell as old as it, signifying that a spell was indeed used to create this immortality magic, ruling out divinity, aliens, and what have you."

Bruno found himself starting with surprise. He hadn't considered either option, let alone others like it.

"There is also some sort of connection to the vampire race, though it's unclear what exactly. And brother, you know how the runes can be..."

"Yes," Albacus said, "inexact when they choose."

"*Précisément.* Either it is too early for us to know this information, or we aren't meant to know it at all."

"As usual, you place much faith in the runes."

"And as usual, it is well placed."

"Go on," Bruno urged before the brothers could get to squabbling again. "What else did you learn?"

Mordecai looked up at Bruno, smiling so wide that both rows of teeth, somewhat crooked in places, were on display. "I learned how to interrupt this immortality magic."

Albacus squealed. Had Bruno not been squatting immediately next to him, he would have sworn such a high-pitched celebration could not come from an old man. But it had.

"How? Tell me how, brother?"

Mordecai waggled his mouth back and forth, pretending to ponder. "Do you promise never again to doubt the runes?"

The delight dancing in Albacus' eyes vanished. "Never is a very long time, brother. You of all people should know that. I cannot make such a promise, and you should not ask it of me."

"Well," Mordecai said on a sigh, "it was worth a shot anyway." He leaned over the runes, unmindful of the proximity of a gory severed arm. He traced the path between several runes, glancing up at Albacus. "You see this and this? And then here?" His finger whipped around the runes; for once, the wizard was moving fast. "Then here and again here? You see, brother? Do you see it?"

Albacus gasped. "I think I do."

"Death magic. That's how we interfere with this particular immortality magic."

"Death magic?" Bruno echoed.

Albacus met his waiting stare. "Yes, and death magic is not to be trifled with, I assure you."

"I never would have thought it would be something to mess with. I have a healthy respect for death."

"Smart man," Albacus said. "I managed to avoid it for centuries, but then that bastard Count Washur stabbed me right through with a sword. Even with all the magic I knew, I couldn't avoid the swift kiss of death."

Mordecai rubbed his brother's back. "A story for another time, perhaps. At least I didn't lose you."

Albacus chuckled morosely. "Only because you gave up your life for me."

"And I'd do it again if I had to."

Bruno regretted interrupting the brothers when they were finally being kind to each other, but after knowing them for only this short while, he understood it might be the only way to keep them on task.

"How will you use this death magic to get Meiling here out of the immortal's dome?"

The brothers studied Bruno with open faces, and at the exact moment said, "Very carefully." Then they laughed, their expressions creasing in similar places.

They are as volatile as the weather during the stormy season, Bruno thought to himself.

As Mordecai scooped up the runes, Bruno asked, "And will you use this death magic to kill the immortals?"

The brothers were slower to stand than they'd been to sit.

"You would sentence them to death?" Albacus asked, gravity riding every word of his question.

Bruno hesitated, but only for a moment. "*Sí*. I would."

"Death is not something that should be decided lightly."

"I agree fully. My pack lives deep in the Andes Mountains in Argentina, isolated from modern society. Every action we take is with a thought to maintain the balance of nature, of life and death."

The brothers nodded as if they understood all that Bruno meant with that simple statement. His pack lived as did the ancient tribes who inhabited the land long before white men invaded. The pack wolves followed the ways of the natives, and in that vein they did not take life unless it was necessary, and then it was only taken after honoring the creature's sacrifice. Not even an insect was taken without need or ceremony, and the Andes shifters regularly made offerings to the Pachamama that supported them so wholly.

It was this same connection to the land and all of nature that led Lara to be such a powerful alpha, and that honed Bruno's intuition so acutely that he rarely questioned it.

It was this deep knowing that connected to something so much greater than he was that led him to say, a hand over his heart, "This particular immortal is evil. He disrupts the balance of life and death without need, without meaning. I know this."

To his surprise, neither wizard so much as blinked at what he said.

"Then he will die," Albacus said simply, helping his brother to his feet.

"Just like that?" Bruno heard Maverick ask Boone.

"Just like that," Boone whispered at a volume that the wizards wouldn't pick up without preternatural hearing. "I told you. They always get there. Eventually."

Maverick chuckled softly. "Though I see they like the scenic route."

But by then Albacus and Mordecai, whose runes were stuffed back in his pocket, were lined up across from Meiling.

"You might want to step back a bit, *chérie*," Albacus told her. "We've never done this before."

"Should I be worried?" she asked, sounding concerned already.

"I wouldn't be," Mordecai said. "It often goes well when we try new things."

Often hung loudly in the air, unspoken by any of them.

Meiling took several steps back, crouching in the center of the dome, where she could be farthest from the glowing red magic on all sides.

Then the brothers joined hands, pointing their free ones toward the dome, which didn't so much as flicker in anticipation, though Bruno's heart began to race. If the wizards could take down the dome that could knock him out in a nanosecond, then they had a real chance at saving Naya.

The brothers glanced at each other.

"We recite the resuscitation spell," Mordecai said.

"Only in reverse," Albacus completed. "And hopefully without the price to pay."

"*Oui.* Death is less complicated than life."

"Let's hope this holds true, brother of mine."

"Let's hope," Mordecai repeated, causing Bruno's palms to sweat even without any understanding of what price might potentially be exacted from the wizards.

When they began chanting, they spoke quickly, their words running together.

Bruno identified that they were speaking Latin, since it was the root of Spanish and easily recognizable. That commonality was sufficient for him to guess accurately at many of the words, but not to follow everything.

They mentioned life and death, balance and imbalance, good and evil, light and dark. He thought they might have even mentioned magic and power, perhaps even vampires, but of this he wasn't certain.

Regardless, he could tell that their spell, whatever its exact terms, was working.

The telltale charge of potent magic electrified their surroundings. From within the dome, Meiling's long hair, pulled back in a thick braid, rose to stand horizontally behind her. The red of her prison crackled and sizzled as if it were a live wire with enough juice running through it to power an entire village.

Unconsciously, Bruno took another step back.

Magic, in the same red as the dome, arced between the enclosure, the severed arm, and the wizards. It looped in a furious frenzy, building in intensity even more, until the buzz of it entirely obscured what the mages were saying—even to Bruno's sensitive hearing.

The charge in the air continued to build until it raced around them in a furious circle, like a storm directly overhead. They stood in the eye of it. Bruno's hair whipped in every direction, lashing against his eyeballs. Brother Wolf paced inside him, ready to spring forth. From somewhere outside, a wolf whined loudly, and Bruno knew the shifters of the Rocky Mountain Pack that waited outside were feeling this too. It seemed impossible not to.

Within the dome, Meiling sat down and crossed her legs tightly against her body. She closed her eyes, and through the rise and fall of her chest Bruno could see the deep breaths she began pulling in, her palms open and resting loosely across her knees.

He had to give her credit; it was probably the best thing she could do if her wolf inside was as nervous as his was.

Then, just as the corrugated steel of the building began to vibrate and ring with a high-pitched whine, and Bruno wondered if the magic the brothers were conjuring might blow the roof right off, the spell's power surged so intensely that the dome burst under its magnitude.

A shockwave raced like thundering horses in all directions, throwing everyone onto their asses. Eyes pinched tightly closed against the sudden brightness, Bruno landed hard, skidding backward a dozen feet.

Before he even opened his eyes, he knew when the magic ceased. The raging storm quieted to a whispered hush. The static charge in the air raced across his skin and was no more. His ears rang and his breathing came heavy.

When he opened his eyes, the dome was gone, Meiling sitting still in the now free space. Her hair no longer flew behind her like a cape, but it still possessed noteworthy volume, errant strands sticking up on all sides of her stunned face.

"Wow," Scooby said from somewhere behind him before anyone else gathered the oomph to speak. "*Dude*, that was fucking awesome!"

Bruno scrambled to his feet and raced to check on the wizards. They lay flat on their backs, side by side, their arms lying limply beside them.

Bruno barely breathed until he was certain they were okay.

He knelt beside their heads. Tentatively, he shook their shoulders, noticing how his hands met the solidity of fabric and the flesh beneath it. But though his hands didn't sink through either of the men, their bodies felt cool and somehow insubstantial to the touch, as if Bruno were attempting to nudge a stiff gust of wind instead of wizards.

"*¿Están bien?*" he asked, before realizing that the shock of the situation had led him to speak in his native tongue.

But the wizards opened their eyes and stared up at him, blinking wildly.

"Are you all right?" Bruno repeated.

"Are we all right, brother?" Albacus asked.

"Are we ever!"

Then both men laughed and laughed until Bruno couldn't help but join in, even if he didn't think he wanted to.

Their festive mood was infectious, and soon all of them were laughing. Amid signs of battle and death all around them, they celebrated a win.

A big win. An important one.

Bruno helped the now chuckling and wheezing men to sit up, kicking Cyrus' arm out of the way, while Boone knelt by their other side.

"You did it!" Boone said, smile as wide as the old wizards'.

"You didn't ever doubt us, now did you, boy?" Mordecai asked.

"Not for a second."

While the others helped the mages stand, Bruno approached Meiling. She smiled up at him and took his offered hand, saying, "Excuse me if I'm a bit stinky. Cyrus didn't exactly provide me with luxury facilities."

In response, Bruno pulled her into an embrace. She wasn't Naya, but she looked just like her, and she was safe.

Safe.

Which meant that chances were good they'd be able to find Naya and save her too.

Already, Maverick was barking orders behind him, sending Scooby off to orchestrate getting a jet ready for immediate takeoff.

Bruno led Meiling over to the others, where the wizards now stood smiling once more like excitable children, though exhaustion also visibly tugged at those smiles.

"On behalf of the entire Rocky Mountain Pack, I thank you," Maverick said, a magnanimous gesture since Meiling wasn't even part of his pack. "I meant it before, and I mean it even more now, if you need anything, you call me, or you have Boone call me. I won't forget what you did for us here."

"Wait," Bruno said, "don't we need their help to get Naya?"

Maverick stared the wizards in the eye. "If they offer it, yes, we need it."

Bruno looked at the two old men, who'd revealed more power than their frames seemed capable of channeling. He willed them to say yes, that they'd help bring back the woman he now understood he didn't want to be without.

"Where would this jet be taking us?" Mordecai asked.

"China," Meiling piped up. "To the Shèng Shān Monastery."

Albacus' eyebrows arched. "That is the vampire monastery, is it not?"

"It is," Meiling said. "It's where I was raised. It's where I think the female immortal, Cassia, took Naya."

"We haven't been there in ages," Mordecai said. "Are you thinking what I'm thinking, brother?"

"I think so."

Bruno sighed, unwilling to interrupt the fraternal back-and-forth the mages had going on now that he saw where it got them—eventually—especially now that they'd become the only wizards Bruno was willing to trust, possibly in the entire world.

When the brothers only grinned some more, new energy brimming in their faces, Boone barked out a laugh. "They're totally going with you guys."

"Wouldn't miss it for the world," Mordecai said.

Albacus held up a finger. "But will there be a place for us to nap on this jet of yours? I hate to admit it, but I just don't spring back as well as I used to."

Maverick chuckled. "Of course. You can have the run of the place."

Mordecai waggled his brow. "This sounds like a fine deal. Especially since we would have flown commercial just to get to play with more immortality magic."

Bruno swallowed his own smile. He was quite certain neither of these men had ever flown commercial anything. He was equally certain that the magic they'd woven to eradicate the immortal's dome had carried dire consequences. The wizards hadn't needed to mention it. The magic that buzzed had said it all. Had the mages been any less competent, none of them would have survived what they'd done.

With them coming along, the chances at rescuing Naya were stronger than ever. Bruno allowed himself to feel hopeful again, and Brother Wolf yipped within him.

"Let's move, then," Bruno said.

"You should stay—" Maverick started.

"I wouldn't waste my breath. I'm coming, one way or another."

"I'm coming too," Meiling said. "She's my sister."

"No," Maverick growled. "We got you out of here because it was the right thing to do, but you're the reason Naya was taken from us in the first place."

"No I'm not. I traveled across the world to save

her from the immortals. I failed, but my intentions were true."

When Maverick paused, seemingly just to glower at her, Bruno shook his head. "Come on. We're wasting time we don't have to waste. We have no idea what this Cassia immortal might be doing to Naya while we stand around arguing. We have to go. *Now.*"

Finally, Maverick nodded. "Fine. We all go."

"I can't," Boone said. "This isn't the only shit-storm brewing in the supe world. If you don't need me, I'm needed elsewhere."

"Go," Mordecai said. "The Magical Enforcers need all the help they can get right now."

Bruno was curious about that, but not enough to drag things out. "*Vamos,*" he barked in the tone that got his pack wolves moving, infused with alpha energy.

It worked. Even Maverick stalked toward the exit without questions.

"Wait," Meiling said after Bruno opened the door for her. "What about the arm?"

Maverick nudged her outside. "Don't worry about it. I have plans."

"What kind of plans?" she asked.

"You'll see," he called as he walked, not slowing or glancing behind him.

But it didn't take long to figure out what he was doing. When they reached the tree where he'd stashed the bag loaded with weapons, he confirmed with Scooby that the building was fully empty while he loaded up the rocket launcher.

A minute later, the warehouse was a ball of blazing fire. An inferno terrible enough to devour the wickedness that had flourished within its entrails.

While Maverick packed the rocket launcher back up, he said, "I don't usually condone careless destruction, but it's a dead industrial zone, and Scooby's already called the fire department. That place just had to go."

When he received no argument, the lot of them continued on to where they'd stashed their cars.

Their rescue team would consist of a few shifters and a pair of half-dead—yet fully eccentric—wizards.

Together, they'd be taking on an entire monastery filled with vampires, all training day in and day out in the most extreme of martial arts.

But none of them would have their motivation.

Bruno would kill whomever stood in his way. He'd have Naya in his arms within a day. All he needed was a little luck on his side to make it happen...

CHAPTER SIXTEEN

NAYA

NAYA COULDN'T BELIEVE what she'd heard, and struggled to contain her reaction to the news. Too many eyes watched her within the throne room of the Shèng Shān Monastery.

As a blond, blue-eyed woman in the midst of a sea of heads with hair so dark it reflected back the candlelight illuminating the vast, windowless room in hues of blue, she stuck out so much she might as well have been an albino. But these people—almost all vampires, from what she could tell—would have been accustomed to Meiling living among them. She shouldn't have drawn that much curiosity.

But Naya could feel the attention of others on her like hundreds of acupuncture needles prickling her skin. She couldn't decide who exactly was studying her so attentively, or how many of them—beyond the obvious in Cassia's lapdog Édouard. This bunch was a dodgy crowd. Their every movement felt furtive and laden with double meaning—with dubious, secret intentions. How Meiling had survived here all those years, she had no idea. This felt like the kind of place where someone might sneak into your room at night and slit your throat while you slept.

Naya missed the security of her pack with a constricting pang. What she wouldn't give to have even one of them here to have her back. Sister Wolf inside her was uneasy.

Cassia had just swept into the throne room as if she were its queen instead of a guest of creepy old vampires. The grand master of the place, Ji-Hun, shadowed her, walking half a step behind her, announcing that Cassia was the most powerful of the two.

But the grand master's deference to Cassia wasn't what had left Naya reeling, though it was unexpected, with the way everyone at the monastery seemed to treat Ji-Hun as if he himself were a god. It had been Cassia's pronouncement that she would accept Master Xiong as a proxy for Ji-Hun after all that had dread gurgling in the pit of Naya's stomach.

Cassia was only out to punish the men because of a lie she told. Ji-Hun hadn't drunk her blood, of course. Naya itched with the need to confess the truth to Cassia, to save Master Xiong's life.

But in saving his, no doubt she'd be transferring his fate to her. She nibbled at her lip.

Édouard was far enough away that, even with his advanced hearing, he shouldn't be able to listen to a word she said if she spoke softly. But he continued to move toward her; the window wouldn't be open for long.

The monk with the kind eyes stayed behind her, a soothing hand touching her back from time to time. He felt the safest amid this den of vipers, but he thought she was Meiling. Would he be the first to betray her when he discovered she wasn't who she claimed to be? What could she whisper to him that might help her plight when she spoke not a word of Chinese?

Swallowing hard, Naya decided she had only one course of action. No one here would be her ally. She needed to get away from everyone and escape on her own.

Maybe while Cassia was busy murdering a master vampire she could take her chance. But then she'd have to live with the death of an innocent man on her back like a two-ton anvil. Could she really allow another to pay the price for her misfortune? For the cruelty of her fate?

No, *she* couldn't.

But what about the fact that the precious blood that coursed through her could save werewolves from extinction? Now that there were three sisters to share the burden, Naya's survival was less crucial. But wolf shifters in general were always hunted. Never safe. And the three of them? Well, they were hunted worse than any of them.

Even if two would survive her, there was no guarantee they'd live long enough to secure the future of all werewolves.

It was possible that she could admit to Cassia that she'd lied about Ji-Hun's tapping her vein and play it off as if she were simply nervous, a believable fact since Cassia was one scary mofo. Precisely because Cassia was a psychotic immortal who didn't value the life of others, however, she might still kill Naya for lying in general.

To fulfill her destiny, Naya had to let the situation play out. Master Xiong would be a sacrifice in the survival of the werewolf species. And Naya would live with the guilt of his death for the rest of her days.

The matter settled, her stomach stopped churning, a deep sadness taking its place. This world was fucking cruel and unfair. Master Xiong would never even know the full extent of his sacrifice, nor the purpose behind it.

Again, she scanned her surroundings. The spectators, already crowded against the walls, pressed further into the lavish tiles of jade, avoiding the large statues of demonic-looking lions and columns displaying elaborate carvings. Candles protruded from sconces above them, casting their faces in sinister shadows.

Most were dressed in the style of clothing that Meiling wore: loose pants and shirts with gaping sleeves, cinched in the back around the waist. The *gis* were in a variety of colors that must have signified rank and mastery. On their feet, they all wore simple, supple slippers. Just looking at how they all stood— relaxed yet strong, in the way of lifelong athletes— Naya had no doubt Meiling had been accurate in her brief recounting of the place. These monks and acolytes were all trained in traditional martial arts that had endured centuries.

Naya had every confidence in her own skill level. She'd pushed and trained and demanded that she excel in everything she studied. Even so, there was only one of her and perhaps a hundred of them, just in this room. And they were largely vampires with preternatural speed. And Cassia ... well, Naya wasn't certain exactly what the immortal was capable of. But given how the grand master deferred to her, Naya knew she had no desire to find out.

"Choose your weapon, Master Xiong," Cassia called out, hushing the excitable buzz that had filled the room. "We will fight to the death in single combat. I'll allow you a few moments to say your farewells. But don't tarry. I'm not a patient woman."

Master Xiong squared his back, clasped his hands behind him, and announced in a heavily accented voice, "I require no weapon, great immortal. I accept my fate and will not fight you. I will die an honorable death as I have been chosen to spare Grand Master Ji-Hun's life."

Had Naya been Ji-Hun, she'd have felt grateful to the man who was sacrificing himself so she could continue living. But if anything, the grand master appeared annoyed, flashing Xiong a fangy—and very much forced—smile.

The pit of dread opened back up in Naya's stomach. The grand master wasn't worthy of such a sacrifice as Xiong was making!

Xiong stood stoically, his long mohawk braid

making him appear more a warrior than Ji-Hun with his fancy stylized hairdo and long nails.

Master Xiong had lived more than seven centuries before Naya showed up.

She needed air. She had to get out of there. She didn't want to watch what Cassia would do to the vampire master when the immortal's smile was so wicked and satisfied.

Naya turned to leave, only to find Kind Eyes' hand tighten on her arm. "No," he whispered so softly that it was little more than an exhale. "You cannot do anything to draw attention to yourself now."

"But..." she began, turning to search out the man's eyes, only then realizing that he was speaking to her in English.

She waited, her muscles tensing in anticipation of a possible fight.

It was his move next, but if he tried to out her, she'd take him down and make a run for it.

"I am Li Kāng," he breathed. "Are you Naya?"

For a long moment, she didn't dare move or say anything, but then she nodded slowly.

So he knew. And he hadn't given her true identity away. But *how* did he know? And why hadn't he betrayed her?

"Turn back around," he whispered urgently.

"Behave as if nothing is amiss. As if you've been here all your life."

Naya turned around to face forward, accidentally meeting eyes with Édouard as she went.

"I won't be able to keep up the ruse for long," Naya murmured out of the side of her mouth. "I don't speak the language. I don't know the customs."

"You will be all right for now. Cassia always forces the rest of us to speak English. To her, Chinese is less civilized."

Of course it is, Naya thought, unsurprised that Cassia would ignore millennia of history and rich culture to declare her personal preferences superior.

"Here," Li Kāng said, "you are only allowed to speak first to your inferiors. To your superiors, you are only permitted to speak if spoken to first. While Meiling has performed well and risen in rank enough that there are several, ah, how should I say, rungs perhaps, beneath her, none of them will be suspicious if you do not speak to them today. Everyone will be distracted by Cassia's killing of Master Xiong."

"We can't let her kill him," she implored, suppressing the urge to turn around and impress Li Kāng with the importance of her plea. "If we do nothing, he will die for my mistake."

"And if we do anything, you will die as well, and Cassia will still kill Master Xiong."

"Maybe not." For the first time, she was hopeful as memories of her conversation with Cassia on the flight over flooded in. Cassia was oddly invested in protecting her and Meiling...

"She wants me to live," Naya said.

"It is true, she may. Over the years, she has shown herself to value Meiling's survival greatly. But the immortal is as changing as the winds she controls. She is quick to anger and, ah, unpredicting?"

"Unpredictable," Naya answered automatically.

"Yes, yes, thank you. Cassia punishes betrayal severely. I do not know what you did, but whatever it was, we cannot rely on her wish for you to survive."

"Perfect," Naya muttered.

Cassia was already facing off with Master Xiong in the middle of the great hall, as much open space as possible surrounding them on all sides, given the amount of bodies crammed into the room. The large double doors behind them had been propped open, and myriad faces crowded to peer inside. They might be quiet, disciplined monks here, but word still traveled fast—somehow.

Ji-Hun had resumed his place in the throne in front, where he sat caressing the dragon carvings beneath his fingers. He watched Master Xiong with an impassive, mask-like face, as if what he were taking in were nothing more serious than a performance. *What a cold-blooded bastard!*

Naya couldn't help but wonder what the vampire had done to inspire such loyalty. Had Naya been Xiong and observed the grand master's ennui, she'd have withdrawn her offer to be his proxy right then and there.

The six thrones behind Ji-Hun were filled, save Xiong's empty seat. At least in this row, the vampire masters' reactions were mixed. Some appeared as disinterested as Ji-Hun, others couldn't fully hide the nervousness ping-ponging around inside them. One of them kept dragging a sharp fang across their bottom lip before seeming to notice it, stopping, then starting again a few moments later. Another gripped the arms of their smaller throne with white-knuckled fingers.

But none of them made a move to interfere. None of them so much as offered Master Xiong a word of sympathy or encouragement. Certainly, there was no gratitude that he should spare Ji-Hun so they wouldn't have to.

"I can't," Naya uttered more to herself than to Li Kāng, but the man answered.

"You must." Then she felt more than heard his hesitation. "Meiling, is she well?"

Was she? Last seen in the company of another vicious immortal, Naya couldn't be sure.

"She's fine," she said anyway. "We're twins. I'd feel if something happened to her." Another fact she couldn't be certain about, but it seemed like the right thing to say. Yes, Naya hadn't known she'd had not one but two sisters her entire life. But now that she did know, she wanted to think that they were intrinsically connected.

"Why did she not come with you? I was expecting her return."

"We got separated. Long story for later."

"How—?" he began, but got cut off. Without preamble, the execution had begun.

Dressed in a long tunic over leggings, Cassia stood with her arms out to either side of her. No one moved save her until Édouard led the rest of her vampire minions to the front of the throng—should they be needed, Naya assumed.

Though not so much as a slight breeze had swept through the hall before, suddenly a gust tore through it, whistling loudly as it circled all of them, whipping at fabric and hair, causing candles to wobble precariously in their holders.

Then the wind traveled around Cassia, circling her over and over again until she was a blur of long raven hair and royal blue fabric. Until she was the one and only center of attention.

Though Naya was nervous for Xiong, the man didn't flinch, not even when his long braid whipped around his shoulder to lash at the side of his face.

The crowd oooohed, and Naya leaned forward to make out the cause of their reaction. But Li Kāng held her back.

The wind howled as it circled and whipped and lashed and sang.

Sister Wolf threw back her head and howled inside Naya. It was a cry of loss and lament, though Naya wasn't entirely sure what her wolf was mourning. It seemed like there were options to choose from. Loss and fear hung in the air; Naya could taste them, tangy like blood.

From where Naya stood, she had a view of Cassia's back and Xiong's front. Even so, the spectacle Cassia was putting on was impressive.

The wind had tightened around her like a cyclone, she standing steadfastly in the center of it.

The force of the air intensified; tapestries that hung far up the wall tore from their fastenings and got sucked up in the current. They swirled dizzyingly as smaller items of the décor joined them—jade and porcelain baubles became lethal shrapnel at these velocities.

Li Kāng's grip on her tightened. She was about to turn around and tell him to keep his overprotective grubby hands to himself when she remembered he was the only friend she had here. So she tapped his hand instead.

Immediately, he let go. "I apologize," he said so softly that the wind nearly picked up the sound entirely and tore it away from her. "I've been caring for Mei since she was an infant. I forget myself sometimes."

She patted his hand in response, grateful Meiling had had someone to look out for her in this snake pit.

"Feel my power," Cassia roared loudly enough to be heard over the storm. "Mess with what is mine and you will feel my wrath."

Naya's brow bunched. Was Cassia referring to her? Thinking she was Meiling? If Cassia considered Meiling her property, things were even worse than Naya realized.

"Disrespect me and the fires of hell itself will rain down on you," Cassia shouted in a voice that seemed to echo with the fury spilling out from inside her. "I will strip the flesh from your bones before claiming your soul as *mine*."

She grit out that last word with a vicious growl, and for the first time Xiong blanched. He glanced quickly over his shoulder at Ji-Hun, but the grand master only stared back at him blankly.

The fine hairs across Naya's body stood on end; it could have been from the woman's words or the static charge that was building in the air. As if her long blond strands didn't make her target enough already, they spread out around her like a sheet, causing Li Kāng to yank his face out of the way.

Then Cassia bellowed and threw her head back. She pointed her open palms skyward.

The currents rocketed upward to follow her direction.

The entire roof trembled under the sudden force.

On the way up Shèng Shān Mountain, Naya couldn't help but admire the rooflines of the monastery. Their concave curves at the eaves made art out of the practical.

Cassia grunted loudly, like a wild beast, and the roof tore off the room entirely. Loud crashing soon followed, suggesting that Cassia had destroyed more than the one structure.

Gasps circled the room as many of the onlookers turned to shield their faces from the sun overhead, scrambling to scurry farther into the shadows that lined the insides of the walls.

These had to be the newly turned vampires. Over the centuries, a vampire's vulnerability to the rays of the sun lessened. And once they were very old, as old as Master Xiong and Grand Master Ji-Hun, the sun didn't bother them at all.

A few more shrieks filled the air as some of the new vamps didn't manage to shield themselves fast enough and the sun burned their faces. A woman nearby locked eyes with Naya while her cheeks and forehead blistered. Naya couldn't look away, nor help but wonder whether Meiling knew the woman. Someone snagged one of the flying tapestries and threw it over her head, sparing her from further damage.

Cassia laughed, a long hollow, eerie cackle that the wind picked up and carried outside.

Naya shivered, though she wasn't cold and she was no longer afraid. All she wanted to do just then was kick Cassia's teeth in. If she didn't carry the burden of an entire race on her shoulders, indeed she might have.

Her blood boiled at so much careless destruction, at so much unnecessary pain, at such terrifying selfishness. Within, Sister Wolf snarled and bared her teeth. In moments like these, she and Naya were of one mind, and Naya yearned to let her wolf free.

Only, she had no control over her shift. Only the moon did, and the full moon was growing near. Naya could feel its impending arrival like a rash about to bubble up on her skin.

Before any of them had had a chance to properly recover, Cassia redirected the currents to circle Xiong. The air whipped and brewed so ferociously that the skin on Xiong's cheeks spread back as if he were traveling at great speeds. His knee-long robe pressed back against his body as if it were glued on, and the pants beneath revealed every curve of his muscles beneath.

That was when Cassia turned to face her audience. When everyone else gasped, so did Naya.

Cassia's eyes glowed red like embers, telling every single one of them that, though she appeared human, there was little human about her. She was wicked and beautiful. Terrible and stunning. Naya couldn't look away even as the woman shot a look like a laser beam at one of the vampires in the front row. The man fell immediately, a single woman stepping in to catch his crumpling body while everyone else took a step back.

The woman who'd caught the man trained her attention on him only, and Naya suspected it was only this stalwart refusal to meet Cassia's waiting stare that spared her life.

Cassia grunted and spun back around.

While the wind kept Xiong locked in place,

Cassia stalked toward him, closing the distance between them too quickly.

Collectively, her audience seemed to suck in an anticipatory breath.

All but Ji-Hun, who continued to oversee from the raised dais, seemed to be rooting for Xiong's survival despite his dismal odds.

When Cassia stepped into the wind circling him, its path enlarged to include her, pressing the front of her body against his, as if they were ardent lovers. Cassia cupped his face in her hands, and as lovers would kiss, she pressed her mouth to his.

The sweep of the wind ceased abruptly. Hair and fabric fell to hang limply against bodies. Statuary plummeted from above, sharp projectiles. Cries stung the air as people zoomed out of the way with the speed of vampires.

But Naya couldn't steer her attention away from that kiss.

Xiong cried into her mouth, where Cassia swallowed his useless protests greedily.

She kissed him until the man began to deflate where he stood.

His body, lean yet obviously limber and muscular beneath his clothing, shrank ... and continued to shrink until he was nothing more than an empty shell in skin too large to house what remained inside it.

Naya sucked in a ragged breath. She couldn't help herself.

Cassia had delivered a kiss of death.

When Xiong's husk was shriveled as if he'd been mummified, she released his face. Lacking all the grace the man had possessed in life, his corpse dropped in one direction first, snapped, then fell in the other, until the bones broke.

Atop the marble floor, Xiong's body seemed to have nothing in common with the man who'd so recently occupied it. There was nothing sacred about the vampire master who'd had the courage to sacrifice himself for another.

Despite all that he'd said, there'd been no honor in his death—though there should have been.

Like a performer, expectant of admiration and applause, Cassia turned in place, taking them all in. Naya swallowed thickly when the crazy immortal's eyes paused on her, and for a brief moment Naya wished she hadn't pushed Li Kāng's hand away. Cassia was enough to make full-grown adults want to suck their thumbs and clutch a soothing blankie.

Cassia was scarier than anything or anyone Naya had ever known—ever heard of, even. She was worse than the hunters who chased wolf shifters around the globe just to experiment on them and kill them. Hunters had only one purpose: to wipe all wolf shifters and werewolves from the face of the earth. And yet they were cuddly teddy bears compared to this woman.

But the predominant emotion racing through Naya right then wasn't fear, but horror for the suffering she caused. Not desperation for her own future well-being, but self-righteous anger and a burning desire to enact vengeance for all these people in here.

Just because their "grand master" was a heartless prick shouldn't mean they had to put up with assaults like this.

If Cassia was going to try to kill her too, then Naya was going to go down fighting. Hard.

She set her jaw in determination.

Cassia thought she was top of the food chain? That no one could touch her freaky, scary-ass self? Maybe. But Naya would make her question her immortality before she was finished with her.

Cassia licked her full, sensuous lips as if she'd just finished devouring a tasty meal, before she flicked her hands in the direction of the empty shell on the floor, so out of place atop the elegant bright marble.

Nothing happened for a beat while the crowd held a collective breath.

Then Xiong's body exploded in a far-reaching

splatter of blood and gore. Pieces of flesh and bone stuck to Grand Master Ji-Hun, and for the first time since this all started, he reacted.

He hissed and cleared his eyes of Xiong's remains, flinging what stuck to his fingers carelessly on the floor at his feet.

Once more, Cassia threw her head back. Only this time it was to laugh. And laugh. And laugh some more.

Since Naya had grown mature enough to understand that she carried a great destiny, that she had to put the survival of her kind above all her personal needs, Naya had understood she was the hunters' greatest prize.

She had known that there were those who considered her their enemy because of nothing more than her relation to Callan "the Oak" MacLeod.

She'd been born with nameless enemies. Her face was a target, and so she'd learned to hide from the rest of the world beyond her pack.

Never before had Naya been able to put a face to *her* enemy...

Until now.

Cassia might look to be one of the most beautiful women Naya had ever seen, but that face would represent all the horrors of this world, all the undeserved cruelty, all that was wrong with the supernatural community and humanity...

Until Naya wiped her from this world.

Cassia might be an immortal, but nothing was ever certain in this life, not even the ability to survive it for eternity.

Naya had trained and prepared her entire life to take on her enemy.

Cassia had set out to make Naya hers? Well, she was in for a nasty surprise.

Cassia stood amid red, pink, and white pulpy bits of Xiong totally untouched, while everyone within a forty-foot radius of her wore pieces of the very much dead master. She believed herself the rose that didn't stink amid the pile of shit she'd created.

Let her believe that.

If Naya had prepared for anything, it was to play the long game.

The hunted was in the midst of becoming the hunter.

When Cassia caught her eye again and smiled like all things wicked in existence could be trapped in that one seductive attempt, Naya smiled back, allowing her teeth to show in a friendly gesture that was anything but.

Cassia's surprise scrawled across her face before she tucked it back away.

That's right, bitch. I'm coming for you.

If Naya didn't have the responsibility of others on her, she might have charged Cassia right then—to hell with it all. But no matter how much self-righteous fury raged through her, that didn't change her duty.

She'd have to bide her time, wait for her chance *... and strike.*

CHAPTER SEVENTEEN

CASSIA

MONKS at all stages of mastery bustled around the monastery in their colored *gis*, gathering the rubble from Cassia's destruction. As they picked up broken tiles, cracked beams, and jagged shards of glass, they glanced her way often, averting their gazes quickly any time she looked in their general direction.

She'd done her job well. Fear hung densely in the air like a storm as she perambulated around one of the inner courtyards with Grand Master Ji-Hun. She purposefully measured her pace to a pleasant stroll so everyone could see that killing Master Xiong hadn't taxed her, that she could kill any of them who opposed her just as easily.

In reality, the performance had drained her some, but appearances were everything. Her reputation as the Kiss of Death was the principal reason she'd survived for more than a millennia.

It was the same reason that she'd refused Grand Master Ji-Hun's request to go freshen up before they talked. Pieces of his subordinate Xiong clung to his robes, stuck to the many spiral braids that circled his head, and generally offended the persnickety vampire. Apparently, though he drank blood to survive, he thought he had refined sensibilities. The gore that clung to him bothered him so much that his eyes, usually cold and steady, flashed with irritation.

She, however, was unmarred, her clothing impeccable.

She smiled, unwilling to hide her pleasure at his discomfort.

"That display was unnecessary," he told her, his tone harsh. But he didn't speak loudly enough for any of the many vampires within the monastery's walls to overhear them. Cassia would be forced to kill him if he undermined her display of authority now.

"No, I don't think it was," she said.

"And you didn't have to destroy my buildings. It's incredibly difficult to get construction materials all the way up here. The repairs will be arduous."

Her smile widened. "Then perhaps you should have thought of all that before you crossed me. Meiling is my ward, and I left her in your care, a handsome payment all the recompense you should ever need to keep your end of the deal. You were to keep her safe and secure—and under constant supervision. I told you that she was to feel free to leave but that she never should."

"And she's been a prisoner since you first brought her here," he snapped. "I did what you asked. There is always someone watching her. She shouldn't have been able to escape."

"And yet she managed it. That is a failing on your part, no matter how you dress it up."

The vampire's cold eyes hardened. "I was in the process of getting her back when you showed up."

Cassia tilted her face up toward the sun; it felt brighter at this altitude. She wondered if it might warm her eternal body. But no, it didn't...

She looked back at Ji-Hun, delighting in the way he scratched at gore that coated one of his cheeks with one of those ridiculous long nails.

"You were in the process of getting her back..." she said. "Are you referring to the way I delivered her to you? How I did your job for you?"

"No, I am not. I sent several of my most trusted soldiers out to find her."

"And yet I see Mage Li Kāng here."

They reached the end of the courtyard in one direction, took the turn, and kept going. The stones that paved their way were as old as Ji-Hun, though they were worn smooth, where the vampire remained as sharp as ever.

The vampire tilted his nose in the air. "Li Kāng wasn't best suited for the hunt. He is a simple mage. My night hunters are far more skilled in pursuit and retrieval."

"Interesting, when the only one I see with Meiling now is Li Kāng."

The two stood off to one side, huddled in deep discussion. Édouard had stationed himself close enough to them that he'd be able to overhear every word they said. Her other minions shadowed Édouard uselessly.

Ji-Hun's nostrils flared. "At my direction, he will be keeping close to her."

"No, at *my* direction, he watches her."

"Yes, well..." Ji-Hun trailed off.

"How did the girl escape?" Cassia asked instead of needling the vampire as she wanted to. She would reserve the *why* component of that question for Meiling and Li Kāng. Ji-Hun was unaware that the girl had sisters, and his ignorance would remain.

Ji-Hun stopped picking at the remnants of Xiong on his skin and clasped his hands behind him. "It appears that she escaped in the night and walked right out our front gates. My sentries missed her."

"And they shouldn't have," Cassia said. Despite the fact that she was intentionally making Ji-Hun feel lacking, he was competent, as was his operation. It was the main reason Cassia had so confidently entrusted the girl to him. For all her mockery of him, it was true that his sentries should have noticed Meiling's comings and goings. From past visits, Cassia knew that only vampires guarded the monastery. The humans who lived among them served largely as blood sources.

"They most definitely should have seen her, especially as I have sentries stationed all the way down our grand stairway. She managed to climb all the way down, unnoticed."

"A feat that shouldn't be possible."

"No, it shouldn't. Not without assistance. She possesses not the skills to do that on her own."

As one, they glanced in Li Kāng's direction. He noticed and met their eyes, nodding his head respectfully at both of them.

"If he betrayed me," Cassia said, "then he has nerve."

"If he betrayed *us*," Ji-Hun said, "he possesses more than nerve. He has lived here with us from the time he was a young child. Before we knew he would be a mage. He has never shown any tendencies that do not align with complete loyalty. No, I do not think it was him."

Cassia frowned. She didn't think it was him either. "Could the girl have climbed down the backside of the mountain?"

Ji-Hun snorted. "Absolutely not. That way is so steep it is almost a sheer drop. Besides, mists keep that rock face slick, and if not, covered in ice. Meiling has become well versed in Seimei Do. She has a natural aptitude for our martial art. Even so, she couldn't escape that way. No one here at the monastery is capable of that level of skill. It's impossible."

"It's not impossible for me."

"There is no one else like you in this world," Ji-Hun said. "Unless you orchestrated her escape, then the only way she could have left is down the staircase."

"Hmm," Cassia said, thinking. "To make it past your guards, she would have had to be both invisible, soundless, and odorless."

Once more, they both glanced at Li Kāng. This time, the mage didn't notice, staring intently at Meiling as he was. Cassia itched to overhear what they said. She had to wrap this up with Ji-Hun.

"That is correct," the grand master said. "That is the only way my guards could have missed her.

Twenty of them were posted in a position where they should have noticed her. None of them reported anything unusual that night."

Cassia's eyebrows arched before she forced them back down. "That is a lot of protection when each of your guards is as skilled as they are."

"That is correct. I take my commitment to *Osculum Mortis* seriously."

"Good," Cassia grunted. "Very good."

"Now that you are reassured of that," Ji-Hun said, "would you consider leaving the book in my care?"

"Oh, let's not be hasty here. You still lost the girl."

"But not from negligence. From extraordinary circumstances that neither of us understand as of yet."

When Cassia didn't say anything right away, he added, "The book is at the center of our religious teachings. What do I need to do so that you'll allow me to keep it?"

She chuckled. "Religious teachings? Are you a religion now?"

His back straightened. "Of course we are. We have been since I founded this monastery. Why else would I have done so? To follow the teachings of others?" He scowled.

"I thought it was to stroke your ego."

"It isn't. Vampires need faith too."

"Faith in what?"

His neck tightened, the cords to either side popping out against his skin. "Faith in deliverance."

"Deliverance from what?"

He sucked in his cheeks before replying. "Deliverance from the darkness."

She stopped, genuinely surprised. "But you are the darkness."

"Exactly." Then he resumed walking, leaving her behind.

She caught up, glaring at him. "This is not the way to convince me to leave you my precious book."

"Our faith will survive without it."

"You said it was the foundation of your faith."

"I am adaptable, or I wouldn't have lived this long."

They had almost rounded the courtyard, nearing where Li Kāng and Meiling stood, apparently waiting for her now.

"If I were to leave you the book, what would you give me in exchange?"

"I will unearth the secrets behind Meiling's escape and make sure it never happens again. She will be safe here with me. If I have to imprison her so she cannot leave again, I will."

"NO, Meiling won't be staying here any longer. She is coming with me when I leave."

Ji-Hun was slow to nod his acceptance of the situation, though he had no choice in the matter. "Then perhaps I might owe you a favor in exchange for keeping the sacred book. One you can call in at any time."

Cassia mulled that over while drawing to a stop where the courtyard opened up paths to the throne room and a few other structures. "That might be satisfactory. And if you were to die before I collect?"

"Die? In all the world, you are the only one who poses a threat to me. If you don't kill me, you'll be able to collect."

Cassia paused, then, "Very well. You may keep the book for now. A favor of my future specification in exchange."

Ji-Hun dipped his head. "Thank you, great immortal."

She smiled down at him imperiously. When she began to walk away, considering their discussion concluded, the grand master said, "Wait."

She faced him.

"Remember, the moon is nearly full. When the girl is touched by the moon, she becomes strong and fierce enough to rival even your power. I recommend that you wait until the moon wanes before leaving.

The girl can spend the time in the cell I had created to hold her when she is a werewolf."

"I will take your consideration under advisement." Then Cassia turned back toward the girl and the mage, who stood too close together, as if they were friends.

Perhaps she'd been mistaken about Li Kāng. Was he foolish enough to wrong her?

She snapped her fingers, drawing Édouard in her direction, walking far enough away that she and the vampire could whisper.

When he arrived, he bowed deeper than usual. The fresh memory of how quickly she could tear vampires apart had apparently served everyone there well.

"Mistress?"

"What have you learned? The two seem friendlier than they should be."

"The mage has only expressed relief that she has returned safely. He has told her that he was worried for her and didn't know where she'd gone."

"But they knew you were listening."

"Perhaps, Mistress."

"Did they speak of her escape?"

"*Oui*, they did. She says it took her all night, but she managed to sneak by the guards on the stairway."

"Hmm."

"Mistress?"

"What do you think of what you heard, Édouard?"

"I'm sorry, Mistress, I don't understand the question."

She waved her hand. "Never mind." She'd taught him too well... "Unless the girl is with me, she doesn't leave your sight."

"Of course, Mistress. And the others?" He glanced at her vampire minions, who all stood clumped together, waiting for direction,

"Send them in pairs to snoop. To eavesdrop. To observe."

"And will they be searching for anything in particular?"

"Anything suspicious."

"Might I remind Mistress that they know very little of her dealings. They might not be able to distinguish what is or isn't suspect."

Édouard had a point... "Then tell them to search for any signs of how Meiling might have actually escaped the monastery."

"And should they also search for signs of how the girl might have learned of her sister?"

"No. That fact remains a secret. No one is to know."

"Yes, Mistress. Will there be anything else at this time?"

"Food. I shall eat soon."

Édouard bowed so deeply he was nearly folded in half, then scuttled away, gathering up the rest of her minions as he went.

Then she trained her sights on the girl and the mage. As if she were peering at them through the scope of a rifle, she aimed, and approached, a wicked smile crossing her face and making both of them visibly start.

Oh yes, the death of Master Xiong had been well dealt...

CHAPTER EIGHTEEN

NAYA

WITHIN THE CROWDED and chaotic throne room, Meiling's friend Li Kāng had warned Naya that their conversation outdoors would be overheard, and, in hushed whispers that were little more than exhales, he'd directed her on what to say. Even though Cassia would learn only what they wanted her to, Naya couldn't help but feel like a fluffy, defenseless bunny rabbit in the sights of a hawk circling overhead.

She forced herself not to react to Cassia's twisted, pleased grin as the immortal sauntered their way.

Naya was no defenseless bunny rabbit. And she hadn't forgotten her vow to end the woman—immortal or not. Where there was true determination, there was always a way.

With the immortal's stunning appearance, Naya

imagined it was all too easy for her to enrapture people and bend them to her will. There was no denying the woman's beauty. Her light violet eyes, dark hair, and creamy skin were alluring, her figure the perfect expression of femininity. But a vicious beast hid inside her, snapping, snarling, and writhing just beneath the surface.

"Li Kāng," Cassia said in a purr of seduction that made Naya's skin crawl. "I'm pleased to find you here."

"Of course I'm here, great immortal," Li Kāng said in a simpering tone that had Naya blinking at him in shock before she remembered that everything she did was noticed.

He dipped his head in a bow. "I've been awaiting your arrival. As soon as my friend here disappeared, I knew it was just a matter of time until we were graced with your presence."

If Li Kāng hadn't so recently been cautioning Naya about the dangerous immortal, she herself might have believed his act; he was that convincing.

Cassia chuckled flirtatiously, and Naya almost believed that the woman hadn't just murdered Master Xiong, decorating the throne room with a splatter of his remains.

"I see your charm is as healthy as always," Cassia said, extending her hand toward him.

Li Kāng took it with a devilish smile and kissed the back of her hand. Several large rings adorned her fingers. A sizable ruby caught the sun in a dazzling crimson flash.

"You are here to entrust Meiling to the care of the monastery once more?" he asked, his Chinese accent very subtle, as if he spoke English regularly.

Regally, Cassia pulled her hand back. "No. Meiling will be coming with me."

Naya's breath caught briefly before she reminded herself to behave as if nothing were amiss.

In the company of a cruel, bloodthirsty immortal and equally bloodthirsty vampires. Yeah, right. Everything was A-okay.

"Oh?" Li Kāng quirked a single eyebrow elegantly.

But Cassia didn't explain herself. Given that her flirtation was very obviously an act, Naya wasn't surprised.

Cassia looked from Li Kāng to Meiling, settling on her. "How did you escape?"

Naya swallowed. "I waited until nightfall—"

"Even though vampires are largely creatures of the night?"

"Yes," Naya said, forcing herself not to hesitate. "The mist was particularly thick then, after a heavy rain. I waited for my chance, and then snuck out the front door and down the stairs."

"I see. And none of the guards noticed you? How did you manage that?"

This was one question that Li Kāng hadn't prepared her for, but Meiling had told her enough for her to be able to improvise.

"I've lived in the monastery all my life. I've trained every single day that I can remember. I might be a werewolf, but I've learned from vampires. I've studied their ways. I know their strengths and their weaknesses. How they think, how they move, how they react. With enough information, there's a way to defeat everyone."

Naya stared into Cassia's eyes for a beat too long, before adding, "I have advanced sufficiently in Seimei Do to have become a viper. You may know that this is one of our highest levels of mastery. I know how to move so as not to draw attention. I know how to slink through the night without being seen or heard."

"And your scent? How did you mask it?"

On the fly, Naya couldn't think of a single believable answer that wasn't the truth: Li Kāng gave Meiling a spell to achieve this otherwise impossible feat.

Naya shrugged. "I took all night to descend the

staircase, moving only when the wind took my scent in the direction that favored me. But mostly, I got lucky. It was possible it might not work, but I decided to take the risk."

"Why? Why did you escape? Have I not provided you with everything you could ever need here where you are safe?"

"I escaped because I wanted to see if I could," Naya said. "I've been challenged and tested all my life. This seemed like the ultimate test." Again, she shrugged.

"I see." Cassia waited, but Naya didn't know what she expected her to say. Naya resisted the urge to look to Li Kāng for direction.

Finally, Cassia asked, "And you ended up in the United States, for what reason? To prove that you could?" Disbelief dripped from this final question.

Naya's heart sank. And she thought she'd been doing so well! But Meiling's life was so foreign to her...

Though Cassia seemed already to think Naya was blowing smoke up her ass, the immortal still believed Naya to be Meiling. In the absence of a better idea, she went with her gut.

"I can't tell you why I ended up where I did because I don't fully understand myself. Something ... was just drawing me there. When I'd challenged myself to escape Shèng Shān Mountain unnoticed, I wasn't fully prepared for succeeding. So when I did achieve my goal, I didn't know what else to do. So I followed my intuition where it led me." Hoping it was the right thing to say, she added, "Li Kāng has always advised me to listen to my guidance. It's the wolf inside me, he tells me."

When Li Kāng didn't appear to freak out, she relaxed, and said, "But then I was captured by another immortal when I didn't know any existed."

Naya was on the precipice of explaining that she hadn't even known Cassia existed when she stopped herself. She was treading in murky water. The fewer details she volunteered, the better, especially when she knew so few of them to be true.

While Naya waited for Cassia to speak, she took in the monks coming and going around them. They had to be frustrated that the immortal had destroyed not one of their buildings, but three, in the throes of her theatrics. But the monks—both the men and women—wore placid expressions beneath long hair that was pulled back in a variety of styles as repetitive as their colored robes. Another signal of rank, Naya figured. They zigzagged amid piles of rubble like industrious ants.

Cassia didn't so much as spare them—or the destruction she caused—a glance.

Those violet eyes were pinned on her.

"So you were willing to risk your destiny to follow your ... intuition?"

Naya inhaled deeply and hoped for the best. Between what she was and wasn't supposed to know, and what Meiling was and wasn't, keeping everything straight had become a challenge.

"I only learned of your existence and my destiny when I woke up on your jet. Before then, I knew nothing of any of it. I didn't know that you are my ... guardian"—Naya tried not to cringe—"before today. And I didn't know how important it was that I survive."

When Cassia didn't appear outraged by her response, she continued: "Had I known my guardian is the great immortal everyone here respects and fears, I would not have attempted an escape. I wouldn't have needed to challenge myself to see what I'm capable of. I would have known you would guide me."

That last bit rang so falsely to Naya's ears that she feared she'd gone too far.

When Cassia stared at her—hard—Naya's neck and underarms began to prickle.

But then the tension seeped from the immortal's face, and Naya breathed again.

"I see now that I should have told you earlier of

your destiny. You are clearly mature enough to understand and respect its importance."

Naya figured that Cassia actually meant that Naya was astute enough to respect and fear *her*.

Cassia turned to Li Kāng. "And you, why did you not notify me earlier of her escape?"

Naya couldn't believe her luck. Did that mean Cassia had actually bought the shit she'd been shoveling? Was she off the hook?

Li Kāng's round, youthful face parted in a carefree smile, when Naya was certain he couldn't have been feeling that relaxed. She'd have to remember what a magnificent actor he was. After all, he was Meiling's friend, not hers.

"I didn't notice Meiling was gone until after the first training session. I escorted her to her room for sleep, as I have every single night of her life. But then, Grand Master Ji-Hun requested my help with the book during the morning training session. So my first opportunity to notice Meiling's absence was after that. Immediately, I notified Édouard, using the solar-powered satellite phone as you've instructed."

He bowed his head another time. "Forgive me, your greatness, for my delay in informing you. Despite my reasons, disappointing you is inexcusable, and something I will labor to never repeat. I am, and have always been, fully loyal to you."

"Your loyalty to me supersedes your devotion to Grand Master Ji-Hun?"

Li Kāng, thespian extraordinaire, didn't so much as hesitate. "Of course, great immortal. Always and forever. Or, rather, so long as I will live."

She glanced at both of them back and forth before finally saying, "Very well. Now that Meiling knows how important she is to me, there will be no more escapes."

Cassia glared at Naya with such ferocity that Naya wondered if she were attempting to brand obedience into her through some use of her magic. Damn, she hoped not. The woman could bend air to her will and suck the life from a vampire who was supposed to be nearly as immortal as she was.

"I would never attempt to escape again," Naya said, even as she wondered how she would accomplish it. Because there was no way—*no way*—she was entrusting her life to this psycho. Destiny to save all werewolves or no destiny, Naya couldn't stay with this woman. Perhaps she wouldn't have the chance to escape right away, but she'd search for it until it arrived.

And then she'd make sure the immortal never found her—or Meiling—again.

"The moon will be full soon," Cassia said. "We'll remain here until your werewolf comes and goes, and then we will depart. Li Kāng, I entrust her to you while I'm otherwise occupied. You are personally responsible for her safety"—in the way prison guards were responsible for their captives remaining right where they were thought to belong, Naya imagined.

"You will shadow her as you've done before," Cassia added, making Naya wonder what kind of life her twin Meiling actually had while here. No wonder she'd been so ready to risk everything to travel across the world to warn a sister she'd never met of dangers she barely understood. Naya would have taken the chance to get out of here too. In fact, Naya was certain she would have escaped without additional reason than ditching this place—and long before Meiling had.

"Great immortal," Li Kāng said with a final bow of his head while a hand settled on Naya's back, beginning to lead her away.

With the burn of Cassia's stare on her, Naya allowed Li Kāng to guide her. Anywhere else would be better than in Cassia's company.

Naya didn't even have to turn to confirm that Cassia's attention had moved on from her. Instinctually, her body relaxed, and the urge to run away eased.

"Come," Li Kāng whispered right next to her ear,

so that his breath tickled her already alert senses. "We have to prepare."

"For what?" Naya mouthed back at him.

"For your escape. You leave tonight."

Her step hitched, and she stared up at him, wide-eyed. "But—"

He pushed against her back so she'd keep moving. "Never mind all that. You must. Or you'll lose your chance."

"How?"

Li Kāng simply shook his head, the small pony-tail at the top of his otherwise shaved head lolling to one side.

"She'll punish you," Naya said.

"Yes. She'll try."

"But then—"

"It will be my atonement. I kept Mei a prisoner of this place all her life. It doesn't matter that I didn't comprehend to what extent until recently. I am guilty just the same."

"No—"

He steered her down another open corridor, taking her away from the bustle of so many people. "Later. Imagine that the walls have ears." He spoke so softly that Naya had to strain to make out the words, though his chest pressed against her back, his cheek touching hers.

"We'll have only one chance. Don't waste it."

She couldn't think of an argument she wanted to make to that, so she allowed him to steer her farther away from the unhinged immortal with a god complex, and the creepy vampire masters.

If she were to escape tonight, she'd have to begin narrowing her focus to that one task only. The full moon was close enough to rising that Sister Wolf was unable to remain still inside her. Soon, the beast within Naya would unleash. There was no stopping her wolf ... or the pain she brought with her.

Whatever Naya was to do, the window was closing fast.

When Li Kāng picked up the pace, so did she.

CHAPTER NINETEEN

BRUNO

HE KNEW he should try to sleep. It was the smart thing to do. The flight to Shèng Shān Mountain was long, and he'd need every bit of his strength once they arrived.

But his thoughts raced with the many ways that things could go wrong, and Brother Wolf was equally agitated.

There was too much at stake.

They were on their way to rescue Naya. And to do so, they were heading into a monastery filled to the brim with vampires, all of whom were accomplished fighters, in addition to possessing the usual preternatural skills all vampires did.

One of the wizard brothers, he couldn't tell which, snored particularly loudly, causing Meiling to smile. She looked as tired and strung out as he was, but when she smiled, she reminded him so much of Naya that it hurt.

He was painfully aware how little sense it made that he should feel this connected to a woman he'd barely spent time with, but he'd given up on arguing the topic with Brother Wolf.

Somewhere along the way, Bruno had surrendered, accepting that Naya was his mate. With how long it had taken him to accept the fact, even when it was *his* wolf that was insisting upon it, he couldn't help but agonize over what Naya would think once he told her.

Annoyed with himself, he slid forward on his seat to stare out a window, rubbing at his eyes. Dense, fluffy white clouds floated around them, casting their journey in a magical, uplifting light he feared it wouldn't actually possess.

One of the wizards snorted loudly, as if coming awake. Bruno glanced the brothers' way in time to see Mordecai—he thought—roll onto his side and begin snoring away once more.

The brothers had reclined their seats so far back they were almost horizontal, falling asleep immediately after takeoff. Lying next to each other, their faces relaxed in sleep, they looked similar enough to be identical twins. All that bushy facial hair probably hid distinguishing features.

"Is it odd that I find them almost cute?" a female shifter from the Rocky Mountain Pack by the name of Cleo asked. "In, like, that they're-so-ugly-they're-cute kinda way. Like a pug or maybe a bulldog, only in an old man way."

"Yeah, that's weird as fuck," Scooby said, another of the pack wolves to come along.

Bruno wasn't sure Maverick chose them and a few others because they were best suited for the job, or because they'd been the ones waiting for him by their cars after they'd left the warehouse where the immortal Cyrus had imprisoned Naya and Meiling.

Maverick had been in such a rush to get them out of there that he hadn't even made time for any of them to clean up or to stop by the pack compound for fresh clothes.

The front and back of the alpha's shirt were still covered in dried blood, making him appear a formidable survivor, or perhaps a bit unhinged in his desperation to reach Naya.

Either way, Bruno wasn't complaining. Every minute that passed was another chance for something to go wrong with Naya in the middle of a bunch of vampires, and in the company of a female immortal who sounded just as bad as Cyrus.

And the power Cyrus had possessed was already more than Bruno was equipped to overcome.

The wizard brothers might not actually be cute, but Bruno couldn't be more grateful they'd chosen to accompany them. When faced with the immortals' magic, they were their only true weapons.

A flight attendant who smelled like a wolf shifter passed through the cabin, topping off coffees and waters, offering food and other comforts Bruno didn't have the headspace for.

Maverick stretched out his long legs with a groan, rolled his head stiffly around his fully healed neck, and stood, taking the unoccupied seat next to Meiling and across from Bruno.

"You too tired to talk?" he asked her.

She shook her head. Her hair, half escaped from a ponytail, stuck out around her face. Along with her bloodshot eyes, she appeared as exhausted as Bruno felt.

"No," she said. "I'd actually like to talk. It will help keep my mind off of ... things."

Things like how Naya might be dead already by the time they got to her. Or that this female immortal Cassia might have powers that differed from Cyrus', and so the mages might not be equipped to deal with whatever she threw at them.

The brothers moved with far more agility than their hoary looks suggested, but they still moved like old men. Mages didn't usually live the many centuries these wizards had. If Cassia engaged them in active combat, would they be able to keep up? Their child-like enthusiasm, as refreshing as it was, wasn't a weapon...

"Don't go there," Maverick said, and it took Bruno a beat to realize the alpha was speaking to him. "Whatever you're thinking, don't do it. There's no point to considering what might happen when we don't know. You'll just torment yourself for no reason."

Bruno nodded and smiled darkly, though Maverick didn't look like he was taking his own advice. His face was drawn and haunted.

He turned sideways in the leather captain's chair to face Meiling. "Tell us more about what we'll be walking into once we get there."

She ran a hand over her head, then pulled out her ponytail, and set to braiding her hair while she spoke. "There's only one place to land a plane that's close enough to the monastery. It's the same landing strip the vampire masters use, so it will be watched. But there are no other nearby alternatives. Anything else will allow us to arrive with surprise, but it will take us a full day, maybe even two, to reach the stairway to the monastery from there."

"We can't spare that kind of time," Bruno said right away.

Maverick frowned. "No, we can't. They'll know we're coming as soon as we touch down. That's not ideal."

"It is possible that they won't have guards at the airstrip," Meiling said. "If we get very lucky. But that depends on whether the vampire masters are expecting shipments, and they receive them all the time. They like to indulge with all sorts of special things they have flown in from all over the world, when we're only allowed to eat a very limited diet. They claim it's for our training, but I don't know. They think none of us know what they're up to, but we do. When you're locked up at the top of a mountain all your life with nowhere else to go, you learn everything there is to know about the place, whether you mean to or not."

"So we'll just have to hope luck is on our side," Maverick said. "But if it's not, what will they do once they spot us?"

"I'm not sure. I've never watched the shipments arrive, it's only what I've heard. But with the rest of what I know about the vampire masters and how they like to run things, I'm guessing that the guards will wait to see if it's maybe a shipment they didn't know was coming. The masters aren't forgiving. The guards will want to make sure they don't attack in case it's some of their prizes being delivered ahead of schedule. I think, anyway. They'll wait to see before attacking."

"So we could pretend we're unloading goods," Bruno said, "then take the guards out before they can call in a warning?" He looked at Maverick. "Is there something on board we could use?"

"I'm sure we can find something."

Maverick called the flight attendant over. She promised to put together something that would pass as a luxury indulgence. At the very least, they had champagne and caviar on board, and though Meiling had no idea whether that was the kind of thing the masters ordered on a regular basis, it would still work in a bind.

"How easy will it be to take them out?" Maverick asked.

Meiling grimaced, sliding her completed braid over her back. "Not very. We all train in the Seimei Do martial arts. We train every single day, and hard."

Bruno leaned his elbows on his thighs. "I haven't heard of that martial art, and I thought I'd at least heard of most of them."

"Seimei Do is one the main vampire master, Grand Master Ji-Hun, developed himself, many centuries ago. Whatever can be said of the vampire, the practice he has designed is incredible."

"You know it?" Bruno asked.

Meiling huffed. "Of course I do. Didn't I just tell you that we all train every day?"

"I didn't realize that would include you. You're a werewolf."

"Yes, I'm a werewolf. *And* I'm a viper in Seimei Do. There are only four levels of mastery beyond where I'm at, and Grand Master Ji-Hun is at the very top. The six other master vampires are one level beneath him."

Maverick said, "Tell us more."

"We begin training as soon as we can walk. The exercises then are very basic, of course. They focus on flexibility, elongating the muscles. By the time we're four, we're all required to be able to stand on one leg with the other behind our heads, as an example. With each year that passes, we're required to hold the position for longer. By age seven, we're required to stand on the crown of our heads without any other support."

"You can do this too, then?" Bruno asked.

Meiling smiled impatiently. "Of course I can. I can do all of it. I don't believe in doing anything halfway, even if I'm obligated to do it. Though I don't possess their speed, I can fight against vampires."

Bruno shook his head. "That seems ... impossible. Werewolves lack the speed and strength of ordinary wolf shifters."

This time, Meiling's smile was tight, flashing a bit of teeth. "I'm well aware. I've had to work hard to get where I'm at. But it wasn't all like you think. Most of the monks in training are human. Grand Master Ji-Hun promises them that if they reach the leopard level, which is the next one above mine, he will offer them the chance to become a vampire."

"That's ... wow," Maverick said. "Does this happen often?"

"Often enough. Less than half of the warrior monks reach the level of leopard. One-seventh of those reach the level of tiger. Most set out thinking they want to become a vampire. At the start, it all seems very glamorous. But by the time they reach leopard rank, not all go through with it."

"Why not?" Bruno asked.

"By then, they've seen too much of what the vampire masters are really like. They are vicious and cruel, though they hide it well."

"And what happens if these tiger-level monks decide not to become vampires?" Maverick asked.

"Then they must fight to the death with one of the vampire masters. If they win, they get to leave. If they don't, they die."

"Humans against vampires?" Bruno asked. "That doesn't seem very fair."

"It isn't, but the masters don't care about fair. They're old too, all of them, really old."

"Which means," Maverick interjected, "that they are very powerful."

"Correct."

Though he suspected he already knew the answer to his question, Bruno asked, "How many leopard-level monks who decide not to be turned leave the mountain?"

"So far, none."

"And they still choose not to be turned?" Maverick asked. "Even knowing they'll die?"

"Yes," Meiling said. "That probably tells you all you need to know about the vampire masters of the Shèng Shān Monastery. And Grand Master Ji-Hun has earned his title as the most important of them all."

After a fresh wave of apprehension ripped through him, Bruno stared at Maverick. "How long until the second assault team arrives?"

"They'll be no more than an hour behind us. River was already getting everything ready to go when we took off. But he and Blake will remain behind."

Because Maverick wasn't sure he'd make it back, and the Rocky Mountain Pack would need continuity in its leadership. It's what Bruno would have done too.

"Okay," Maverick said. "We're heading into a shitshow. Any advice on how to get in and get out with Naya, and without dying?"

"Yeah," Meiling said. "Move fast. Assume everyone's trying to kill you. Strike first and go for the kill strike. Take no mercy, because not a single one of them will have mercy on you."

Bruno's brows drew together. "Even the acolytes? Surely, they're innocents?"

"Maybe. But they'll still try to kill you. It's what we're taught to do. Seimei Do is more about offense than defense. The fastest way to disable and kill while taking the least amount of damage. And if it makes you feel better, just think that you're saving them from a lifetime of struggle and hardship."

"It doesn't," Bruno said. "Don't you have any friends there you want to see live?"

"Of course, but there's only one that I *need* to live, and that's Li Kāng. He's the mage who helped me escape."

"All right," Maverick said. "So how will we know him by sight?"

"Don't worry about him. He won't let you see him. He has invisibility magic."

One of the wizard brothers snorted a disruptive

snore just then, as if, even in sleep, the two were drawn to unique and different magic.

"Give me a minute," Maverick said, pulling out his cell phone and typing furiously into it before tucking it back away. Sending instructions and warnings to River and Blake, no doubt.

The alpha leaned back into his seat, appearing relaxed, though Bruno didn't buy it. Maverick asked Meiling, "Why did you set out to find Naya?"

"Because my friend Li Kāng told me she was in trouble. Someone who wanted to hurt her had found her. He helped me escape, so I did."

"Just like that?" Maverick's mouth was a tight, skeptical line.

"No," Meiling said. "Li Kāng told me what I was, and what it means for me to survive. I didn't know before then."

"I see," Maverick said. "But then after you found out about how important it is that you live, you decided to risk your life anyway?"

Meiling swiveled in her seat to fully face the alpha. "Yes." After a few moments that sizzled with her ferocity, she added, "Wouldn't you have done the same? If you'd just found out your entire life was a lie? Besides, Li Kāng told me I was in danger if I remained there."

"You believed him?"

"Yes. He's the only one I trust there. Even others I consider my friends would turn on me if it benefited them. It's how it works there. It's what the vampire masters teach us."

"*Que hijos de mil puta*," Bruno muttered, bringing out one of the worst insults in his native tongue for the vampires that apparently deserved that and so much more.

"Why does this immortal, Cassia, think you are Naya?" Bruno asked Meiling.

"This I've been wondering. I'm not sure. But I do know that the other immortal man, Cyrus, he hid me when Cassia came. I don't know what he did, I felt the same, but Cassia didn't see me. She only saw Naya."

"What does Cassia look like?" Maverick asked.

"Beautiful. Terrifying. She moves like a dragon. Like every one of her next moves might be a kill strike."

Bruno nodded in understanding. Cassia was a predator.

"And physically?" Maverick asked. "How will we know when we see her?"

"Oh, you'll know," Meiling said. "Without a doubt. But she has waist-length black hair, very odd-colored violet eyes; they are bright, like candlelight illuminates them from behind. A nice mouth, nice face, nice body. She is young-looking, maybe in her mid-twenties."

Bruno was watching Maverick, not Meiling. The alpha's face, already pale from the blood loss and shock of nearly having his head ripped off, was suddenly sallow as if he might faint.

Bruno rose from his seat and crouched beside him. "What is it? What's wrong?"

When the alpha didn't answer, Bruno pressed urgently, "Maverick, tell me what's wrong. Now."

"I know who Cassia is. I've seen her before."

CHAPTER TWENTY

CASSIA

THE GIRL WAS LYING to her! The fact was blatantly obvious.

What an ungrateful brat.

And to compound her offense, Meiling was treating Cassia as if she were an idiot who'd been born yesterday instead of more than a thousand years before.

Meiling escaped the monastery and traveled to the United States following nothing more than her ... intuition? A mere hazy feeling had led her to abandon the only home she'd ever known and trek across the unfamiliar world alone? Cassia scoffed as she lowered herself onto a decorative parapet off to one edge of the courtyard that bordered the throne room. As with everything she did, she'd chosen her location strategically. Out here, she'd remain in sight of all the busy bees coming and going, cleaning up the piles of rubble, while she meditated—or rather, while she pretended to meditate. She'd never had much use for stillness. Not when there was always so much action to be taken.

But seeing her, eyes closed, seated in a lotus position, appearing for the monks to be at complete ease with how she'd killed Master Xiong, would inspire a healthy dose of ill ease. Of fear.

Since power was as much about appearances as actual strength, it was the perfect way to think things through. For the first time in a long while, Cassia wasn't certain what to do.

If she didn't have need of the girl, the solution would be straightforward. Meiling would be dead already.

But with her sister Davina out of the equation, Cassia couldn't afford to waste any of the other three girls. She needed every chance for her immortality magic to take. She *would* become the first true immortal werewolf. She'd done too much and come too far not to see her brilliant plan through now.

But she itched with the desire to punish the girl. She couldn't allow Meiling to get away with her treachery. She wasn't even supposed to know about her bogus origins and her connection to Callan "the Oak" MacLeod, the legendary ancestor whose value lay within Cassia's imagination. It never ceased to amaze her what people were willing to believe without objection. When they saw what they thought they were supposed to, they didn't question the minor facts that wouldn't hold up under objective scrutiny.

"The Oak" MacLeod was now a fundamental part of werewolf lore. He was one of their revered heroes. Some of the clans had even taken to celebrating the man's birthday every October twenty-second, with absurd fanfare.

There'd been a werewolf by that name who'd lived in Wales centuries before. In an odd twist of chance, Cassia had even met him, well before she knew she'd have need of him. And though he'd been perhaps a remarkable man, and by all accounts a competent and respected leader of his pack, there was nothing noteworthy about his blood. He'd had several children the usual way. Certainly, his ancestral line encompassed hundreds of descendants by now—and none of them were Cassia's girls.

Though Meiling's connection to the man was a fabrication, Cassia had ordered that Meiling not be told about it. That the girl's ancestry remain a "carefully guarded secret." Cassia figured that someone would let the news slip eventually, and that the intrigue surrounding it would only serve to add depth and believability to her little tale.

Someone had obviously informed Meiling of this carefully guarded secret. That wasn't what concerned Cassia. Much more importantly, someone had told Meiling that she had at least one sister. And no one—*no one*—should have known.

Several people within the monastery possessed knowledge of Meiling's supposed origins, of how important it was that she survive long enough to pass on her ancestry to the next line of werewolves, blah, blah, blah. Beyond Ji-Hun and Li Kāng, she was certain other monks were also aware of Meiling's importance. No one kept secrets fully. This was as true then as it had been when Cassia was a child. People talked.

But ... not a soul within the monastery walls should have known that Meiling was but one of several. Of the creatures currently roaming the monastery, the only one who knew the extent of Cassia's plans was Édouard. Had the vampire betrayed her? Was his sniveling *mistress this* and *mistress that* all an act? Cassia didn't think so, but neither did she know who else could have betrayed her.

Briefly, she considered the value of killing Édouard, Li Kāng, *and* Ji-Hun, the likeliest sources of at least part of the leak. But she liked Li Kāng, and Édouard was a useful servant. Ji-Hun, however...

He was arrogant and prideful. His vanity had led him to develop an entire religion around a set of beliefs that placed him directly at their center. Yes, he claimed the "sacred" book as the basis of this religion, but, oh how convenient, he was the sole interpreter of the text, divinely appointed.

Though the grand master vampire left a bitter taste in her mouth, he was powerful in his own right. Cassia might not have a specific use for him now, but that could change in a century or two. It would better suit her to leave some allies around to call on in the future. With how much Ji-Hun desired her book, she could get him to do just about anything for her.

The brat had even lied about Ji-Hun drinking her blood! What was the purpose of that deceit? Meiling must have known Cassia would confront the grand master about it. Why would the girl lie when it was so easy for Cassia to find her out? None of it added up, and Cassia couldn't help but feel that she was missing something glaringly important.

Her nostrils flared as her immortality magic whirred and spun inside her erratically, setting her teeth on edge.

Cassia was the only one allowed to have secrets. The only one who could plot and plan and deceive.

She was the one true immortal here. Even amid ancient vampires, she was the only one who nobody atop that mountain could kill. She could raze it all, and she'd be the sole survivor.

If Édouard were feigning his subservience to her, then he was the most skilled thespian she'd ever met. And Édouard didn't strike her as the most skilled at anything—other than servitude perhaps; he was quite good at fulfilling her orders.

She liked Li Kāng. That in itself was a rarity. There were few people on this planet she liked enough to care whether they lived or died. She trusted him, an even further rarity.

But Li Kāng *was* a mage, and everyone knew mages were unreliable, as changing as the seasons and as fickle as magic itself; they could shift their allegiances on a whim.

Perhaps Cassia should kill him after all.

She had tasked him with watching over Meiling, with ensuring that the girl remain safe within the monastery.

He'd failed at his assignment. Whether or not further betrayed her, he'd already earned his death sentence squarely.

Cassia huffed in irritation, her eyes snapping open. She caught a monk staring at her, his body half concealed behind a column—as if that were any kind of protection against the likes of her.

She snarled at him. He squeaked like a field mouse and ran, stumbling over a pile of broken tiles, falling to his knees, then rising and scampering away.

She smiled, feeling better already.

She began unfolding herself from her seat before she realized she'd come to a decision. Of all of them, Li Kāng was the least likely to serve her future needs should she let him live. Yes, she liked him the most, but he had failed her. And since she couldn't kill Meiling, she'd kill him.

With the way she clung to him like a drowning rat in a vast ocean, it was clear the girl liked him. She felt safe with him.

Cassia's smile grew. Li Kāng's death would most rattle Meiling. Especially if Cassia told Meiling that she was responsible for the man's death. If Meiling understood that her escape and lies had cost the mage his life.

Meiling would never attempt to betray her again.

Even so, Cassia would use Meiling next. She'd have her scientists meet them at her estate in Southern France. She was in the mood for its warm sunshine and fragrant flowers.

For now, Lara and Naya were secure enough

where they were. Naya was back with her pack. Lara had never left hers.

Cassia would infuse Meiling with her immortality magic next.

But it was time to harvest all the girls.

Now that they were of an age resilient enough to withstand the intensity of her magic, there was no reason for further delay.

Cassia couldn't shake the feeling that she was missing something that was staring her straight in the face.

It was time to minimize risks and maximize payoffs.

Standing, she surveyed her surroundings. She had to give Ji-Hun credit for one thing. His monks were industrious little ants, carrying out orders without question. Perhaps there was something to this religion he'd established and the fanatical devotion it inspired.

She was as akin to a god as would ever walk this earth. If this pompous vampire could garner this many followers willing to dedicate their lives to him, she was certain she could do the same and more.

Perhaps once she became the only wolf shifter immortal to ever exist, she'd found her own religion. Hundreds of people to worship her and cater to her every whim? That didn't sound bad at all...

Cassia set off in the direction of the monks' dormitory, where Meiling had a small, austere room all to herself. This was probably where Li Kāng had taken her. The girl was in desperate—and fragrant—need of a shower and fresh clothing.

Cassia would kill Li Kāng in front of her, then lock her up in the wolf-proof cell to reflect on what she'd done while she awaited her transformation into a beast.

After that, Meiling would be putty in her hands. She'd board her jet without complaint and all but beg for some of Cassia's magic.

Lost to her thoughts, it took Cassia a moment to register that Édouard, along with a row of the other vampire minions she'd paid so handsomely for, stood to the side of the open corridor she walked, waiting for her to acknowledge him.

"What is it, Édouard?" she snapped, annoyed to be interrupted now that she'd finally decided on a course of action. Bouts of indecision always left her in a foul mood.

"I've discovered something I think Mistress will be quite interested in," he said, bowing his head to her.

Cassia studied the vampire she'd known for centuries, concluding that his subservience was not feigned. The man was truly loyal to her.

With a flick of her hand, she dismissed the other vampires. They jumped and immediately began walking away before one stopped to glance over his shoulder at her. He bit his lip, a fang pressing into the tender skin. "Um, Mistress?"

Cassia's face scrunched in distaste at hearing the term only Édouard ever used.

"Yes, what is it?" Her obvious annoyance made the vampire look back at his comrades, but none of them so much as acknowledged him, staring vacantly off into space instead.

Their survival instinct was strong.

"Wh-where would you like us to go?" the man finally spit out.

Cassia rolled her eyes. "Good help is so hard to find these days," she muttered under her breath. With their preternatural hearing, they were sure to have heard her anyway. "Go far enough away that I don't have to see you."

As they zoomed out of her sight, Cassia closed the space between her and Édouard, lowering her voice. "What did you find?"

"It's the ... friendly one ... that Mistress likes. Somehow he has discovered..." Édouard met her eyes. "...the connection to the one in Colorado."

So Li Kāng *had* betrayed her several times over.

The desire to end him raged through her as she forced herself to focus.

"How did he find out?"

"Of that, I am less certain. It appears likely that it was through some sort of scrying or other tool of divination."

"He used his magic to find out, then."

"It would seem so, Mistress. I elicited the news from a chambermaid who is infatuated with him. She watches him closely. She overheard him speaking with the girl, telling her what he'd learned."

Édouard chuckled as softly as his whispers. "The chambermaid is hopeful that you will dispatch with the girl after learning of this news, but she begs that the man not be touched."

Cassia huffed. "As if it's in her power to decide that."

Édouard shrugged and offered Cassia a conspiratorial smile. "She didn't need to know how you'd react to this information."

Of course Édouard would have a good guess at what she'd do.

"Did he tell the main one?" Cassia asked.

Ji-Hun wouldn't be the supreme grand master he claimed to be if he didn't use spies throughout his compound. Just because it didn't appear that they were being overheard didn't mean their every word wasn't being recorded and relayed back to Ji-Hun himself.

"In order to answer that question, I will have to probe more, Mistress. I wanted to report back these findings immediately before continuing on. But as of now, it appears the friend was acting alone, conspiring only with the girl."

Cassia sized Édouard up. Over the recent decades, his body had softened almost as if he were affected by age. He was a vastly different man now from the one she'd rescued from the streets of Paris. Then, every part of him had been hard, vicious, driven by savage bloodlust.

"You've done well," she told him, and his eyes, flat like a shark's, sparkled for once.

He bowed. "You honor me with your praise, Mistress."

Here was a man capable of appreciating his blessings. Meiling could learn a thing or two from him.

"If you discover more, find me and let me know right away."

"Of course. Without delay, Mistress." He glanced up at her. "And where will I find you?"

She grinned, as savage and vicious as she'd ever looked. "Where do you think?"

CHAPTER TWENTY-ONE

NAYA

SHE STOOD in the middle of Meiling's bare, diminutive bedroom, staring hard at Li Kāng—not trying to make sense of what he was saying since that were clear enough, but rather to determine whether he was truly trustworthy after all.

Especially since he was all but shoving her out the narrow window of Meiling's room—which opened onto a treacherous sheer drop more than four-thousand feet down.

"I'm not suggesting it's going to be easy," he was saying. "It won't be. There is a very good reason why the masters don't bother guarding this way down from the mountain."

"Yeah, like that it's far too dangerous," Naya said. "I'd be free climbing a fucking straight drop I'm completely unfamiliar with, when my wolf is already riding me hard. The full moon's close. If I don't make it down before the shift comes over me..."

Then *splat*.

She'd be dead as dead got while her precious blood drained into the mountain. No one would ever recover her body. She'd become a part of the landscape of Shen Shang Monastery forever.

"You'll also possibly have to deal with gusts of wind at times, and the mists that embrace the mountain like smoke ... they make the rock slick. There's also a waterfall that might moisten the rock face—"

"So your awesome plan is to send me climbing down a death trap." Naya walked to the open window and peered down ... and down and down, until the mist that Li Kāng mentioned obscured her view.

"I'm good, okay?" she said. "I know I am. I'm probably one of the best climbers in the world. But I'm not that good. No one is. I'd have to at least know the terrain. And it's not like the crazy immortal allowed me to pack my climbing shoes when she kidnapped me." She looked down at the boots she was wearing, provided by said crazy immortal. They were cute and fashionable—and clunky without a chance at a good grip. She'd be better off going down barefoot.

"It's also cold up here," Naya said. "I'm a werewolf, not a regular wolf shifter. I don't have their resilience to cold."

"But you are better suited to the cold than a human, or than a mage like me."

"Of course I am. That fact won't keep my fingers and toes from getting stiff."

"There isn't ice on the mountain this time of year."

"Doesn't mean the rock won't be colder than the immortal ice queen's dead, blackened heart."

Naya turned her head this way and that, studying how difficult it'd be to get out of Meiling's window. There was no ledge outside the opening, no easy surface onto which Naya could lower herself. The window was an unadorned cutout in the stone wall.

She started shaking her head even as she pulled it back in through the window. "No. I'm not gonna do it. I may as well fling myself out the damn window and save myself some effort. Climbing down is way too risky."

"It's either that or death," he said, his accent thickening the more his panic mounted.

"Why the sudden crazy hurry? What changed? Why do I have to leave right this second?"

"Because something changed with the circumstances. We did have more time. But we don't anymore."

Naya sighed and lowered herself onto Meiling's bed. It was as firm as a mountain ledge. She crossed her arms and really studied the man before her.

The mage was young, perhaps in his early thirties. His dark hair shone in the candlelight he'd lit to illuminate the depths of the small room, but it was his brown eyes that held her attention. She didn't think he could fake that kind of concern.

She kicked her feet out in front of her, crossing them at the ankles, wondering if she'd be insane enough to attempt the climb.

"You say the circumstances changed, but you've gotta tell me more. You can't expect me to just hurl myself out the window without any idea why I'm doing it."

"Cassia is coming."

Naya sat up straight. "What? Now? Why would she be coming now? She just sent us away."

"I don't know what her reason is for coming, but I know the effect of it will be your death."

Naya didn't move a single muscle as she waited for him to continue.

"Maybe not today, maybe not even tomorrow, but if you go with her when she comes to get you, you will die soon."

"Wow, okay. And how exactly do you know all this?"

He glanced back at the closed door of the room as if Cassia might walk through it at any moment. "There isn't time. You need to leave. Now."

"That may well be, but I'm not risking my life in a major way without understanding more. *How* do you know all this?"

He hesitated, looking at the door once more.

"You're wasting precious time," Naya pressed.

When he whipped back around, it was to glare at her, an uncommon expression on his smooth, placid face. "You're as stubborn as she is."

Naya smiled, though there was scant little to smile about. She hadn't had much chance to figure out how she felt about suddenly having a sister, but she liked knowing they were both determined.

Li Kāng walked over to Naya, crouching in front of her on the bed to hold her gaze while he spoke. "I've lived in the monastery as long as I can remember. Amid vampires who are pleasant in appearances only. Behind the masks they wear, they are cruel and dark of heart."

"That's pretty obvious to me just by looking at them."

"Listen," he said sharply, "there is no time for commentary."

She scowled at him, but held her tongue.

"They drank my blood for a long time, thinking I was human. They only stopped after I could no longer contain my powers. When my magic first began revealing itself to me, it was unstable, and with no other mage here to teach me how to master my natural abilities, I didn't have much control at the start. I would have preferred to keep my true nature hidden from them, but that wasn't possible.

"All this for you to understand ... I honed my abilities as I could best figure out on my own. My focus was on survival. I was cast into a den of hungry lions who already had my scent. I trained in the Seimei Do martial art like everyone else here. Without any better way to figure out my powers, I trained myself in my magic in the same way. I practiced, over and over, until I figured out what I was capable of. And then I kept practicing until I was so good at what I did that I could control my every move.

"My main focus while I've lived here has been to make it to see another sunrise. It came as no surprise that my skills were in invisibility, limited control in elemental magic, and what I've come to call intuition magic—the skills most suited to helping me survive.

"I don't get all the details, but I receive the messages I need to heed for my survival ... and that of those I love. I don't love you, but I do love your identical sister."

Naya could see the truth of his love for Meiling spark in his eyes. His brow bore down with the intensity of his sincerity.

"I don't know how you will die exactly or when, but I am certain that if you go with Cassia now, you *will* die. And it won't be a pleasant death."

"Dandy," Naya whispered under her breath.

"It is my magic that tells me this. I feel it, in here." He pressed a closed fist to his heart.

"Can you tell whether I'll survive the climb down the mountain?" Naya asked softly.

"No, that my magic does not show me. But my magic is always right." He paused with another urgent glance at the door. "Mei trusts my magic. I felt that she had a sister. It made little sense to either of us, but she trusted me and my feelings enough to leave here and go looking for you. I didn't know your name or your precise location. All I could tell her was that you were in the Rocky Mountains, living in a wolf pack. She had to figure out the rest on her own. She's intelligent and knows how to watch and learn without being seen.

"She endangered her life because my magic told me that *your* life was in peril. I'm sure she would want you to do whatever you had to in order to survive now."

Naya frowned at him. "I'm not hesitating to make the climb because I'm scared." Though maybe she was, just a little. "I'm not throwing myself out the window because I'm not sure I'll make it to the base of the mountain."

Li Kāng stood, shrugging. "You either try and hope to live. Or you stay and you die."

Naya squeezed her eyes shut. How had it come to this?

"How long do I have to decide?"

"Cassia is almost here. You either go now, or you seal your fate."

Naya rubbed her hands across her face quickly, then began rapidly tying her hair back into a braid. If her hair whipped in her face at the wrong moment, she'd lose visibility.

"Can you manipulate the air element? Like Cassia does?" She began kicking off her boots and pulling off her socks. "Can you help me down? Or at the very least help keep me pressed against the rock face as I climb down on my own?"

"I could, but only so long as you remain in my sight. But I won't be able to help you at all, not even at the start."

Naya stood, stretching out her neck and arms,

circling her wrists while flexing her fingers. "Why not? Don't wanna help out a lost cause?"

She brought one heel to her butt, then the next, wishing she at least had the chance to properly warm up before she attempted the most unreasonable climb of her life.

"You will need me to fight off Cassia," Li Kāng said, beginning to stretch his own arms out. "If I don't buy you time, you'll never make it."

Naya swallowed, hesitated, then ran over to give him a quick embrace. He surprised her by squeezing her back instead of hurrying her off.

"Thank you for helping me," Naya whispered into his chest.

His chin rubbed against the crown of her head in a nod.

"I never got the chance to tell Mei that I love her. Will you please tell her for me?"

Naya pulled back to stare him in the eyes. "Tell her yourself," she snapped fiercely. "Get yourself out of here and come find us."

His smile was mournful. "I won't ever see her again. I should have told her before, but she's so precious, I never wanted to burden her with my admission."

"You didn't want to burden her with your *love*? That's stupid."

Li Kāng chuckled darkly. "Yes, yes it is."

Naya began to walk away before looking back at him. "Is it your magic telling you that you won't survive today?"

The sad smile returned. "No, it's not. Cassia is the great immortal who has lived a thousand years. She sucks people dry of their life force. I am a simple self-taught mage. I am no match for her."

Naya ran back to him in a burst of anger. She poked him in the chest, fully aware of how obnoxious she was being. "Don't you think that way. *Don't you dare*. You will never survive unless you think you have a chance. The mind and the imagination are the most powerful tools in our arsenal. See yourself winning, surviving. See yourself telling Meiling how much you love her, and then, only then, will you have a chance."

Li Kāng didn't say a word. He just stood there, his shoulders heavy, resigned to his fate.

Naya shoved him, and he stumbled back. "Snap out of it. Don't just stand there like some mopey kid who just lost his puppy. *You have to fight*. You have to believe that you'll live hard enough that it can happen."

He didn't move.

Naya stared into his eyes, willing him to accept what she was saying, to see a spark in his eyes that told her he would fight for himself. "Tell me you understand me."

His smile grew, but it remained the saddest fucking smile she'd ever seen.

"Li Kāng, get your shit together. Right now. In life, in magic, in love, in all of it, most of the battle is won in the mind. In our thoughts. In our beliefs. Don't you dare let Meiling down by giving up on yourself."

He hesitated.

"Can I tell her that you fought to survive until the very end? That you're going to do absolutely everything in your power to make sure you make it out of here to see her?"

Another pause they surely couldn't afford.

"Li Kāng," Naya barked savagely. "Can I tell her that you are fighting for your love for her? That she has a chance to see you again and tell you she loves you back?"

Naya had no idea whether her sister loved the man or not. But right then she didn't care if it was a flat-out lie. If it got the man to do what he had to do, then it would be worth it.

"Can I tell her that you didn't give up on her? That you didn't give up on yourself? That you kicked some serious immortal ass?"

"Yes," he said, but it was so soft that the sentiment was barely there.

"Can I motherfucking tell her that you love her enough to get your head out of your ass and fight for your life, dammit?" she growled like some deranged drill sergeant.

His docile eyes grew wide at language he might have never heard used before.

Good.

She squeezed both his shoulders and lowered her voice. "Don't let these asshole vampires and immortals dictate the terms of your life. You're as worthy of a magical life as they are. Claim your power. Right now, Li. Right this motherfucking second, you own all that power this world has given you. Kick Cassia's ass so hard she never thinks to come near you again."

That last part might've been a bit much, but Naya's words had finally lit a fire in the mage's eyes. *Now* he had a fighting chance.

"Good," she said, nodding, pressing a peck of a kiss on his cheek. "From Meiling. You get a full-on sloppy tongue kiss from her when you make it out of here."

At the window, Naya looked back at him. "Thanks for helping me."

"You're welcome. Now *go*. She's almost here. I can feel it."

Naya nodded, took a breath to steel herself for the hell of a climb down she was about to begin, and stepped out the window.

Before she dipped below it, she caught sight of the mage's body wavering ... until it completely disappeared from view.

His invisibility magic; it had to be.

The very moment after Naya lowered herself below the window, clinging to the depressed groove of grout between stones, she heard the door of Meiling's room open with a loud crash.

"Where's Meiling?" Cassia demanded in a savage whip of force.

But then a howl of the wind rose from within Meiling's room, obscuring whatever Li Kāng said, if anything.

Naya trained her focus only on getting down this mountain as fast as she could.

The mage was on his own now.

As was she...

In a race against the moon, a psychotic immortal, her own stamina, and the unpredictability of down-climbing an unknown mountain so high up that the elements were all accentuated, each gust of wind more severe, every degree in temperature deciding, every step and hold a matter of life or death.

But as she'd advised the mage, Naya trained her

mind fully on her success. It was the only way she'd live to experience another shift.

To discover if there was anything to her dreams of Bruno.

To see Clove and the rest of her pack again.

In her mind, she chanted, over and again, *I've got this. I was made for this,* all while she held on tight to the feeling of arriving at the mountain's base as if it alone could be her salvation.

Craning her neck down, she sought immediate handholds and footholds, while purposefully ignoring how she could see nothing beneath her but open space and mist.

She allowed her body to glide through moves she'd practiced thousands of times, motions that were as familiar and easy to her as breathing. Not to think, and definitely not to fear. Not to linger on the astounding height at which she dangled. Not to wonder whether Li Kāng would be able to buy her enough time ... or whether Cassia would soon pop up, floating beside her.

"Give me all the time you can," Naya whispered to her wolf, her words instantly yanked away by a stiff breeze whipping violently at her clothes, trying to pull her away from the rock face. She doubled down on the strength she channeled through her fingers, sticking the holds.

Naya would need every second her wolf could give her.

When Liv's face popped into Naya's mind, she forcefully shoved it away. Her client had died because she'd lost her focus.

I've got this. I was made for this.

One foot after another, one hand and then the next, Naya made steady progress downward.

Thirty feet down.

Far too many left to go...

CHAPTER TWENTY-TWO

BRUNO

"WHAT IS IT? WHAT'S WRONG?" Bruno asked Maverick when the alpha stopped walking a few feet from the jet and tilted his head, as if he were picking a specific sound out of their rapidly darkening surroundings. With the fresh wave of nerves rolling through him, Bruno's accent was more pronounced than usual; he'd even had to remind himself to speak English.

Before they landed on the remote airstrip in the middle of a dense Chinese forest, he hadn't liked a single thing about Naya being in the company of a vicious immortal, at a monastery filled with equally ferocious vampires. Now that they were out of the plane, he had to force himself to wait, to listen, to take measured steps toward her rescue. The enemy could be anywhere now that they were in their back yard.

He wanted to tear up the steps to the monastery as if his next breath depended on his immediate arrival.

"Well?" Bruno barked at Maverick.

In response, Maverick growled menacingly at Bruno, no doubt trying to put him in his place, but Bruno didn't care. His Brother Wolf was as powerful as Maverick's. He'd given the alpha the respect due to him from a beta of another pack, but if the alpha didn't start moving fast in the next three seconds, Bruno was going to take charge, and damn the consequences.

"I'm picking up the presence of vampires," Maverick finally said after he allowed another few torturous moments to tick by.

"Their scent will be everywhere," Meiling said as she stepped up next to them, her eyes darting in every direction, not even bothering to alight on the two men in front of her. "That doesn't necessarily mean they're here right now."

But her words were soft, in case they did have an audience, and the jittery energy rolling off her made Bruno even jumpier than he already was. If he were a gun, he'd be loaded and cocked, the slightest depression of the trigger all that was needed for him to kill.

His vision was sharp enough to track a rabbit's movement from a hundred feet away, but vampires could remain still like the dead, not even breathing while they hid. Just because Bruno wasn't picking up anything moving around them beyond the usual forest critters did *not* mean that they were alone out here.

Silently, Scooby, Cleo, and a few other wolves from the Rocky Mountain Pack, circled them, facing outward as if to protect their alpha.

However, the alpha wasn't the most important person here. Without the wizard brothers, they had no chance at taking down the immortal and freeing Naya.

For all its remoteness, the airstrip was set up to receive multiple planes. Already, two were parked to the side of the runway, and there'd be room for the secondary assault team to park theirs as well once they arrived.

Surely, though, their presence would be noted by vampire sentries. Airplanes weren't exactly inconspicuous.

"I don't like it," Meiling said on an out breath while they waited for the eccentric mages to emerge from the jet.

The brothers had slept most of the way, and it had been a *very* long flight, the longest of Bruno's entire life, compounded by the fact that every passing minute diminished Naya's chances of survival.

He'd attempted to sleep several times while the wizards snored away like hibernating bears, but Brother Wolf wouldn't settle enough for him to shut off the urgent thoughts looping through his mind.

Bruno's body was exhausted, fueled solely by adrenaline and determination.

"Could we really have gotten this lucky?" Meiling asked, suggesting she was as suspicious of this fact as he was.

With someone as important to the survival of the werewolf species within their compound, wouldn't the vampires be expecting them to come?

That wasn't the only thing that didn't make sense. Why would Cassia care so much about securing the future of the werewolf species?

She knew *exactly* who Naya was and why it was so important that Naya survive at all costs. That one fact alone had been the main reason sleep had never finished claiming Bruno.

Maverick turned to watch the jet, perhaps as ready as Bruno to charge back in there to see what could possibly be taking the brothers so long. They'd had a flight nearly fourteen hours long to prepare for this moment.

With a quick glance at their alpha, the pack wolves spread out, heading into the thick trees. Their alpha must have used the pack link to silently give them orders.

Maverick waited until they were out of easy hearing range before shaking his head, speaking softly. "I still can't believe it..." It was a sentiment he'd repeated many times to Bruno and Meiling since he first arrived at a terrible and haunting conclusion...

"How could Cassia be the same woman who delivered Naya to me when she was a baby? How could she care for her enough to save her then ... and endanger her life now? Could she somehow think ... she's helping Naya?"

Maverick had spoken of little else since he recognized Cassia from Meiling's description.

How could the immortal have gone to such extraordinary lengths to save not one infant, and not even two, but *three* babies from certain death, only to endanger one of them now, delivering Naya to a nest of ruthless murderers. Meiling had nothing encouraging to say about the ancient vampires and their many acolytes, killers in training.

"No wonder Cyrus had known right where to

find Naya. Cassia must've told him." Again, Maverick shook his head, as if he simply couldn't shake the depths of his disbelief. "She was never safe in the pack. I was deluded."

Maverick was reeling from shock, it was the only explanation. Had the alpha had more presence of mind, he would never voice such vulnerabilities aloud, even if he had sent all of his pack wolves away.

"There is no way that woman is doing anything without having a plan," Meiling said. "Cyrus had a healthy respect for her, it was obvious. He was so careful with her that it reminded me of dynamite. Like Cassia was one wrong move away from *kaboom*."

"She could still be thinking she's helping Naya," Maverick suggested, though his tone implied not even he truly believed this alternative.

"No way," Meiling said. "She feels worse than Grand Master Ji-Hun, and he frightens me to my bones. And I don't get frightened easily."

That much, Bruno could readily believe. Despite their circumstances, and the fact that Meiling would be swarming the monastery as a part of their team—as the enemy to the vampire monks—she'd never once indicated any concern for herself, only for the sister she barely knew.

"Your pack must have a spy," Bruno told Maverick, and the alpha tensed all over. But it wasn't a conclusion the alpha himself hadn't arrived at.

"I know," he eked out like a leak in a steel drum. He ran a hand through his hair, rubbing at his neck. "Dammit, I know. It has to be. Cassia might've brought Naya to me, but she's had no contact with me since. She'd have to have some other way to get updates on Naya, to know that she was still there. For all she knew, I could've moved her to some other, safer location."

"That doesn't necessarily mean there's a spy in your pack," Meiling said. "Remember, Cyrus took us, not her. She only came to pick Naya up after Cyrus let her know he had her ... or me." Meiling sighed, louder than any words she'd said. "Cassia probably still thinks she has me. This is all my fault. I should have stayed here. Then maybe Naya would still be safe with her pack."

Bruno squeezed her shoulder for a moment. They'd already been over this too. But nothing Bruno said made Meiling feel better.

Just as nothing anyone said put Bruno at ease.

"There are too many things that don't add up," Bruno said. "It's likely you have a spy, Mav, though it isn't guaranteed. And it seems almost certain that there's at least one person feeding Cassia information at the monastery."

"That part doesn't surprise me," Meiling said. "I didn't feel safe a single moment I lived here. Never."

"Let's get Naya out of here," Bruno said. "Then we worry about making sense of everything else."

"Yeah," Maverick agreed, but he still sounded distracted. As if he couldn't accept the fact that Cassia had manipulated him to one extent or another, a conclusion that seemed all but inescapable now.

"What the hell are they doing up there?" Bruno grunted. "Redoing their braids? *Mierda*, how could two old men take so long to descend a plane? They don't even have to walk down. They could just float ... or whatever it is they do."

Meiling pursed her lips before saying, "I'm going to check on them." And she didn't wait for anyone's agreement before she walked back across the airstrip to do just that.

The men waited in silence, their eyes tracking their surroundings, their unease as noticeable as the descending twilight.

"We don't have time to spare," Bruno grumbled, though none of this would be news to Maverick. "If the moon rises before we can get to Naya..."

Then Meiling wouldn't be able to guide them into the unknown territory. She'd be lost to her werewolf's transformation.

And Naya would be lost to her own shift. She'd be out of control for three days, until the moon began to wane again.

It would make getting her out of there safely that much more difficult, and there'd be no chance of sneaking her out without alerting the entire monastery of their actions.

Werewolves weren't known for reason or subtlety; they were physically incapable of it.

"Have you been able to reach her?" Bruno asked after another pause.

Maverick huffed in evident annoyance. "Do you really think I wouldn't tell you if I'd been able to reach her through the pack link? If for no other reason than to get you off my ass?"

Bruno waited.

The anger seeped from Maverick; it had never been intended for Bruno in the first place. They were all on edge.

Maverick shoved his hands forcefully into the pockets of his jeans. After a few beats, he pulled them back out. *On edge.*

"It was one thing not to be able to reach her after we figured out she was on her way to China. But now that we're nearby? I should absolutely be able to fucking reach her."

"So the immortal must be interfering with your connection to her somehow," Bruno said.

"It looks like it. I couldn't reach her after that Cyrus fucker took her either. When she was passed out, under his thrall or whatever, it made a certain kind of sense. Now?" He jammed his hands back in his pockets. "Now, I don't know what to fucking think."

"But you'll keep trying?"

"Of course I will," Maverick snapped. "I'm her alpha. I'm her protector. But I like to think I've been more like a father to her. I'll keep trying until she's standing right beside me. I'll never give up on her."

"Neither will I." It made no damn sense, but it was an inescapable truth; Bruno knew it.

Maverick had even stopped questioning his intentions.

Even Bruno had tried to reach her. Mate bonds allowed telepathic communication between the two partners. It was well known that the bond only activated after a full mating occurred, linking the two wolves together forever.

That hadn't stopped Bruno from trying.

Silence had been his sole response, and it had been devastating.

"If they don't walk out of that plane right now..."

Maverick grumbled, and Bruno grumbled wordlessly back in response.

As if the wizards felt the menace directed at them, they *finally* emerged from the plane.

Brother Wolf paced incessantly, snarling and ready to charge up the steps. Bruno moved toward the wizards, wanting to do anything in his power to shorten the distance. He watched them hover down the steps as slowly as if they were walking them. "What the hell took you two so long? You'd better hope Naya is still alive."

Bruno actually liked the strange wizards, but he couldn't help himself. Any control he'd held over himself was quickly slipping. If he didn't think it'd be foolish to run up to the monastery himself, he would have done it already. But he couldn't alert them of their presence if the vampires didn't know they were there already. All of them together had a better chance at getting her out of there alive. He wouldn't do anything to endanger her, no matter how much he was tempted to be unreasonable.

The mages hovered to a stop in front of him as Maverick and Meiling circled them.

"It was my brother and his runes," one of them said, telling Bruno this had to be Albacus. "He insisted on throwing the runes after you disembarked. I told him we didn't have time."

Mordecai scowled. "There is always time to ensure one is on the right path. That is actually considered *saving* time, not wasting it, *brother*." Mordecai's eyes narrowed into crinkles as he glared at Albacus.

"If I hadn't taken the time to consult the runes, we'd be heading in the wrong direction right now—"

"What wrong direction?" Bruno asked before Mordecai finished speaking.

"We planned on heading up the mountain."

"Yes," Maverick said, drawing the word out. "And that's still what we're planning on doing."

"It's a mistake. The runes are clear."

Albacus' nostrils flared, and he waggled his head to a chorus of twinkling beads. "Brother of mine, don't make me force the words out of you..."

"As if you could. You—"

Bruno interjected. "Please. I'm losing my mind. I need to get to Naya. Tell us what the runes say. What should we do?"

Mordecai and Albacus ceased all their glaring at each other to smile warmly at Bruno.

"Young love," Albacus said. "There is little better. Even after all these centuries, it remains one of the best experiences in life."

"And to be mates..." Mordecai added, causing Bruno's Brother Wolf to yip at the recognition.

"The bond between wolves is said to be extraordinary."

As thrilled as Bruno was to hear validation of the bond that continued to feel insane even to him, he was flexing and unflexing his fingers at his sides, doing what he could to keep himself from wringing the explanation out of the mages already.

Eventually, when Bruno's patience was so frazzled he could barely think straight, Mordecai jiggled the pockets of his long robe, making the runes tinkle as they clinked together.

"Naya is on the move," the wizard said with a solemn nod.

"What does that mean?" Bruno asked right away. "Did we get it wrong? Is she not in the monastery?"

"Is she on the mountain?" Maverick added. "Is she with the immortal woman?"

Mordecai held up a restraining hand. "All good things come to those who wait, *n'est-ce pas, mon frère?*"

"*Oui,*" Albacus said. "But in this case, my brother, if you don't spit out what you know, I think these two fine wolf shifters might kill you all the way. And since I'm half dead already, I'm not certain I'll be able to revive you as you did me."

Did the men use the long way round to say everything?

"The runes don't tell me everything I want to know," Mordecai said. "They tell me only what I need to know."

"Plus," Albacus added, "they are open to interpretation."

"But," Mordecai said with a pointed look at him, "when in the hands of someone as experienced as I, they are an incredible resource that we would be wise to heed."

Bruno couldn't wait any longer. In a controlled tone that belied how close he was to losing it, he asked, "What do the runes say, Mordecai? Tell me or I will lose my mind, right here and now."

Mordecai frowned, but spoke: "She is near, but she isn't where we thought. She is moving, but not moving fast enough. The moon almost rises."

"That much is true," Meiling said, while she cast a worried glance at the sky. The moon wasn't up yet. The sun had only just set. But it wouldn't be long—certainly, not long enough.

She looked between Bruno and Maverick. "When I ... shift, you'll be able to keep me in check?" Her brow furrowed and she nibbled on her lower lip. "I wouldn't want to hurt anyone, and I don't know what I'm doing when I'm in my wolf form."

Bruno would have offered to help, but he had to find Naya.

Maverick settled a hand on one of her shoulders. "I'll assign Scooby and Cleo to you. They'll make sure you don't hurt anyone, and that you remain safe too. I don't want any harm to come to you either."

Meiling smiled her thanks shyly as if genuinely moved, and Bruno once more wondered what kind of environment she was used to at the monastery.

The monastery that held—*or didn't hold*—his mate against her will.

"So where is Naya?" Bruno asked Mordecai.

"I can't tell you exactly." He held up a gnarled hand. "And no, it's not because I don't want to, it's because the runes didn't tell me. However, she is moving very fast and covering a vast distance in a short time."

"What?" Bruno's jaw went slack. The monastery was on a freaking *mountaintop*. "What could she be doing? Is she coming down the stairs? Did she escape already?"

His face a mask of grave concern, Mordecai said, "What she is doing is extremely dangerous. Also..." He faced Maverick. "You cannot reach her because your link to her is blocked. That will soon change."

"Now? Why? How? Who?" Maverick asked rapid-fire.

But Mordecai was shaking his head. "The runes didn't give me those answers."

"It is likely the immortal," Albacus said in a knowing tone Bruno had no desire to dispute. "If she is anything like the magic of the immortal man Cyrus we encountered, she is very powerful. Her magic may extend so strongly that it interferes with yours, Alpha."

"So what are we going to do?" Meiling asked. "We can't just stand around here and wait. If the guards haven't seen us yet, they will soon, and then we won't be able to pretend we're here for a delivery. That option is gone already."

And they'd had the caviar and champagne setup all ready, just in case...

"Should we just start climbing?" she continued. "Even with your speed, the trek up is long."

Mordecai frowned as if in deep thought and looked at his brother, who frowned back.

"I know that look," Albacus said.

"As you should," Mordecai said.

"What are you thinking?"

"That the runes didn't say to go up. But nor did they say to go down."

"We can't go down," Meiling interjected.

"If we can't go up," Mordecai said.

"Or down," Albacus added.

"Then we must go—"

"Around!" Albacus said triumphantly.

Mordecai grinned, the bushy hair on his face rising with the gesture.

Bruno scowled. "Around? Around the mountain? But the monastery is at the top of it, and the back of the mountain is inaccessible."

Upon approach, Maverick had instructed the pilot to loop around the mountain while maintaining a reasonable altitude so as not to alarm the vampires. It was a risk, but they'd needed to examine the terrain beyond what outdated satellite images could provide.

The back of the mountain was mostly a cliff...

"Oh fuck," Maverick breathed. "I know where she is."

"Where?" Bruno asked urgently.

"Oh man. It's not good."

"*Where*, Mav?"

"I'd bet my two balls on her climbing down the back of the mountain."

Meiling gasped. "No, that's not possible. The vampires don't even bother guarding it because no one can survive that climb. Not even other vampires."

"If anyone can do it, Naya can." But Maverick didn't sound reassured in the least.

Bruno knew precisely why. That face of the mountain appeared sheer, with waterfalls shooting across it in parts. The monastery was so high up that it was shrouded in mist like clouds that allowed gaps only to reveal more bare mountain. Barely any greenery dared to attempt to live on it.

"No one can get down that way," Meiling insisted. "It's not that it shouldn't be done. It's that it *can't* be done. No one would try that unless they have a death wish, and Naya wants to live."

"Which is exactly why she might try it," Maverick said. "She doesn't know we're on the way. If she thought her chances were better trying to escape than staying with a killer immortal, then she might do it."

"She'd be crazy to try it."

"Naya's one of the best climbers in the entire world, even if no one knows her name. And I know her. I've known her all her life. She's a fighter to the end. If she thought she had to, she'd do it."

An uneasy, dread-filled silence settled across them all, interrupted only by the calling of birds as they prepared for nighttime.

Finally, Bruno studied the mages. Both of their nearly identical faces were pressed into grim, *accepting* lines.

"You think this is what the runes were trying to tell you?" he asked Mordecai.

"I can't think of any other explanation."

Deep inside him, Brother Wolf threw back his head and howled.

There was no doubt Naya was formidable. Bruno had seen enough of her movements in the ring to believe she was capable of nearly anything.

But Meiling was right.

No one—*no one*—could survive a climb down four-thousand-feet of sheer, cold, slick mountain.

Not even her.

Not even his mate.

His heart cracked a little and he forced his face not to react as he felt the pain of losing her before he'd had her at all.

CHAPTER TWENTY-THREE

NAYA

THE SAVAGE WIND WHIPPED at the fabric of her tunic; she'd wished a hundred times already that she'd removed it instead of keeping it on to protect against the cold. She'd assumed tucking the shirt into her leggings would be enough. It wasn't.

The air lashed at her entire body, cracking the skin across her knuckles and making her eyes and nose water. She longed to wipe at her wet face.

But she couldn't afford even a second of distraction. Nothing that might cause her to lose her balance. No missteps that could send her careening down the mountain, tumbling and smacking against the stone until she finally ceased falling, arriving at the place from which she'd never move again.

Her bare feet were cold and her toes slightly numb. Far from ideal when the holds on the mountain were sparse and shallow. The only saving grace was that the rock held up without crumbling. The stone was solid. So long as she could make her way down, it would hold her weight.

Her scalp was also itching like a mofo. It was perhaps the nerves of all that was at stake. Or maybe it was the knowing that Cassia was possibly right on her tail, already seeking her out.

All Naya could do was push the many discomforts away and train her mind on one thing.

One thing only.

The base.

It was all that mattered.

She couldn't help anyone she cared for right then. All she could do for them was survive.

Every time her thoughts started to wander—to Li Kāng, was he still alive, had he given his life for her, would he ever get to see Meiling? to Clove; to Mav and the rest of her pack; to Bruno, the man who invaded her dreams as if he were a real part of them —whenever her thoughts began to drift, she yanked her concentration back so hard she felt as if she were actually pulling on her brainstem.

Focus had been easier at the start, when the adrenaline pumped through her body like a blood transfusion. When the sounds of Cassia's arrival at Meiling's room had echoed as if they were as eternal as their creator. When Li Kāng's sacrifice had still felt all too real.

Now, exhaustion was creeping up on her.

The climb was simply too long. The pressure of knowing there was no rope to catch her should she fall was too great. And the knowledge that Cassia might snatch her off the mountain to kill her anyway was too inescapable.

Naya might not be allowing herself to think of all that could go wrong or all that depended on each step down, on every hold she chose, but it weighed down her muscles.

She was climbing down a sheer mountain somewhere in the middle of a dense Chinese forest with a silverback gorilla clinging to her back, doing everything he could to pull her away from the rock.

And all that was *before* she took into account the fact that night was quickening, darkening her view of the rock, causing the wolf inside her to stir and stretch and prepare for her emergence.

Naya and her wolf were as connected as any werewolf was to the beast inside them. Naya was certain her wolf understood all that was on the line if the shift should overcome her when she clung to a few tiny knobs and indentations in the mountain.

But the wolf couldn't help her nature any more

than Naya could help the fact that she was a were-wolf, beholden to the cycles of the moon.

Naya imagined that her wolf would give her all the time she could—that she'd purposefully delay Naya's transformation as long as was physically possible—but in the end, Naya's beast would over-take her. And if Naya was still clinging to the moun-tain when it happened ... well, she and her wolf would die. Simple as that.

Her shift was too painful and too prolonged. Her transformation into a wolf wasn't instantaneous as it was with most wolf shifters in her pack. Had that been the case, then *maybe* the additional resilience and advanced healing of her wolf could survive a fall from a hundred feet up, perhaps even more. But Naya had never been graced with that ease, and she was much higher than a hundred feet up.

She had no idea how far she'd managed to climb, or how much mountain she still had to traverse. Was she halfway down? A third? Less? More?

When she'd begun the climb, she'd estimated that she had somewhere around three or four hours before the moon would be visible. Maybe even five. It still wouldn't be enough for this much mountain to descend. But she might get close enough to the bottom that she'd have a chance.

All Naya knew for certain was that her forearms

and triceps had begun to shake. Her shoulders ached, and her thighs were about to begin trembling too. She could feel it happening.

This was the time when she should have sought out a ledge to rest. To wait out the three days of her wolf before climbing the remaining way down.

She could survive a few days without water and food.

Of course, there was no ledge to pull into. No spots to rest, not even for a quick moment. She didn't even have a chalk bag to aid her grip. She'd been wiping her hands on her clothes at regular intervals to keep her palms dry. Once the shakes really set in though, no amount of chalk would help her anyway.

Picking out each new hold was even more challenging than before under the rapidly consuming darkness. The full moon would be rising over some ridge before long.

At least her vision was better than an ordinary human's, though nowhere near as precise as a regular wolf shifter's. Still, she could see better than most, thank fuck.

Her body told her to slow down, to stop. Naya sped up, beginning to pick her hand and foot holds more rapidly, and therefore taking more risks that one might not be ideal, might not be enough for her to hold on to.

But she'd reached the point where time was as important a consideration as caution.

Tears overcame her suddenly, pricking obnoxiously at the back of her eyeballs. With punishing severity, she blinked them away, sniffling, setting her jaw hard in her renewed determination.

If she succumbed to fear, exhaustion, or emotion, she'd be sealing her fate. She'd die.

So she ignored her body's warning signs as she also ignored the way she wanted something to be fucking easy in her life for fucking once! She wished it with a desperation so ferocious that she tasted it on her tongue as if she were sucking on a tangy penny.

She pushed on. She moved as fast as she could, not thinking, not considering, just climbing, not allowing herself to feel a thing beyond what she couldn't avoid. She shut down as much of herself as she could, leaving only those parts vital to her survival. One hold, then the next, then the one after that. She channeled the ease of a monkey or a spider. Hell, right then, she'd even take the grace of the crazy-ass mountain goats that scaled rock faces no one in their right minds would attempt on purpose.

She *moved*.

She climbed faster than she'd ever climbed before. She pushed beyond every limit she'd ever encountered.

Her muscles trembled, but she still locked them down, still forced them to obey her commands.

Her fingertips were sore—raw—and the bones in her fingers ached now every time she bent them to grip another protrusion in the rock.

She pressed on.

Her heart clenched from the demands she'd had to place on herself since she was a little girl first becoming aware of the weight of her destiny. Of her ancestry.

Her heart squeezed as it reached for Bruno, a man Naya hardly knew. Unreasonably, she yearned for the comfort of his embrace.

Naya shut her heart down even harder and just *moved.*

Where's the next foothold? Yes, good. That one. And what handhold follows that?

Down, down, down she went, the full moon pressing down on her like a lioness lining her up in its sights before charging in a lethal attack.

Give me as long as you can, Sister Wolf, Naya pleaded. Seconds counted. Every breath was borrowed.

Another foothold, another handhold. Naya's forearms vibrated so terribly that her muscles visibly bounced.

More, more, more. Naya kept going down. She'd

push until her body or her mind or her heart gave out on her. Or until her wolf claimed her.

It was a race as to which would bring about her demise first.

Naya had forgotten about the vicious immortal a while ago. Her only enemy now was herself, her skill, the elements, and time.

Come on, Ni, she whispered to herself, wondering if she'd truly spoken aloud. Her lips were numb, as were her cheeks.

Everything was quickly converting into a surreal scene. She wasn't even sure if she was still in control of her body. It felt as if she were observing herself from the outside, watching her actions with objective disinterest.

Somewhere along the way, she'd detached from herself, from her desire to endure. She was simply following the momentum of the actions she'd sent in place, the intention she'd decided on as she exited Meiling's window.

Robotically, she experienced her body running through the motions it had to.

Down, ever downward she went, abstractly wondering if she'd make it—from a place that felt far away.

Her fate was out of her hands. All she could do

was her part. The rest ... well, the rest would be decided independently of her wishes.

From her birth, her life and her destiny had been beyond her deciding.

The mist and empty space gaped open beneath her, ready to embrace her—or swallow her whole.

Bruno

Once he was certain Mordecai wasn't going to alter his interpretation of the runes, Bruno had whirled on Meiling. *What is the fastest way to the back side of the mountain?* To the sheer drop he couldn't imagine any creature of any sort climbing down safely.

Even as Meiling had raised a hand to point out the direction he should follow, Bruno was stripping out of his clothes with practiced swiftness, and he'd been out of them and running before anyone could try to stop him.

He'd shifted into his wolf while he ran, hearing Maverick calling him back as he did so. To just wait a fucking second. They'd come up with a plan together!

Bruno didn't so much as pause or hesitate.

Maverick wasn't his alpha. Bruno didn't have to follow his commands.

And Naya was his *mate*.

That bond superseded any deference Bruno might have wanted to show the alpha of another pack.

He'd been separated from Naya too long already. While she was in danger. *When she needed him.*

Brother Wolf whipped through underbrush, weaving between tree trunks and leaping over fallen logs and debris so fast that his surroundings blurred.

Bruno's wolf sniffed the air, searching for Naya's scent. He perked his ears, scanning for any sign that she was nearby. He ran and ran, willing his muscles to elongate to their furthest, to extend every stride, pushing to arrive faster, *faster.*

The mountain's diameter at the base was wide. He had many miles to cover before he reached the cliff Naya was attempting to scale down. Could the wizards be right? And did Maverick really know Naya well enough to predict that she'd try a move so ... suicidal?

From the plane, Bruno had studied the terrain closely as they circled it from above. Clouds and mist enshrouded the mountain and the large monastery complex perched atop it, but through gaps in the obstructions he'd glimpsed stone so vertical and so forbidding that it had made perfect sense why the vampire masters didn't bother guarding it.

No one could escape or infiltrate their compound that way. *No one.*

Or so he'd thought then...

Could Naya really be capable of such an extraordinary feat? A total defiance of gravity and the limits of the human body?

Or would he find her remains on the forest floor ... finally within his physical reach but out of his life forever?

His heart thumped awkwardly at the thought of losing someone so wholly irreplaceable.

Wolf shifters mated for life. There was only ever one person to come along to perfectly match the other's heart and mind.

Naya was the only chance he had at fitting together with someone as if they were long lost puzzle pieces finally joined as one.

Bruno had no idea yet what he'd do once he reached the back side of the mountain, bare of stairs and any other aid to attempt a climb down—or up.

But if Naya was truly coming down, then he'd find a way to reach her. He simply had to.

He didn't bother counting how far he traveled, only how much farther he had to go. He was growing closer, but so was the full moon rising. Between what

Meiling and Maverick had shared with him on the flight over, he understood that Naya would be unable to resist her change once it started, and that her wolf would be beholden to the moon's influence as soon as it became visible over the mountain ridges.

The single saving grace of their location was that the moon would be slower to rise here than over flat land.

Maverick also told him that Naya's shifts were painful and long. If her Sister Wolf were to emerge during the climb, there'd be no way for her to hold on.

For the first time ever, Bruno felt the moon's rising as acutely as any werewolf. Urgency pricked across his fur, igniting his muscles, guiding him to bound across unfamiliar terrain as if he'd been running through these forests all his life.

Critters scurried out of his way, but he didn't even bother watching them go. His focus was pinned on one goal only.

Reach Naya before the moon rose.

Her face filled his mind. Her smile more brilliant than any he'd ever seen.

Though Bruno had known Lara all his life, and the alpha was undoubtedly enchanting, the pull to her was nothing like what it was to Naya. Now that he understood why, he didn't question it. He just hoped with every loop of breath that he'd arrive in time—that she was as good a climber as Maverick claimed her to be, as Howie and Jeb said she was.

The forest was alive with the signs of diurnal animals preparing for sleep, and of nocturnal creatures arising for a night of prowling. But not a single one of those sounds and scents was from Naya.

Another wolf was following him. Running fast to catch up.

Maverick.

Bruno scented more wolves farther behind him, but not Meiling.

She'd have remained behind, wary of her own oncoming shift.

Bruno had been in the process of trying to reach Naya through a telepathic link—one they hadn't forged yet—when panic surged through Brother Wolf so suddenly that it commandeered his entire being. He couldn't pull in a complete breath.

He skidded to a stop, sucking in air. Out of nowhere, his limbs had begun trembling violently, and he felt as if the weight of the blasted mountain itself were pressing in on his chest.

Then, without warning, reprieve arrived.

Maverick had nearly caught up. His footfalls were closing in.

Brother Wolf tore off again, kicking up fallen

leaves as he pushed off, more frenzied even than before to reach Naya.

That desperation, that panic that had overwhelmed him, it hadn't come from anything he'd done.

She was close! She had to be.

He was in the middle of bounding over a large rock in his path when he heard her.

He heard her!

He'd never witnessed her in her wolf form before, but when the loud whimper reached his ears, he knew without a doubt that it was his mate.

He touched down, lighter than a feather, and kept running with absolutely everything he had in the direction of her whimper.

Then another arrived.

More alarmed, more high-pitched. *Pained.*

Her cry sliced through his entire body as artfully as a carving knife.

He pivoted and adjusted course now that he had her to guide him to her—

A thud that sounded too much like a soft, breakable body smacking into unforgiving stone stilled his heart. The cruel hand of fate reached into his chest and squeezed the rapidly beating organ.

Bruno the man couldn't focus on a single thought; anguish rolled through him thickly, viscously, suggesting he'd be forever consumed by it. Brother Wolf registered that Maverick and the other pack wolves keeping pace with him had also stopped running.

Urgently, with a feverish desperation, Bruno reached into Brother Wolf's senses. Was there any sign that the body, if it was Naya's, still beat and breathed and lived on?

Only the usual sounds of a forest met his ears...

¡No, Dios, no! Por favor, no, Bruno pleaded, the well of his grief making Brother Wolf wince and snarl.

The howl that rent free from him next was filled with a desperate longing—and hope. Bruno would never give up on Naya. He couldn't.

He howled out the song of his mate, unsure how he even knew it. But he called for her. And then he howled again, promising that he'd be there for her forevermore.

The moon, yellow and bright, was cresting the mountains surrounding them, its round, pregnant swell illuminating the night.

Bruno howled again, his heart seizing and cutting his cry short.

He sprinted toward her.

To his mate.

It was all he could think to do.

He ran faster than he'd ever run before.

Barely breathing while his heart shattered inside his chest, he gave his search for his beloved every single piece of himself he had.

Naya. Ahora vengo, he promised.

But he didn't receive any sign that she'd heard him at all...

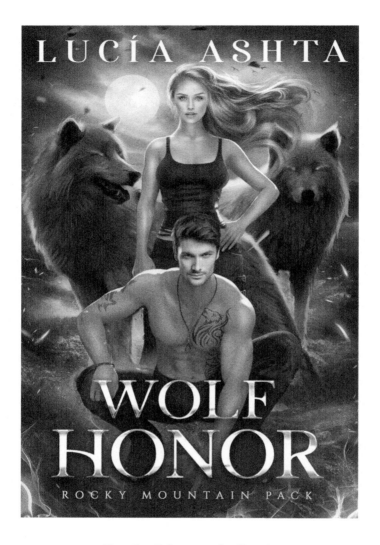

Rocky Mountain Pack

Book Three

Wolf Honor

Continue the explosive adventure with Naya, Bruno, and Cassia in **WOLF HONOR**, the next book in the Rocky Mountain Pack series.

BOOKS BY LUCÍA ASHTA

~ FANTASY & PARANORMAL BOOKS ~

WITCHING WORLD UNIVERSE

Magical Enforcers
Voice of Treason
(coming soon)

Magical Dragons Academy
Fae Rider
(coming soon)

Six Shooter and a Shifter
When the Moon Shines

Pocket Portals

The Orphan Son

Rocky Mountain Pack
Wolf Bonds
Wolf Lies
Wolf Honor

Smoky Mountain Pack
Forged Wolf
Beta Wolf
Blood Wolf

Witches of Gales Haven
Perfect Pending
Magical Mayhem
Charmed Caper
Smexy Shenanigans
Homecoming Hijinks
Pesky Potions

Magical Creatures Academy
Night Shifter
Lion Shifter
Mage Shifter
Power Streak
Power Pendant
Power Shifter

Power Strike

Sirangel
Siren Magic
Angel Magic
Fusion Magic

Magical Arts Academy
First Spell
Winged Pursuit
Unexpected Agents
Improbable Ally
Questionable Rescue
Sorcerers' Web
Ghostly Return
Transformations
Castle's Curse
Spirited Escape
Dragon's Fury
Magic Ignites
Powers Unleashed

Witching World
Magic Awakens
The Five-Petal Knot
The Merqueen
The Ginger Cat

The Scarlet Dragon
Spirit of the Spell
Mermagic

Light Warriors

Beyond Sedona
Beyond Prophecy
Beyond Amber
Beyond Arnaka

PLANET ORIGINS UNIVERSE

Dragon Force

Invisible Born
Invisible Bound
Invisible Rider

Planet Origins

Planet Origins
Original Elements
Holographic Princess
Purple Worlds
Mowab Rider
Planet Sand
Holographic Convergence

OTHER WORLDS

Supernatural Bounty Hunter

(co-authored with Leia Stone)

Magic Bite

Magic Sight

Magic Touch

STANDALONES

Huntress of the Unseen

A Betrayal of Time

Whispers of Pachamama

Daughter of the Wind

The Unkillable Killer

Immortalium

~ ROMANCE BOOKS ~

Remembering Him

A Betrayal of Time

ACKNOWLEDGMENTS

I'd write no matter what, because telling stories is a passion, but the following people make creating worlds (and life) a joy. I'm eternally grateful for the support of my beloved, James, my mother, Elsa, and my three daughters, Catia, Sonia, and Nadia. They've always believed in me, even before I published a single word. They help me see the magic in the world around me, and more importantly, within.

I'm thankful for every single one of you who've reached out to tell me that one of my stories touched you in one way or another, made you laugh or cry, or kept you up long past your bedtime. You've given me additional reason to keep writing.

My thanks also go to my reader group and advance reader team. Your constant enthusiasm for my books makes every moment spent on my stories all that much more rewarding.

ABOUT THE AUTHOR

Lucía Ashta is the Amazon top 20 bestselling author of young adult, new adult, and adult fantasy and paranormal fiction, including the series *Smoky Mountain Pack, Witches of Gales Haven, Magical Creatures Academy, Witching World, Dragon Force,* and *Supernatural Bounty Hunter*.

She is also the author of contemporary romance books.

When Lucía isn't writing, she's reading, painting, or adventuring. Magical fantasy is her favorite, but the romance and quirky characters are what keep her hooked on books.

A former attorney and architect, she's an Argentinian-American author who lives in North Carolina's Smoky Mountains with her family. She published her first story (about an unusual Cockatoo) at the age of eight, and she's been at it ever since.

Sign up for Lucía's newsletter:
https://www.subscribepage.com/LuciaAshta

Hang out with her:
https://www.facebook.com/groups/LuciaAshta

Connect with her online:
LuciaAshta.com
AuthorLuciaAshta@gmail.com

facebook.com/authorluciaashta
bookbub.com/authors/lucia-ashta
amazon.com/author/luciaashta
instagram.com/luciaashta

Printed in Great Britain
by Amazon